AFTER BATHING

D.J. Taylor was born in Norwich in 1960. He is the author of three novels, *Great Eastern Land* (1986), *Real Life* (1992) and *English Settlement* (1996), and two works of criticism, *A Vain Conceit: British Fiction in the 80s* (1989) and *After the War: The Novel and England Since 1945* (1993). He is currently working on a biography of Thackeray. He lives in London with his wife and their two sons.

BY D. J. TAYLOR

Fiction

Great Eastern Land
Real Life
English Settlement
After Bathing at Baxter's

Non-Fiction

A Vain Conceit: British Fiction in the 80s
After the War: The Novel and England Since 1945
Other People: Portraits from the 90s
(with Marcus Berkmann)

D. J. Taylor

AFTER BATHING AT BAXTER'S

Stories

VINTAGE

Published by Vintage 1997

2 4 6 8 10 9 7 5 3 1

First published in Great Britain by
Vintage, 1997

Vintage
Random House, 20 Vauxhall Bridge Road, London SW1V 2SA

Random House Australia (Pty) Limited
20 Alfred Street, Milsons Point, Sydney
New South Wales 2061, Australia

Random House New Zealand Limited
18 Poland Road, Glenfield,
Auckland 10, New Zealand

Random House South Africa (Pty) Limited
Endulini, 5A Jubilee Road, Parktown 2193, South Africa

Random House UK Limited Reg. No. 954009

A CIP catalogue record for this book
is available from the British Library

ISBN 0099779218

Papers used by Random House UK Ltd are natural,
recyclable products made from wood grown in
sustainable forests. The manufacturing processes
conform to the environmental regulations of the
country of origin

Typeset by Deltatype Ltd, Birkenhead, Merseyside

Printed and bound in Great Britain by
Cox & Wyman, Reading, Berkshire

A VINTAGE ORIGINAL

RACHEL'S

CONTENTS

ACKNOWLEDGEMENTS

Many of these stories originally appeared elsewhere, and I should like to thank the various editors involved for permission to reproduce them. 'Dreams of Leaving' first appeared in *P.E.N. New Fiction I* (1984). 'After Bathing at Baxter's' was first published in *P.E.N. New Fiction II* (1987). 'At Brackus's' appeared in the *London Magazine*, in *Best Short Stories 1990* and was broadcast on Radio 4. 'La Grange' was published in *Signals* (1991) and broadcast on Radio 4. 'Disturbance at the Heron House' appeared in the *London Magazine* and was broadcast on Radio 4. 'Seeing London' was broadcast on Radio 3 and appeared in *Telling Stories One* (1992). 'Final Payments' was broadcast on Radio 4 and appeared in *Telling Stories Four* (1995). 'Summer People' was broadcast on Radio 4 and appeared in *The Oldie*. 'Fantasy Finals' appeared in *Perfect Pitch*. 'Taking an Interest' was first published in *The Oldie*.

'Cuts', 'Saturday Night at the Jenks Motel', 'McKechnie's Diner, 9 A.M.', 'Looking for Lewis and Clark' and 'Essex Dogs' were originally broadcast on Radio 4.

I should like to acknowledge the help and encouragement of the many people who accepted or commissioned these stories, in particular Peter Ackroyd, Giles Gordon, David Hughes, Richard Ingrams, Simon Kuper, Allan Massie, Duncan Minshull, Alan Ross and Pam Fraser Solomon.

AFTER BATHING AT BAXTER'S

FOR QUITE A long time – longer in fact than either of them could remember – Susy and Mom had canvassed the possibility of an extended summer vacation. Late at night in the apartment, Mom listlessly fanning the dead air, Sunday mornings coming back from church along the side of the freeway, over long, slatternly turn-of-the-year breakfasts their conversation turned inevitably on the single topic. Sometimes, Susy thought, Saturday afternoons mostly when she lay on her bed smoking and contemplating the rigours of the past week, it was only this activity that gave their lives any purpose, that without the brightly coloured travel brochures, the timetables advising coach journeys to Des Moines and Kansas, life here in Tara City was bereft of meaning. Mom incubated similar ideas, seldom expressed. 'Nothing keepin' us here,' she had once remarked, with uncharacteristic acumen, and then more pointedly, 'Ain't as if ya had a career or anything'. It wasn't. Susy had rather resented the stricture about careers (there had followed an argument on who the fuck did Mom think paid the rent?) but she appreciated the distrust of milieu. Lulu Sinde, who had married a local dentist, reckoned she had put down roots in Tara. 'Yeah. Like in fuckin' concrete,' Susy had retorted, half jokingly. 'Like I was born here,' Lulu had said, dimly aware that her husband's decision to run for mayor demanded a certain patriotism. Susy had not said anything. Driving back down the freeway, past the first strew of advertising hoardings and the neon sign that read WELCOME TO TARA CITY, she had said a great deal.

Mom and Susy were not people who did things in a hurry. Last time the apartment needed painting it had taken a year for them to decide on the appropriate shade. The installation of a central heating system (two radiators and an immersion – shit, this was Tara) trailed thirty months of low-spirited bickering. It was not to be expected that such a momentous step as removal would be entered into without a period of procrastination. Three years back when they had been on the point of vacationing in Florida Mom had recollected that coach journeys disagreed with her and in any case what was the point in going two thousand miles just so that you could lie in the sun? The picturesque leaflets of Tampa Bay and the virid swamps were consigned to the trashcan. Eighteen months back Mom had floated the idea of staying with Aunt Berkmann in Tucson, had sought and obtained Aunt Berkmann's approval, had even, with unusual foresight, made arrangements for letting the apartment. Two days after that the fast-food chain owner to whom Aunt Berkmann acted as personal assistant decided to go to Europe. It was, Aunt Berkmann's letter explained, 'too good an opportunity to miss'. The episode had annoyed Mom considerably. 'And she fifteen years older'n him,' she had remarked, both appalled and envious. Yet Susy thought she detected relief behind the bluster. It was possible to speculate that the late-night poring over guide books, the posters of shimmering Californian beaches, were merely an elaborate piece of camouflage.

While Mom vacillated, stuck metaphorical toes in water and pulled them out, Susy found her sense of purpose continually resuscitated. Just walking down the main street did that. Tara City had only one function as a population centre. It was a place you moved out of. Doctors fresh out of medical school who thought they fancied a year or two seeing the sights of the mid-west stayed a month and then applied for hospital jobs back east. Ranchers whose social pretensions advised the purchase of a town house took one look at Tara and thanked God they were hoosyar boys from the flatlands. Curiously, this revulsion rubbed off even on casual visitors. The bikers

who sneaked in off the freeway and cruised the streets
looking for dope and tail saw within a few minutes that they
wouldn't find it in Tara. Licence, even of the home-grown
variety, was scarcely encouraged by the row of gloomy bars,
the run-down amusement arcade and the single enervated
cathouse that made shift as civic amenities. The local weirdos
and bomber boys went east if they wanted diversion, to
Denver and Castle Rock. There was too much respectability,
and too much decay. Reagan-voting, gun-toting, its cinema
screens cleared of anything that might cause offence to tender
sensibilities, its library shelves relieved of the weight of tomes
immoral or unAmerican, its streets populated by Godfearing
rednecks just itching to pump lead into the asses of Jews,
queers and liberals, Tara City nevertheless harboured more
subtle depravities. The niggers were moving in; longhairs,
Ricans – 'yaller trash' Mom, trained in Southern schools of
prejudice, would murmur whenever an Hispanic loped
silently towards them down the street. At night the apartment
block resounded to the thud of hectic jungle jive. Mom cried
a little every time she walked past Trapido's and saw the
Ricans clustering round the green baize tables, monitored the
nigger kids drinking Seven-Up on car bonnets. Pa had taken
his beer in Trapido's every day for twenty years, back in the
days when the buck occasionally stopped and (as Pa used to
say) you could still buy something with it. Distant days, of
which Susy preserved only a few recollections: swimming in
Tara Creek with Artie Tripp, watching the hippy convoys
heading west, coming back across the railway line, Artie
Tripp saying as they blundered through the dusky scrub that
in ten years they could get married and what did Susy think
of that?

Artie Tripp, Susy had decided – a reflection prompted by a
decade's marginal straying inside her consciousness – was a
paradigm of what Tara did to you. Artie Tripp, Susy thought
as they sat in McKechnie's Coffee Piazza, *had been talking
that shit for eight years*. Susy remembered a sixteen-year-old
Artie Tripp who had stolen rubbers off his father and driven

3

the latter's Ford Pontiac with negligent abandon, an eighteen-year-old Artie Tripp who featured as the shit-hot quarterback angling for a football scholarship, a twenty-year-old Artie Tripp who had talked about evading the draft and heading off East, looked across the table at a twenty-five-year-old Artie Tripp who had spent the last nine years working the forecourt of his father's gas station. 'Yeah,' Artie Tripp was saying, as he shovelled ice-cream through mild, uncombative jaws, 'I told him how it was, you know, politely, that you know I oughta think of changing things. I really gave it to him,' Artie Tripp went on, giving a swift, nervous little grin, spoon halfway from his plate. Susy gazed out of the window at the clotted high-summer streets, wanting to say *like fuck you did Artie Tripp*, wishing that Artie Tripp had turned out different. As he approached maturity a strain of nervousness, hitherto unobserved, had proved to be the principal feature of his character. 'Hell,' he said, as a blob of ice-cream flicked airily on to the sleeve of the blue sports jacket he wore on afternoons off from the gas station. Susy watched dispassionately. 'So I guess,' Artie Tripp went on, still dabbing gingerly at the vermilion stain, 'I'll be heading East soon. Pa's promised to give me a start, like with money and stuff.' Yeah, like with twenty dollars and you can kiss my ass, Susy thought. She said: 'That'll be nice Artie. Guess I can come and see you sometimes.' 'Reckon you can,' said Artie Tripp, showing his teeth as they walked into the molten sunshine. Five years ago, or even three years ago, the remark would have been enough. As it was, when Artie Tripp half an hour later drove her back to the apartment block she said: 'You can keep y'fuckin' hands off. OK?' Crestfallen yet resigned, Artie Tripp had backed away. Curiously, Susy found that this craven acceptance of her decision only increased her contempt. What else, she wondered, could you expect from a man who had spent nine years tending his father's gas station, or for that matter from Tara City?

But then it did not do, Susy thought, to condemn. By condemning others, implicitly you condemned yourself. Arid,

4

airless mornings in the flat, Mom making interminable phone calls to Larry Vosper, Susy leafing through expensive designer magazines, lodged this fact irrevocably in her consciousness. Larry Vosper was a fat, elderly cowboy run to seed who owned a ranch twenty miles west of Tara. This, however, was not the only thing that Susy had against Larry Vosper. There was the fact that he was five foot six and wore built-up high-heeled boots, the fact that his first action when Mom opened the door was to hand her a bunch of carnations and holler: 'How's my best girl?', the fact that after supper he went to sleep in front of baseball games on the TV. Larry Vosper, in short, did not have a great deal going for him. One thing Larry Vosper did have going for him was that Mom rather liked him. 'When ya get to my age,' she had once remarked, 'ya'd settle for a lot worse than Larry Vosper.' Susy, eyeing the quarter-inch of foundation, the miracles of corsetry stemming a tide of adipose tissue, could believe it.

And if Mom had Larry Vosper – who had twice proposed to her, once on the sofa after dinner, once during the course of a day trip to Salt Lake (Mom was not averse to coaxed confidences) – Susy supposed that she had her job. That was, if you could call the three days a week she put in at Rosati's delicatessen a job. Rosati's delicatessen lay in a grimy sidewalk that ajoined the main street and sold pizza to truck-drivers too shell-shocked to travel the extra quarter-mile that took you to McDonald's. Trade, inevitably, was bad (there was hardly any trade in Tara that could positively be described as good), the schoolkids and garage hands who slouched in at lunchtime indifferent to the delicate strands of tagliatelle, the pert blobs of tortellini that Mr Rosati arranged with some artistry in his window. 'Animals,' he would say, as another trucker sniffed suspiciously at a tray of bubbling lasagna before moving on to finger the discus-shaped pizzas, 'fuckin' animals. For Chrissakes. Give those bastards a truffle and they'd probably think it was a fuckin' meatball.' Susy, stationed behind the counter in a pinstripe waitress's mini-skirt, blue cap askew athwart her right temple, found these performances acutely embarrassing. Generally they were of short duration and he would disappear upstairs to apply himself with deep loathing to the accounts, leaving Susy to wiggle her backside at exopthalmic bikers and juggle with the change. On one occasion, however, a *pasta con funghi* of generous dimensions and enviable texture having failed to attract sufficient custom, Mr Rosati had gone outside and thrown it against the side of a passing truck. 'That,' he had been heard to remark subsequently, 'was a fuckin' *art statement*.' In a small way the gesture established him as an ally.

Summer wore on. Larry Vosper took Mom on a trip to Yellowstone which culminated – Larry Vosper's shiny estate car having negotiated the winding mountain highway – in a tour of the Vosper ranch. Mom had been impressed. 'Thirteen hundred head of cattle,' she reported, 'a nigger houseboy and ya can walk for three hours and the land ain't nobody's but Larry's.' 'Great,' Susy retorted, 'Larry Vosper has a nigger houseboy. Is that any reason to haul your ass over there?' This had been sufficient to silence Mom, but it was not enough to silence the feeling of disquiet. From afar came other signs of the essential instability of the middle-aged. Postcards came from Aunt Berkmann in Amsterdam, Helsinki and Freiburg. Though Susy rather disliked Aunt Berkmann (whom she had once described to Mom as a fat klutz), this itinerary awakened her envy. There was a world out there, outside of Tara City and the hills, in which things happened; a world in which Susy felt, obscurely, she was being denied a role. Susy tried explaining this to Lulu Sinde over afternoon tea in Lulu Sinde's smart little chocolate box of a house, a house whose portals you were not allowed to cross without wiping your feet. 'For Chrissakes,' Susy had said, 'you never used to be like this.' 'Paul says I have to smarten up a little,' said Lulu Sinde. 'Like he says it's a personal and a social responsibility.' 'Cock,' said Susy. 'No, I agree with him,' said Lulu Sinde defiantly. It was hard to evoke sympathy from Lulu Sinde, dumbly awaiting the arrival of the dentist's progeny. 'And Christ the *names* of

6

places,' Susy instructed. 'You ever realized how weird they are? How'd they get there. I mean, Kentucky, Missouri, Michigan . . . You ever been there?' 'I been to Missouri,' said Lulu Sinde, curving the palm of her hand over the slight bump of her stomach, 'yeah with Paul, two years back, I remember, I was awful sick . . .' Susy gave it up as a bad job, went home to dream long, comfortable dreams of US road maps in which squat, green-coloured states went on for ever like the squares in a patchwork quilt.

Halfway through August Larry Vosper bought Mom a plunging black cocktail dress which he wanted her to wear for a party at the Vosper ranch. 'It's kinda nice ain't it?' Mom asked doubtfully as together they manhandled the stretched fabric into place. 'You look about a hundred,' Susy told her and then, relenting slightly, 'Shit, you look OK. Enjoy yourself.' That night Susy allowed Artie Tripp to take her to a movie, Christ, just like it was eight years ago and Artie Tripp still the same octopus-handed youth who had tried to get fresh with her in the back of his father's car. Though she had allowed Artie Tripp to put his hand inside her blouse the expedition was not a success and went unrepeated. Most evenings Susy spent in her room, the view from whose window presented a vista of leprous concrete and cunning piccaninny kids playing baseball, reading Kerouac and thumbing through her record collection. 'What you doing in there?' Mom would enquire through the door about once an hour and Susy would reply: 'Just shiftin' the stale air around Mom,' and slide over to the record deck to whip another disc out of its sleeve. Sixties music. 'Hippy junk' Artie Tripp used to say in the days when he ventured opinions. The sixties and Susy went back a long way: The Dead; the Airplane; Steppenwolf singing 'Born To Be Wild'. Thus:

> Catch your motor running
> Head out on the highway
> Looking for adventure
> Whatever comes our way

7

Susy discovered that the loud electric music cutting through the empty air had a strangely galvanic effect. As the song reached its crescendo ('And the night's gonna make it happen/ fold the world in a love embrace /fire over the guns and watch them/ explode into space' *da dum thud*) she drifted round the room, propelling her limbs with jerky, ataxic movements. At times like these it was possible to imagine that you were seventeen again, smoking dope at weekend parties, screwing Artie Tripp on his parents' wide double bed with the flock mattress, thinking that any day now Peter Fonda would be sailing over the horizon on a Harley Davidson 950, just waiting to light out with you, engines gunning, into the sunset. The illusion seldom persisted. Christ, Susy thought, sometimes when you were twenty-four and a half years old and your experience ran only as far as Tara City and Artie Tripp then imagining yourself as a biker's moll was pretty goddamned funny. In fact it was about the funniest thing Susy could think of.

Saturday was a bad day in Tara City, though it possessed its consolations. Prominent among these was the fact that Mr Rosati let her have the afternoon off from the delicatessen. Things were at a low ebb in Rosati's. The fans, suspended so uncompromisingly from the ceiling that customers ducked instinctively as they approached the checkout counter, rasped lackadaisically. A monstrous *lasagna alla buoni* lay unregarded in the window. Two apprentice street hoodlums – baseball caps and wrapround sunglasses – sat drinking 7 Up by the door. Mr Rosati perched by the till, a thin, saturnine Italian with greying hair and a resentful expression. Occasionally he would raise his head and snap his eyes at the *lasagna alla buoni*, a glance that mingled the pride of the creator with the contempt of the entrepreneur . . . 'Peasants,' said Mr Rosati, not looking up as Susy, changed out of the waitress get-up into slacks and a ZZ Top T-shirt, lingered in front of the counter. 'Better put it back in the cooler,' Susy advised, 'sure as hell won't last in this heat. Hey, you got a

8

match?' She leaned over the bar, whipped a box out of the bulging shirtfront and lit a drooping Marlboro.

'For Chrissakes,' said Mr Rosati, a shade more amiably. 'Buy your own goddamn matches.'

Taking a rise out of Mr Rosati was an activity from which Susy derived inexhaustible pleasure. 'Hey,' she said. 'You wanna see me dance?' Mr Rosati shook his head. 'Guess I'll show you anyway.' Beneath his indifferent gaze she described an inelegant pirouette, hands raised above her head. 'Waddya think?' 'Shit-awful,' said Mr Rosati. 'Anyway,' Susy went on, 'you owe me twenty dollars,' 'Monday,' said Mr Rosati defensively, eye flickering for a moment over the two baseball caps and then returning to rest on the *lasagna alla buoni*, 'pay you Monday.' 'Well *fuck you*,' said Susy.

Outside in the street it was appallingly hot, the interior of Rosati's seen through the green plate-glass strangely aquarium-like. Susy stared back sullenly at the neon sign, experiencing a sudden stab of hate at whichever fate had ordained this monotonous thraldom. Much was made in Tara City of Mr Rosati's idiosyncrasies which were thought possibly to compensate for more obvious disadvantages. As Susy saw it, she had been taking shit from Mr Rosati for too long. About three years too long. Leaving Rosati's behind, a blur of green glass and reflected sunlight, she set off in the direction of the main street, past the accumulation of loping mongrels, fat woman in out-of-date frocks and gook kids that were just part of the scenery at this time of the day in this part of Tara fucking City.

In the foyer of Baxter's she flashed her membership card at the blonde receptionist. 'Swimming or solarium?' enquired the blonde receptionist. 'Swimming huh? Honey it's seventy-five degrees in there, the water I mean, so it won't make much difference.' Susy nodded, stood a while on the faded red carpet reading the noticeboard, her nose wrinkling slightly at the faint smell of chlorine. Baxter's gymnasium and solarium represented all that was lustrous and go-ahead in Tara City. When a local politician talked about civic amenities the chances were that he meant Baxter's. Prompted by a half-

9

hearted public wrangle about facilities, nearly stifled by a committee that had sat for eight years, its funding frozen or misappropriated by a succession of suspicious mayors, Baxter's had – rather to its own surprise – emerged into the glare of public scrutiny. Nominally it was a sporting club. Which was to say that you paid your fifteen dollars a month and could swim, work out, flap ping-pong balls across green baize to your heart's content. But the crop-headed youths and the gap-toothed girls who clustered round the bar drinking coke out of plastic cups didn't come to Baxter's to play table tennis. No. Baxter's was a social catwalk. If you were anyone in Tara City – that's to say if you weren't a nigger or a pauper or congenitally insane – you came to Baxter's to see and be seen. Susy had met Artie Tripp there, light years ago when the world was green and Artie Tripp's Pontiac the nearest thing Tara City possessed to Dennis Hopper's dirt-bike.

In the women's changing room Susy traded gossip with Lulu Sinde who was glumly cramming her breasts into a somewhat otiose bikini top. 'Jesus,' said Lulu Sinde, 'my tits are swelling up, I can feel it. Hey, waddya think?' Susy prodded the profferred torso without interest. 'I guess you have to accept that sort of thing.' 'I guess you do,' said Lulu Sinde, squatting her rump on a nearby radiator while Susy changed into her one-piece bathing costume. 'Christ. The *heat*. I nearly passed out out there on the sidewalk. But Paul said I ought to take some exercise: I guess he was right.' 'I guess so,' said Susy, wanting to say: For God's sake *shut up* about your fucking husband. Together they walked through the chlorinated footbath towards the swimming pool.

The pool was deserted, apart from a couple of kids torpedo-diving off the springboard at the far end: twenty yards of calm, sticky water. Susy swam a couple of lengths on her back, dived downwards to touch the palms of her hands on the bottom, rose to the surface. Lulu Sinde was wading resentfully through the shallows, hands clasped over her stomach. 'Hey,' she called, 'd'ya think it's showing?' Susy dived, swam three or four strokes under water to end up within clutching distance of one of Lulu Sinde's bolster

10

thighs. 'Hey,' said Lulu Sinde nervously, several hundred cubic feet of water away, 'be careful.' Susy relinquished the fistful of flesh, wondered about upending Lulu Sinde, thought better of it, contented herself with directing cascades of water in her direction. 'You be careful d'ya hear?' squeaked Lulu Sinde. Susy floated on her back, gazing skywards at the scalloped overhang of the ceiling, remembered long-ago excursions to Baxter's, a fourteen-year-old Lulu Sinde shrieking in terror because Artie Tripp had threatened to snatch off her bikini top, drinking coke with Lulu Sinde, short-skirted and expectant in the bar, Lulu Sinde saying she thought she was pregnant and was her father going to get mad or wasn't he? As the water swirled and receded above her head, the lineaments of the pool veering jaggedly in and out of focus, Susy contemplated a Lulu Sinde whose pregnancy was indubitable, legal and approved and felt a swift, sharp pang of regret. 'Paul said I ought to take care,' Lulu Sinde confided from the pool's edge and Susy twisted and dived like a versatile eel down into the murky water, wanting to get away from Lulu Sinde, from Lulu Sinde's foetus, but most of all from this disturbing, unheralded vision of the past which the two of them had managed to engender.

It was this image that remained afterwards in the changing room as Lulu Sinde conjectured that she might be about to throw up, persisted as she declined Lulu Sinde's offer of a drink ('just a coke you know') and strode out into the sunlight. Outside Baxter's the street was empty, apart from a Rican on a skateboard and, on the far side, a fat cadillac with white-wall tyres. For some reason, probably the mental activities of the past half-hour, this prompted Susy to think contemptuously of Artie Tripp. As she watched, the car's engine revved and in an elegant semi-circle it came to rest beside her. Rather to Susy's surprise Artie Tripp leaned out of the window.

'Hiya Suse,' he said. There was an odd jauntiness in his manner that Susy could not remember having seen before. 'Like the car?' 'Sure,' said Susy, 'sure I like it.' 'Well get in,' said Artie Tripp easily. He was wearing his blue shirt and a white BMX biker hat. There was a suitcase, Susy noticed, lying on the back seat. 'So where are we going?' asked Susy warily as they bowled down the High Street (Please God, am I dreaming? Artie Tripp in a cadillac?), one eye on Artie Tripp, the other on the clouds of dust that swarmed out on to the sidewalk. 'Out East,' said Artie Tripp. 'Out East?' 'Like I said,' he went on, 'I couldn't take that shit from the old man any more.' They flashed past Trapido's so that the nigger kids scrabbling in the dirt scuttled for safety, watched wide-eyed as they passed. 'You want to get out?' Artie Tripp asked. Susy shook her head. Afterwards she was only able to remember it as one would a scene from a film: the empty street, the girl turning to meet the car, and beyond (fire over the guns and *explode* . . .) the open road and Artie Tripp, his enormous forearms resting on the steering wheel, beside her.

Subsequently, if you had asked Susy to recall the details of what passed in the ensuing weeks (and Mom at least made the effort), they would have existed merely as single, isolated images: sharply focused snaps pulled at random from an interminable roll of film: standing on the hills above Baton Rouge watching the Mississippi stream away towards the Gulf; an open-air concert at Jefferson where they walked airily through the fringes of the crowd as the evening sky turned the colour of blue velvet; driving through Alabama at night with Artie Tripp continually falling asleep at the wheel and having to be nudged awake, until in the haggard light of dawn they hit Montgomery and crashed out in the back seat of the car in the middle of a municipal car-park.

Crackling, moving pictures: with soundtrack. Susy saying *freedom is the road*, Springsteen singing 'Born To Run' out of the car radio above the din of the freeway, Artie Tripp getting mad with a bullet-headed Arkansas straw-chewer who had given Susy the eye in Little Rock, Susy in a diner call-box outside of Nashville saying to Mom that honestly it was OK honestly it was and Mom not saying anything at all and finally hanging up and going out to be comforted by Artie Tripp who put his arms round her and hugged her while families in Hawaiian shirts and sunglasses looked on with prurient interest.

And always the road – the wide, eight-lane Missouri highways, winding mountain motorways that took them out of Colorado and into the wheatfields beyond, tiny Godforsaken dirt tracks that snaked along parallel to the freeway and you could travel for hours without sighting another vehicle – going on for ever, south and east to the Ocean.

So where did they go in these weeks of late summer and early fall? Eastwards of course. 'So what's so fuckin' great about California?' Artie Tripp had demanded. Through Cheyenne and across the South Platte towards Kansas. Late August found them in Oklahoma, cruising on towards the Ozark mountains, the view from the cadillac window a bewildering mixture of flat fields and undulating hills, of movement and inanition, of things going on and things not happening at all. At Clarkesville they fell in with a hippy convoy heading north towards the Lakes where there was supposed to be a free festival in the spring. Susy had wanted to go with them, finding in the buckskin-clad babies, the karma-chewing docility, something that transcended simple curiosity, but Artie Tripp dissuaded her. They left the hippy camp one morning in September, waved on by a regretful crowd of long-haired children. A week later they were in New Orleans, holed up in a cheap motel while they went on daytrips to Breton Bay and Grand Lake. The day they went to Grand Lake it rained – the first time it had rained since Tara City – and Susy stood looking at the sky in disbelief.

Throughout these days of ceaseless travelling, this frenetic dash from the northwestern corner to the southeastern extremity of this great nation of theirs, the question of motive remained curiously unresolved. Two weeks, three weeks into the journey Susy could not have told you for what purpose the grey cadillac sped eastwards through field and town and mountain, could not have told you at dawn where they would fetch up at dusk. Artie Tripp remained strangely taciturn. 'Reckon on making Tulsa this evening,' he would remark as they unfurled stiff limbs from about each other in

13

the grey, early-morning light, the prelude to long, abstracted silences and the consultation of road maps. It did not occur to him as necessary to explain the provenance of the cadillac, just as it did not occur to him to reveal its ultimate destination. Sometimes he talked about getting a job in the East, 'New York, Chicago, someplace – I got references.' At night Susy, watching the intense, white body purposefully gyrating above her, occasionally wondered if he were a little mad, wondered whether nine years on the gas station forecourt had done something weird and irrevocable to Artie Tripp's (admittedly negligible) mind. But then the sixteen-year-old Artie Tripp had begun to recede from vision, so much so that Susy often found it safer to pretend that he had never really existed.

From the outset Susy had always incubated a sneaking suspicion that it wouldn't last. They started off staying in halfway decent hotels, whose receptionists eyed the 'Mr and Mrs Arthur Tripp' that Artie signed with a flourish in the visitors' book with tolerant disdain, progressed to roadside motels full of teenagers balling their girlfriends and glassy-eyed English tourists (the pound was having a bad time against the dollar that summer). Late September found them holed up in grubby rooms above freeway diners where the hum of car engines could be heard outside the window until dawn. Artie Tripp said nothing about this decline in the quality of their accommodation. It could not be that he was running out of cash. The twenty dollar bills, Susy noted, still flicked across the station forecourt when they stopped for gas. Oddly, or perhaps predictably, it was only at gas stations that Artie Tripp became talkative. 'Look at the dumb bastard,' he would grin, as the garage hand lurched towards the car, 'Well he can kiss *my* ass goodbye.'

October, as they turned northwards and New York became not just a speculative talking-point but a possibility, a real-live name up there on the distance boards, the weather broke. Baltimore remained in Susy's mind as a confused impression of wet concrete and endless avenues of dripping trees. In Baltimore they had an argument, a grinding night-long

14

argument at the conclusion of which Artie Tripp told her how he had come by the money and the cadillac. 'All of it?' questioned Susy incredulously. 'You mean to say?' 'Uh huh' said Artie Tripp proudly. 'A week's takings outta the till. What the fuck? He owed it me.' 'Christ,' said Susy, thinking of Peter Fonda and Dennis Hopper, 'some fuckin' wild man you turned out to be.' 'I got a hundred dollars left,' said Artie Tripp nervously. 'It'll last till the end of the month.' His hair, which was wet and had not been barbered since leaving Tara City, hung limply down either side of his face. 'You can give me twenty dollars to see me home,' said Susy, 'to see me home, because this is where I quit.' Though it was the last thing she expected Artie Tripp handed it over without a murmur. Susy checked out of the hotel at first light, trudged in tears through the moist streets to find a Greyhound bus depot. Although it had been possible to predict that it wouldn't last and that Artie Tripp wouldn't last, nothing else in her whole twenty-four and a half years had ever made her feel this sad.

Tara City, glimpsed through the rain-streaked window of a Greyhound bus early one leaden Sunday morning, did not seem outwardly to have changed. Inwardly Susy, checking off the features of the main street against the mental kaleido-scope of the last two months, found it had shrunk: that Trapido's, display-case for so much local éclat, was no more than a glorified dime store, that Baxter's – outside whose porch it now seemed impossible that Artie Tripp had ever lingered – was no more than a second-rate sports club. Walking into the apartment Susy found Mom and Larry Vosper sitting together on the sofa, a spectacle so unusual as to defer more obvious questions and explanations. 'So what's he doing here?' Susy enquired, examining Larry Vosper's brilliantined hair and stacked boots. 'We're getting married next month,' said Mom. 'Anyhow,' he's got a *right* to be here.' 'Susy baby,' said Larry Vosper, Adam's Apple working up and down his throat like a tomahawk. 'Eat shit,' said Susy. For the rest of the day she refused to speak either to

15

Mom or to Larry Vosper. It was not, when you thought about it, a particularly auspicious homecoming.

In Rosati's delicatessen the warm reek of overcooked spaghetti rose impenitently to the ceiling. 'Shit,' said Mr Rosati quietly as Susy slammed a plate down on an adjacent table, 'that ain't no way to serve an order.' 'You wanna see me dance?' said Susy, twitching her ass at him. Mr Rosati shook his head. It was curious, Susy reflected, considering the past week, the way in which things changed, how, bolstered by external camouflage, inner mechanisms simply ground to a halt. Mr Rosati was an altered man, his window bereft of exotic pasta, himself resigned to dispensing pizza to undiscriminating gooks. There had, it transpired, in Susy's absence been a regrettable incident in which Mr Rosati, disgusted by public indifference to a stupendous *canneloni alla Campagnola* had pushed a customer's face into a plate of lasagna and been bound over to keep the peace. Susy thrust her head close up to the till. 'Hey,' she told him, testing this newfound good nature, 'you owe me twenty dollars, remember?' 'For Chrissakes I remember,' said Mr Rosati. Just as there had been other changes, small yet significant, to the complexion of Rosati's delicatessen, so other aspects of the known world had not escaped alteration. Lulu Sinde, unable to contemplate the rigours of parturition, had had an abortion. Aunt Berkmann, jilted by her lover in favour of a Swedish hotel receptionist had returned from Europe ('and serve her dam' right' in Mom's opinion). Susy felt that in some way her return was a small example of the past fighting back in the face of present assaults, that while accepted matter-of-factly it possessed deeper implications. 'About fuckin' time,' Mr Rosati had said, but there had been a painful gleam of recognition in his eye. 'Shift your ass over there,' he shouted as Susy, stirred from rapt contemplation, heaved a plate crosstable into the midriff of a waiting diner. Obscurely the thought comforted her. Outside the rain rattled on the windows. 'OK. OK,' Mr Rosati was saying. Susy thought for the last time of Artie Tripp, framed in the doorway of

Baxter's, the gleaming Iowa cornfields, before turning to consider the more pressing details of Mom's wedding suit, the expression on her face half fretful resignation, half dreamy content.

DREAMS OF LEAVING

THE WALLS OF the studio had been whitewashed a fortnight ago and the raw scent of ammonia still hung in the air. Fuchs unscrewed the cap of the zoom lens and snapped a fresh reel of film into place. Mr Van Oss said: 'OK. So give us the fuckin' works, whydoncha.'

Someone switched on the arc lamp, drenched the room in pale-white light. 'Fuck those asshole bulbs,' said Mr Van Oss. Somewhere in the background a fan began to rasp. The two girls, one black, one white, who had spent the last five minutes shivering behind the canvas screen, removed their robes and began listlessly to belabour each other's rumps with dull, heavy slaps. The smoke from Mr Van Oss's cigarette wreathed their breasts, hung in dense clouds over the camera. Fuchs tried to shoo it away with his hand.

Fuchs had seen it all. Guys and girls. Guys and guys. Girls and dogs. Brawny dykes romping in thigh-high bracken. Banana shots. Fladge. He had graduated from taking twenty-dollars-a-reel pictures for the kind of magazines Mr Van Oss thought 'there ought to be a fuckin' law against' to a staff job on a Brooklyn glossy called *Cocksure* and thence to Mr Van Oss. 'And you can cut out that back-street crap,' Mr Van Oss had told him, when he had suggested a few variations on the usual display of Technicolor pudibunda. 'Jeez, do you think I'm some kind of fuckin' pervert? That stuff with cripples, it's depraved, it's for sickos. What sells this magazine is *class*.'

Fuchs snapped a few pictures. The white girl, having finished chastising her partner, allowed her breasts to be fondled while emitting gusty sighs. The bodies clinched,

18

broke apart, came together again. 'OK, OK,' said Mr Van Oss impatiently. 'OK. So you had the hors d'oeuvre. So make with the fuckin' main course.'

Fuchs sometimes wondered why he took this sort of picture for this sort of magazine. For Mr Van Oss was not classy. The studios up at Staten Island or on the Bronx were classy, where the models arrived in Bentleys, had stockbroker boyfriends and cooled you out if you made a pass at them. Moreover, Fuchs found the sight of so much female flesh, so freely available, strangely unnerving. Fuchs had tried telling this to Ellen. Ellen had dismissed this as 'just what a porno photographer would say'.

Fuchs tried to stifle the yawn of boredom that rose in his throat. Before him the two girls began to lick each other's goose-pimples. 'Yeah, OK,' said Mr Van Oss. The white girl, spreadeagled like a starfish, writhed in simulated ecstasy. Her nipples, Fuchs reflected, looked like coathooks. He remembered the conversation he had had the previous night with Ellen, at the end of which Ellen had announced her intention of leaving 'this whole motherfucking east-coast asylum' and by implication Fuchs as well. This conversation had been calculated to impress Fuchs with a sense of his own insignificance. Oddly, it had left him almost jubilant. He had felt so good, he remembered, he could have reached out and pummelled the sky.

The girls were by now amusing themselves with a curved, ebony dildo. Fuchs trained his camera on the black girl's hand as it caressed, without interest, her partner's mottled thigh. 'Fuck it,' said Mr Van Oss. 'Cut.' The girls disengaged, looked at him sheepishly. 'Waste my fuckin' time, whydon-cha,' said Mr Van Oss bitterly. He looked suddenly woebegone. 'OK. Same time tomorrow.' There were, Fuchs reflected, good days and bad days. This had been a bad day.

Sometimes Fuchs thought (thinking it now as he wandered back to his apartment on the fringes of Harlem, where giant spades surveyed you coolly from street corners) his problems were a result of his name. Checkout assistants sniggered when he handed them his credit cards. Postmen smirked as they delivered his mail. For a time he tried to get people to pronounce it 'Fookes' or even 'Futch', had even gone so far as to ask Mr Van Oss to call him Ralph, but Mr Van Oss had just said, 'Aw, fuckit Fuchs, whydoncha.' Fuchs gathered that the amusement Mr Van Oss derived from his name was one of the principal reasons for Fuchs's employment. He had tried explaining this to Ellen one night, after the third successive occasion on which he had failed to achieve an erection. 'Jesus, why are you so hung up?' Ellen had said and Fuchs had wanted to reply 'Because I take dirty pictures for a living. Because my name is Ralph Waldo Fuchs. Fair enough, wouldn't you say?' Instead he had not said anything. 'Maybe,' Ellen had suggested unkindly, as a reminder of past infidelities, 'maybe you should try making it with one of the broads at the studio.'

But Fuchs had long ago given up attempting to score with the models. You could never be sure of their predilections. Fuchs remembered how a casual invitation from a Swedish girl and her friend had led to some very unpleasant tripartite goings-on (no thank you). Half of them wanted you to beat them up, and the other half wanted you to let them beat you up. Fuchs remembered. He remembered them all, the one who had wanted him to dress up in feathers, the one who had produced a cache of wooden phalli. Fuchs couldn't take it any more. He remembered especially a girl called Rosa Russo, Mr Van Oss's 'Lay of the Month' in three successive issues who, it transpired, had never laid anyone in her life. 'So Jesus why didn't you tell me?' Fuchs had demanded. 'You never asked,' Rosa Russo had said after she had smacked him across the face. And Rosa Russo had been a speed-freak into the bargain. There were some girls, Fuchs thought, who were just not cut out for the modelling business.

'OK Fuchs,' said Mr Van Oss the next morning. 'So I want three reels of fuckin' A-Grade kiss-my-butt film.' It was so cold in the studio that Pedro, the Rican who did the lighting, had brought in a twin-bar electric heater which he placed in the corner with an injunction to Fuchs to 'keep y'fuckin' hands off it turdass'. Fuchs's breath rose to the ceiling in mushroom clouds. They were filming a short sequence based on 'a mutha of an idea' that had come to Mr Van Oss the previous evening, to be called 'Women in Uniform'. Two brunettes dressed in GI battle fatigues prodded each other experimentally with dummy sten-guns, sat astride them, finally (having removed the battle fatigues) clasped the barrels between their breasts. Fuchs bobbed between them, sinking to his knees as the girls slipped into a prolonged horizontal clinch. 'Fuck me,' said Mr Van Oss, 'if this doesn't give Joe Public one hell of a horn.'

Fuchs found himself, as he found himself most mornings, mentally checking off the reasons why he hated Ellen. Because she wore vast maternity smocks while remaining adamantly unpregnant. Because she lay in the bath like a great white whale reading Gurdjieff. Because she had been abroad. Because she expressed dissatisfaction at the ideological shortcomings of Fuchs's job. Because Fuchs couldn't fuck her enough.

Fuchs slammed a new reel of film into the camera, wondered about using a filter (Mr Van Oss like those crepuscular, fumbling in the shadows shots) and decided against it. Five shots into the second reel Mr Van Oss clapped his hands together with the suddenness of a cap-pistol. 'OK. Cut,' said Mr Van Oss wearily. 'Look, we have to rethink this thing.' The girls stood around, hands on hips, while he rifled through a back number of *Penthouse* for exact situational details (most of the major magazines found themselves being ripped off in this way sooner or later). Fuchs, unlit Marlboro scooped under his lower lip, asked Pedro if he had a match. 'Don't smoke, asshole,' said Pedro amiably. 'You forgot, huh?' Fuchs watched the back of Mr Van Oss's neck as he bent over the glistening pages. It reminded him of red tyre-rubber.

Fuchs collected travel brochures, some of the West Coast and the Rockies (Fuchs had never been further west than Cincinatti) but mostly of England. Misty, early-morning shots of the Cotswolds. The Norfolk Broads (Hell, Fuchs thought, what a title for a picture spread). His favourite brochure had on the cover a picture of St Paul's Cathedral looming up behind the words 'London in July'. Fuchs had a feeling that he wanted to see London. He had a vision of himself drinking beer in some quaint English pub, checking out (from a purely professional angle) Soho. Mr Van Oss was properly dismissive of English competition. 'Amateur crap,' he had been heard to say. 'Like some photographer gets his girlfriend to wave her fanny about and they call it "Vixens at Play" or something.' Fuchs had often wondered about the price of an air ticket. Fuchs had been wondering about the price of an air ticket since Watergate.

'OK Fuchs, let's hit it,' said Mr Van Oss. Pedro flicked a few switches, bathed the stage in lurid, blood-red light. ('Yeah,' said Mr Van Oss, 'tasteful.') The girls, naked except for peaked caps and buckle belts, began to march up and down. A dummy machine-gun was brought out and fingered. Fuchs monitored the arched backs, hovered anxiously as one of the girls straddled the barrel. 'Yeah, yeah,' said Mr Van Oss as if he were singing the chorus to a Beatles number. Outside the rain spattered on the window in translucent, coin-sized blobs. Fuchs bent his head over the tapering cylinder of the zoom lens.

Fuchs tended his collection of brochures and posters better than most people did their pets. His bedroom, in fact, was a sort of shrine to the places he had never been to. It was one of Ellen's favourite apophthegms that you couldn't see the wallpaper for pictures of exotic camouflage – gauchos busting steers, llamas teetering on Nepalese mountain passes. There was a line of squat, plastic-backed box-files, divided up by continent, running along the top shelf of one bookcase and a map of the world (a 'political' map borrowed from one of Ellen's friends so that the NATO alliance countries were shaded electric-blue and places like Ghana had per-capita income statistics printed alongside) bluetacked to the door. Fuchs spent a lot of time in there, slicing pictures out of the

National Geographic with a Stanley knife, reading illustrated travel books, bringing the box-file card index up to date. It was a good feeling, this having the world at your fingertips. Hell, Fuchs thought, it was like being a Pentagon hawk, the globe staked out in front of you, lacking only the ability to punch a few buttons and send that map on the wall shrieking up in flames.

Mr Van Oss, Fuchs realised, was losing his grip. For every reel of film shot by Fuchs that ended up on the page, underwritten with prurient captions, approximately five went into the garbage can. This fundamentally stemmed from Mr Van Oss's inability to handle temperamental models. There had been the time when the famous Cindy Lu Win, imported at great expense from a studio on the Bronx, had concluded one session by asking him who did he think he was, fuckin' Van Gogh or something? (Miss Lu Win had further disgraced herself by telling Fuchs 'that goes for you too, pervert'). This meant that the studio was having to rely on inferior models, high-school girls who thought that all you had to do was take your clothes off and pout. Hence Mr Van Oss's gloom, hence it was hinted falling sales – not, Fuchs thought, that the readership had any particular discrimination – hence, more importantly, a cut in Fuchs's salary. Hence too a series of late-night conversations between Fuchs and Mr Van Oss in various down-town bars. Mr Van Oss unquestionably needed a confidant. 'It's like this, Fuchs,' Mr Van Oss had said morosely, 'I get these ideas, you can't expect an ordinary model to handle them at first. That's why we're wasting so much film. Hell, that's art, I suppose. If we were one of those get-that-camera-halfway-up-her-ass studios I wouldn't mind.' Gradually the confidences became personal rather than professional and Fuchs had heard the tale of Mr Van Oss's first wife whom he had married fresh out of high school ('Hell, we were just kids') and whose centrefold appearance in *Up Front* had made Mr Van Oss's reputation. Fuchs sympathised. In fact, Fuchs was prepared to sympathise almost indefinitely. He enjoyed Mr Van Oss's reminiscences of his picturesque past, the stationing in the South China Sea during 'Nam, the hitching across Europe. Fuchs had asked Mr Van Oss what he thought of England and Mr Van Oss had looked at him solemnly and said 'It is a goddamned shithole, Fuchs' and Fuchs had nodded, inwardly disagreeing. The drinking sessions snowballed. Afterwards Fuchs went back to his apartment light-headed with alcohol, listened to Ellen extrapolating her horoscope, smoked dope, lay on his back trying to bite the head off the twisting darkness.

One day Mr Van Oss said, 'Hell, Fuchs, if the studio goes I'll see you're all right.' It was true that twenty minutes and another aborted photo session later Mr Van Oss had called him a 'goddamned shit-stabbing motherfucker' but on the strength of this Fuchs went to his favourite travel agent's on 53rd and treated himself to an unusually lavish selection of brochures.

There remained the business of telling Ellen. 'So you want to go to England?' said Ellen incredulously, eyes darting like fish behind her aquarium spectacles and then, when she realised what Fuchs was getting at, 'So you want to go to England without me?' 'Sure,' said Fuchs, trying to sound reasonable, 'sure, I want to go to England without you.' 'Fine,' said Ellen, 'if that's the way you want it.' Fuchs gazed out of the window at the pale, early-evening light, suddenly hating America so much that he wanted to smother it. Three hours later he discovered Ellen lying in the bath, nervously contemplating the two-inch razor blade with which she had halfheartedly nicked herself. 'Oh Ralph,' she said mistily, 'oh Ralph, you shouldn't have said that. You just shouldn't have.' Fuchs called an ambulance, stood in the kitchen thinking of the early times with Ellen, concerts, Zappa and the Mothers at the Filmore East in the early seventies, the day Carter got the Democratic nomination and Ellen saying that she always preferred Kennedy and anyway where was he on women's rights. It all seemed a very long time ago.

In the studio the air was already a smoky blue, though it was

24

barely eleven o'clock in the morning. Fuchs lounged by the electric heater. Pedro said in an amphetamine monotone: 'Yeah, I been to Cal, man, Frisco, but that whole West Coast scene is dead.' Two kimono-clad strawberry blondes sat in the corner under the arc-light, one painting her nails, the other reading a paperback. Mr Van Oss said suddenly. 'Yeah I got it' to no one in particular. A light bulb fizzed and then went dead. Fuchs thought of Ellen staked out on the hospital bed in Central, surrounded by levees of friends, each of whom regarded Fuchs with thin contempt. 'Yeah,' said Pedro. 'The surf out there. Coming through the breakers, man . . . it's like fucking.'

Mr Van Oss clapped his hands. 'OK,' he said. 'I got it.' He began to run his fingers through his sandy, greaseball hair, capered crazily in the middle of the floor. 'Yeah, this centrefold, no make it a whole fuckin' series (Fuchs get off your ass and grab that camera).' The room lurched into activity. Fuchs wearily manhandled a tripod. Mr Van Oss went on: 'Right. We call it "Dreams of Leaving" see. This chick, her boyfriend's away and she's lonely.' He began to pace up and down, punched the empty air. 'So she looks at his photograph, right – first frame – then she starts packin' suitcases: close-ups. Oh Fuchs – I want that camera so near you can count the goddamned stitches on her appendix scar!'

Fuchs felt himself sweating, yanked his tie so the knot hung low on his neck. Tonight he thought, tonight he would collect Ellen from the hospital, hell, maybe even fuck her for old times' sake. He felt good. He felt like superman. 'Shit,' said Mr Van Oss, suddenly deflated. 'Gonna take us a day to get the props. Hell though, we can wait. This one's gonna be a mutha.' But Fuchs, who had run his eye over the morning's mail, whistling shrewdly through his teeth over the two biggest bills, hoped that it wasn't going to be a mutha, hoped, in fact, that it was going to be absolute crap.

Fuchs went home that night to find Ellen, her left wrist still bandaged, hunched rheumy-eyed over a bottle of Bourbon. She appeared not to notice him. Fuchs tiptoed past, spun on his heel, snaked into the bedroom, stopped dead. The walls gleamed at him palely. Cascades of torn paper arched over his feet, undulated as he moved. A gawky pile of ransacked, split-open box-files lurched against the bed. Fuchs twitched the coverlet, discovered beneath it the greater part of the world, shredded and curling at the edges, Washington DC and Surinam lodged in uneasy juxtaposition. From the kitchen came the sound of keening. Fuchs dragged himself into the bed, fully clothed, and sobbed himself to sleep.

'Sheeit. Wow!' said Mr Van Oss the next morning. 'Ten minutes OK. Then we shoot.' Fuchs watched, resentfully, the assemblage of props, a chintz sofa, a framed photograph, a set of sleek leather suitcases and handgrips. Too many studios, Mr Van Oss explained, scrimped on the accessories budget. Fuchs, whose career had begun when the only accessory you needed was a bed, could believe it. Doors opened and slammed shut. Pedro ripped the plastic seal off a batch of 100-watt bulbs, plaited hanks of Rapunzel-hair fuse-wire. 'OK,' said Mr Van Oss. 'Hit it.' One of the strawberry blondes appeared on the stage dressed in a lacy if exiguous peignoir, clutched the framed photograph, after first holding it up to the camera for inspection, to her breast. Fuchs took a deep breath, the thoughts piling up in his head like windfall apples, took some pictures, obsessed by the memory of the previous night's reconciliation. 'Oh Ralph, lay it on me,' Ellen had sobbed and Fuchs had laid it on her strenuously yet with diffidence, as if he had been fucking an armadillo. The fan rasped. Pedro, unfurling a copy of the NYT said, 'Mandate my ass.' Mr Van Oss said, 'OK. Great.' On the stage the other strawberry blonde draped herself over an empty suitcase, arched a finger over the downy lining. Mr Van Oss said, 'Man, this is one way to pay the fuckin' bills whydoncha.' Fuchs remembered the puzzled look on Rosa Russo's face as he had backed away, thought of all the places he would never see, realised derisively how little he cared, and glared like a malignant sibyl down the aperture of the zoom lens, his eyes smouldering like dying suns.

SUMMER PEOPLE

THE SUMMER PEOPLE began arriving in May. They came in small, rickety trains on the branch line from Cromer, in smoking cars, or were disgorged from charabancs and coaches in the marketplace. From his vantage point at an upstairs window Julian watched them toil to the crest of the hill, where the rows of holiday cottages began: framed by his moving hand they re-emerged as perspiring, red-faced men awkwardly manhandling cases, children in the skimpy clothing their parents had thought suitable for a Norfolk summer, frozen by the wind. There was a pattern to their migrations. May brought young, childless couples who loitered hand-in-hand along the front or turned over the bric-à-brac in the sixpenny arcade. In July came holidaying families who foraged over the rock-pools for crabs and crayfish; in late August a few pensioners who drowsed in the end-of-season sun. By September the town had reverted to its antique state: rain falling over the pebble-dash houses, sending the high street shoppers scurrying for cover beneath awnings or into the porch of St Peter's Church. In the distance cloud hung over the long grey spar of the sea.

As the town's second-largest newsagent-cum-stationer, Mr Holroyd could not afford to despise the Summer People, but he allowed himself sardonic remarks over their choice of newspaper – which, for example, preferred the *Guardian* to *The Times* or the *Daily Telegraph*, or declined to place sixpences in the box held up by the imploring blind boy. Once, in distant days, a man had requested the *Morning Star*. Mr Holroyd had pushed it with his own hands through the narrow holiday-home letterbox, so great was his disgust. The Summer People irked Mr Holroyd. He disliked their grainy Midlands accents, the too-easily earned five-pound notes picked up in the engineering shops of Wolverhampton and Dudley which they flicked over the counter in exchange for cigarettes and ice-cream, and he suspected them of sexual irregularity, or what passed for sexual irregularity in Sheringham in the 1960s. But he made an exception of Miss Hoare, who arrived in the town halfway through July, rented an expensive property on the cliff and spent fifty shillings on sketching pads on her first visit to the shop.

'A very personable woman,' he informed the silent breakfast table audience of wife and son. 'She was staying at the Saracen's Head, but apparently the light wasn't what she wanted.'

The Saracen's Head was the most expensive hotel in Sheringham. The town's masonic lodge met in its back-parlour on alternate Thursdays. Mr and Mrs Holroyd occasionally took afternoon tea there in a rather ostentatious way on winter Saturdays.

Julian first caught sight of Miss Hoare two days later in the shop, where she was making a fuss about cartridge paper. She was a large, fat but undoubtedly stylish woman in early middle age, her clothes of a kind not generally seen in Sheringham: a billowing dirndl skirt, white blouse patterned with sunflowers, wide-brimmed Panama hat. Stepping suddenly from the street into the cool interior, Julian heard her say: 'Of course the A4 is no good at all. Would it be possible to get the A3 do you think?' Unexpectedly, Julian heard his mother agreeing to this request: similar demands, made by sun-cured old men for obscure angling magazines, had not been so kindly received. 'This is Julian,' she said in a slightly subdued way, as he moved further into the shop towards the counter. Miss Hoare gave him a frank, appraising stare of the kind that old farmers at the County Show bestowed on horses, 'Oh yes,' she said. 'You're the young man who's so keen on art,' and Julian smiled wretchedly, not wanting his private experiments with watercolours and charcoal to be known to a pale-faced woman of forty with cropped hair and scarlet lipstick. 'I'll call again then, about the paper,' Miss Hoare said briskly to his mother, gathering up a little pile of purchases that included three packets of Park Drive cigarettes and a sophisticated women's magazine in which Mrs Holroyd made occasional scandalised forays.

When she had gone, mother and son sat on the low stools behind the counter in a space made smaller by her absence, as motes of dust danced in the sunlight of the open door and shadow fell over the rows of shrimping nets and water pistols. Eventually the silence was broken by a gang of children squabbling over the ice-cream chiller. 'I expect we can get the cartridge paper from Norwich,' Mrs Holroyd said vaguely. 'She needs it for her work, you see . . .' Mrs Holroyd added as an afterthought. 'That lipstick . . .'

It was a hot summer that year. Julian drew salmon-skinned children who romped on the worm-casted sand beneath the pier, or shrieked at the Punch and Judy. Old fat women swimming sedately like porpoises in the shallows. Mrs Holroyd chided him affectionately, small things and large things mixed: the condition of his room, the length of his hair, his self-absorption. Impending O-level results, she implied, were no excuse for sequestration. In the end he embarked on long, futile cycle rides out along the North Norfolk flat, towards Wells and Blakeney. These, too, had their Summer People: well-groomed schoolgirls playing tennis on windswept courts overlooking the sea; civil young men in boats. Miss Hoare turned up frequently on these excursions: seated, sketch pad on knee, in rock crannies on the cliff path or arranging her easel on the beach. Occasionally she smiled or waved a hand from which cigarette smoke trickled slowly into the dense air. Once Julian found the easel unattended halfway up the stone escarpment flanking the putting course. He had time to register an enticing impressionist's vista of frothing waves and shipwrecked mariners before the sound of footsteps from below drove him away.

Each night at supper Mr Holroyd uncovered the little cache of lore which the day's traffic had afforded him. 'I asked about that Miss Hoare. At the Saracen's Head.' They ate Cromer crabs, shrimps, salad, dyspeptic hunks of white bread. Mr Holroyd was an advocate of 'plain English food': a birthday dinner had once been ruined by the intrusion of alien sauces. 'Apparently she's made quite a name for herself. Exhibitions and so on. At any rate she seems to make a living out of it.' Julian bent his head at the implied rebuke, which was, he knew, intended to emphasise the distance between an Art sanctified by commerce and feckless bohemian daydreaming. Later that evening Mrs Holroyd sought him out in a bedroom lined with neatly-executed Airfix kits and pictures of the England World Cup squad. 'You mustn't mind your dad,' she said. 'He just wants what's best for you.' The letter from Julian's headmaster, pressing the claims of the sixth-form science course and stating the necessity of a speedy decision, lay on the sill next to the *Collected Drawings of Aubrey Beardsley*, which Mr Holroyd had looked through with tolerant disdain. 'And you could always keep up your drawing,' Mrs Holroyd suggested timorously, 'as a kind of *hobby* . . .'

Once, the summer before, Julian had disappeared on his bicycle for an entire day, returning only at dusk, an hour after Mr Holroyd had telephoned the police. 'Why did you do it?' his father had asked, shocked and puzzled out of his evening routine of checking the stock cupboard and bundling up unsold copies of the *Daily Mirror*. 'I did it to get away from you,' Julian had answered, which was honest but scarcely sensible. Memories of this incident still rankled.

The next evening his father said unexpectedly: 'I saw that Miss Hoare the other day.' 'Yes?' 'A very interesting woman, that. Who was it she was telling me about? Some artist chap or other that she knew . . . Anyway, the upshot of it was that she wondered if you'd like some help with your drawing.' 'Perhaps,' Julian heard himself saying, 'she could have asked me herself.' But Mr Holroyd was absorbed in the correspondence columns of the *Cromer Mercury*. 'I don't think there's any call for that kind of remark,' he said absently.

Julian had little experience of women in early middle

30

age, let alone artistic ones. Mrs Arkwright, the school's art department, specialised in Norfolk landscapes populated by vast, Stubbsian horses. A spinster friend of his mother's routinely dispensed faded, self-painted watercolours as Christmas presents. Miss Hoare, etching in the corners of her tumultuous seascapes, seemed infinitely removed from these pale exemplars. She painted putting courses filled with giant golfers waving their irons like weapons, a vortex of wind, debris and flailing black birds descending on the spire of St Peter's church. 'You can be honest with me,' she told Julian. 'Do you like them?' 'I don't *dis*like them' Julian replied truthfully. 'But in the sea picture you've put the gulls in the wrong place. You see, they always alight on the highest point.' Miss Hoare was delighted. 'A very good answer,' she said. 'If you'd said you liked them, I wouldn't have believed you.'

Conscious of their roles as native and interloper, they strolled around the town in search of vantage points: the gallery of the church, the high ground to the north, the tiny station with its dozing porter. 'Why Sheringham?' Julian asked at one point. 'I mean . . .' He stopped for a second, crimson-faced. 'I thought artists went to the South of France, places like that.' 'So they do,' Miss Hoare said judiciously. 'But my dear, I've had enough of Menton and Nice to last me a lifetime. Full of hopeless Englishmen thinking they're Pierre Loti.' Reaching the front again, they turned into the high street. Here the characteristic high summer smells hung in the air: fried fish, candyfloss, oil, each mixed with the pervasive tang of salt. 'Do you suppose,' Miss Hoare wondered, 'there is anywhere we could get a drink? A proper drink, that is.' 'Not a chance,' Julian told her cheerfully. 'Everyone knows I've only just turned sixteen. If I went into a pub and ordered a half of cider they'd probably telephone my father.' 'Oh well, if *that*'s the difficulty,' said Miss Hoare. At the bar of the Saracen's Head she loomed brazenly above a knot of Summer People in khaki shorts and sunhats and announced: 'Two glasses of white wine. And this young man is my nephew.' Later, as they sat in an alcove looking out over the humped keels of upended crab boats, she said: 'Will it matter? Saying you're my nephew, I mean.' 'I shouldn't think my father will be very pleased.' 'Will he find out?' 'Oh, I expect someone will tell him,' Julian told her, elated by the wine and not caring very much. 'They usually do.'

August came, with flaring skies. An old man had a heart attack on the beach, and an air-sea rescue helicopter came to ferry him away. The O-level results were due in a week. 'Exams,' Miss Hoare pronounced, 'are the curse of the educated classes.' They were in the Saracen's Head again, whose staff, curiously, had yet to complain to Mr Holroyd. 'Are you still set on Art?' She enunciated it as one would the name of a favourite relative or a honeymoon destination. 'I don't know,' Julian wondered, realising that for all his disparagement of mathematics, physics, chemistry and the dreary people who taught them, he really did not know. 'There's an art school at Norwich,' he explained. 'Or even at Lowestoft. And then . . .' Miss Hoare beamed back at him. Reckoning up the number of glasses of white wine she had consumed, Julian calculated it at six or perhaps seven. 'You must lend me those sketchbooks of yours,' she said. 'Let me look at them and see what can be done. It may take a day or so because I've got a friend arriving, but then I'll have a look and we'll see what can be done.' And Julian, glimpsing his face suddenly in the glass of the window, felt the kind of wild excitement he had once experienced as a child watching the Lancaster bombers veer inland from the sea towards the RAF stations of the Norfolk plain.

Mr Castleton, Miss Hoare's friend, was a thin, red-haired man in an outsize purple blazer and a cravat, who made himself unpopular in the town within half-an-hour of his arrival by parking his car across a narrow street entrance and then remonstrating with the people who tried to remove it. Subsequently he antagonised Mr Holroyd by asking for a copy of *Health and Efficiency*. 'I told him,' Mr Holroyd reported testily, 'that if he wanted pornography he could go to Cromer for it.' He and Miss Hoare dined noisily at the Saracen's Head and were seen picnicking on the cliff. Once, passing them in the crowded market square, Julian was certain that they saw him, but the wave went unacknowledged. No word came about the sketchbooks.

The O-level results arrived on a grey Saturday morning. Julian felt his hand tremble a little as he turned over the brown, rectangular envelope he remembered addressing to himself six weeks before. He need not have worried. 'An excellent set of results,' Mr Holroyd crowed. 'And especially in Science. I must confess I'm gratified.' With some ceremony he presented Julian with a creased ten-shilling note. Knocking at the door of Miss Hoare's cottage, an hour later, Julian realised that he had still made no decision, that the tangle of contending paths still ran away before him. Some time later the door was opened, with bad grace, by Mr Castleton. He wore a pair of ancient, buttonless pyjamas and was smoking a cigarette. Mr Castleton examined Julian without interest. 'It's your artist friend,' he said over his shoulder. Back in the belly of the house came the noise of vague, indeterminate movement. 'She's sozzled,' Mr Castleton said ruthlessly. 'Pissed. You understand what I mean? One over the eight. Here. Better take these while you're here.' Stooping to retrieve the sketchbooks in their brown wrapping Julian saw, a room away, the lurching figure: nightdress awry, wild, staring face, one eye blinking in confusion. 'Go on, piss off,' Mr Castleton said equably.

Towards lunchtime, as the wind whipped up, he stood on the low, rocky promontory overlooking the station, where Summer People with bags and suitcases laboured towards the waiting train. Then, with one of those sharp, decisive gestures that define our lives, he began to tear up the books, one by one, casting each fragment out onto the swelling breeze. Later the rain came in, noisily, across the long bar of the sea.

TAKING AN INTEREST

MY MOTHER LIVED in the Breckland for thirty years: at Brandon, Feltwell, Northwold; always in the same rackety houses looking out over the heath. During that time she devised theories about her neighbours: theories of closeness, obduracy, idiosyncrasy. Trammelled by poverty, inertia and isolation, she suggested, the Brecklanders reverted to an inbred, primordial oddity. My mother told stories of elderly men bicycling twenty miles to Norwich on a whim, middle-aged sisters found together in a bed that also contained their father's corpse, lawless children running unchecked through a landscape of virid sedge.

Few of these legends survived. Returning to the western seam of Norfolk a decade after her death, I found a world grown matter-of-fact. The tied cottages, refurbished and extended, housed Cambridge dons and their families; the farm workers had migrated to the soft fruit factories near the coast; shiny new estates edged out the pre-war warrens. A handful of the bicycling old men endured, but they did so with extreme self-consciousness, as vain and dignified as artists' models. Even then, though, I was not discouraged. I knew how slowly time passes out there on the windblown heaths, in the lee of the fens, and, sure enough, only a month had passed before I turned up Thetford Jim.

'Always take an interest,' my mother had said of her dealings with the Breckland people, 'never interfere.' To this end she had patronised village charities, exhibited cakes in draughty barns and church halls, and very occasionally – for my mother was a liberal-minded woman – circulated leaflets

34

on contraception. Thetford Jim loomed into view late one Saturday night at a pub talent evening in Brandon, in the slipstream of two stand-up comedians and a xylophonist, when a deedy-looking ancient clambered onto the makeshift stage to announce 'Here's something for you old-timers to enjoy'. There was a smattering of applause and a short, spare man in middle age began to sing in a reedy tenor, accompanying himself with a limping acoustic guitar. The first half-minute of the performance escaped me, so absorbed was I with the singer's appearance: knobby forehead, horn-rimmed glasses, disappearing hair; an ageless peasant's face, toothy, preoccupied, innocent and conniving by turns. To begin with he played a couple of country and western numbers, but there was a song called 'The Squire's Walk', about harvesting in the 1930s, so far as I could deduce, another called 'We Got Married in Church', with a chorus of *a register office woudn't suit for her ma*. He had a clipped west-of-the-county accent which pronounced 'do' as *du*, and the songs were clearly self-penned as I noticed he had a handwritten lyric sheet unravelled on the sidetable next to his half-pint of Adnams.

Who to ask for information? The vicar had been there for four years, a grain in the hourglass of this remote, rural life. The local lore accumulated by the handful of solicitors and bureaucrats with whom I was on nodding terms rarely exceeded the London train timetable. Fortunately Mrs Nokes, who cleaned for me two mornings a week, had the story. 'It was a shame really, that Jim – and his name's not really Jim, it's Trevor, Trevor Bell. His dad used to work over at Watton in the painting and decorating line. His mother, she was a Fisher, big local family they was sixty or seventy years back, all gone now. But Jim's dad, he died young, and Jim's mum, she took on over Jim. Never would leave him be. He joined the Navy once, but he came back in three months on account of she said she missed him. And then when she died, five years back, people thought Jim wouldn't stand it. Rode that motorbike of his round the place at all hours. Calmed down a bit now, Jim has. Still lives in the old house,

but I hear he does carpentering work out Garboldisham way.'
I saw it all, or I thought I did: the slow, intent life, the long-burning fuse suddenly exploding. I remembered, too, a few subdued remarks heard in the pub. 'Did they? I mean . . .' Mrs Nokes shrugged tolerantly, in the way that I recalled my mother shrugging when confronted with a broken gate, a badger killed on the swarming roads. 'You don't want to believe talk,' she pronounced. 'Jim was struck on his mum, and they was close as peas in a pod, but that's as far as it went and don't let anyone tell you different.' I had the feeling that Mrs Nokes was holding something in reserve about Jim, some prized nugget of data not to be vouchsafed to writers in four-bedroomed houses with city minds.

Take an interest; never interfere. It was difficult to establish where these injunctions broke apart from one another. Once a bundle of my mother's leaflets from the Brook Advisory Clinic had been pushed back through her letter box, doused in petrol and set aflame. After that I began to notice Jim, a small element in a wider tableau suddenly foregrounded by ulterior knowledge. I saw him astride his elderly Triumph motorcycle, labouring along the county backroads, buying groceries in Northwold. He had that vague, dreamy country-man's look, the kind that does not so much see through one as round one, a nod that might have been an acknowledg-ment or a dismissal. On the pretext of wanting some shelves, I even drove over to the cottage, a mile out of Feltwell, halfway along a lane that went nowhere, crowded out by osiers and long-dead elms. He was cagey but affable, admitting that he did 'carpenteering', that shelves 'wouldn't be no trouble'. At close hand, I saw, his face had even more that rapt, simpleton's stare. The cottage was small, dark, meekly furnished. From mantels, tables and wall-brackets, parched Norfolk faces stared out of their frames: old men in caps flanking dray horses, a labourer with pitchfork flung over his shoulder like a gun. Mrs Bell hung above the fireplace: bolster figure, the same vague eyes, set in brick-red nutcracker features. Jim's guitar lay propped against the table edge.

Putting up the shelves took a couple of visits. He came

early in the morning, tapping on the hall door at half-seven, quarter-to-eight. I imagined him caught in the old fieldhand routines mandated by his mother forty years before: rise at dawn, main meal at midday, bed at sunset. While he worked he smoked tiny, pungent cheroots: the inside of his right index finger was a long, mahogany smear. He was friendly enough, but I fancied that he half-despised me, wondered at the cossetted, idler's life that could contract out the putting up of shelves. On the second visit I asked him about the songs. As I suspected, they were his own compositions, or at any rate familial. 'My old dad now, he was a singer. Sung in the pubs, Watton way. Lot of them I got from him. Others are my own. "Sheringham train takes a fine long time", now. I did that years ago, back when they were thinking on cutting the service.' He pronounced it *sar*vice, in a way I hadn't heard for twenty years.

By degrees I discovered a context in which Jim's songs lived and grew. The county radio station sometimes featured what it called 'local entertainers'. They had stage names like Dandelion Joe or The Buttercup Boy, dressed up in smocks and other yokel appurtenances, sang irksome songs about shovelling muck and cows' udders, and conducted beauty pageants at the village fêtes. Set against this tide of bucolic idiocy, Jim looked like a folk poet, a gentle elegist of bygone rural decencies. In amongst the book reviews and the grinning 'middles', I was writing a column for a Sunday newspaper called 'Country Retreats'. I put Jim in it, talked about a few of the songs, mentioned some contemporary folk singers with whom I thought he could stand some kind of comparison. The piece was headed 'Norfolk Voices'. Later, there was a clutch of letters, from people who wanted to buy records or claimed to have heard him singing in pubs. On the Monday morning I put a copy of the article through Jim's rusting letterbox. Passing me on the road a day or two later he made a definite salutation, arm raised stiffly in greeting like a flipper.

Mrs Nokes approved of my interest. 'There were folks used to reckon Jim was simple,' she explained cautiously. 'Kids

37

mostly. They used to stand in the lanes and shout at him when he went past. But you have to make allowances. Jim's dad now, he could hardly write. And the old mawther, well, she'd die sooner than have to fill in a form. Come election time you couldn't get her to vote for love nor money.'

Another piece in the jigsaw of Jim's early life clicked into place. Even now, I realised, beneath the surface old patterns of existence ran on, like black hounds under the moon. An old woman died in Watton that summer, aged eighty-seven, carrying a tumour on her abdomen that weighed eleven pounds. 'We didn't want to go bothering the doctor,' her daughter was reported as saying.

The shelves had been up a fortnight now. The topmost one was slightly askew. I put it down to a craftsman's disdain of perfection, a humility before the absolutes of wood and metal. But something still irritated me about Thetford Jim: a talent not recognised, an ingenuousness not rewarded. A producer I knew on Radio Norfolk was non-committal, but he agreed to investigate. There was another talent night a week later at the pub in Brandon. As the teenaged impressionist gave way to a staggeringly inept magician, I saw the producer's eye list desperately in boredom. But he cheered up at 'The Squire's Walk' and a song I'd not heard before, a plaintive and sentimental number about a village cemetery. 'It's authentic,' he said. When I looked inquisitive, he went on: 'You wouldn't believe the kind of thing that passes for Norfolk these days. Had a character in my office last week called Sid the Ratcatcher. You know how they get themselves up – smock, shepherd's crook – Christ knows what that's got to do with ratcatching. Sang a song about sheep dips. It turns out he's an accountant, lives near Lynn. Does the Rotary Club and the after-dinner circuit. But this one reminds me of the Singing Postman – you remember, the little chap with the glasses who used to sing about ha' you got a light boy? Do you suppose he's ever played to more than twenty people?'

Two days later I met Jim in Northwold high street with a large black labrador loping resignedly at his heel. 'This here dog is my cousin's dog,' he explained. 'I'm seeing to him on account of she's away.' I explained about the producer. 'Uh ho. The radio and that. They wouldn't want me to dress up funny or nothing?' he asked tolerantly. 'I shouldn't think so.' 'OK,' he said, and he articulated it *ooh-kay*, with a satirical glint of the eye. 'I reckon I'll sit myself down and do some practising.' I watched him amble away down the street, the dog dragging at his ankles, fearful of the gulf that separated us. My mother would have known how to deal with Thetford Jim; she would have drawn him out, conquered his reserve. I was simply a fantastic alien who wrote about him in newspapers and wanted to put him on the radio.

There was a Sunday afternoon show on Radio Norfolk, squeezed up between *Memories of my Golden Years* and the religious slot, called *Bandstand*. It was supposed to be live, although in fact the majority of the show went out on tape and only the announcer's feed-ins and the 'star guest' admitted a margin of error. They had him booked in for the Sunday before Christmas – 'Thetford Jim: the sound of Norfolk' – and a photographer came over from Diss to take his picture for the *Eastern Daily Press*: myopic, mild-eyed, gazing out from under a peaked cap he sometimes wore. I was in London, as it happened, seeing an editor or chasing a profile, but the story kept warm. On the Friday before the show someone peppered the downstairs windows of the cottage with buckshot. Puttering down the lane the next morning, Jim ran into a trip wire stretched at shoulder-height between two dead elms and broke his collar bone. Of various local informants only Mrs Nokes offered an explanation. 'All on account of that Tracy Sutton. Just after his mother died.' The name meant nothing. 'Only fourteen, she was. One of those ones that look seventeen. And act like it, too. Who do you blame? In they end they only gave him a suspended sentence, but Tracy's dad always swore he'd get even.'

They discharged him from hospital two days later, and I called round. The door was locked and stayed unanswered, though light burned from the upstairs shuttering. Then in the New Year, out on the bike again coming back from a job at Northwold, he careered across the road and into a file of schoolchildren. No one was badly hurt, but they kept him at Brandon police station overnight 'for his own protection' as the desk sergeant I spoke to put it. After that he disappeared: off to the far side of the county, people said, working at Channings jam factory near King's Lynn. Mrs Nokes, who had access to this kind of information, reported that he was living in a Salvation Army hostel. The look in her eye hinted that I shouldn't visit. An elm smashed against the side of the cottage in the March gales and knocked half a wall away: no one came to repair it. And then, idling in a newsagent's queue with Mrs Nokes, I saw a vast, sandbag-shaped girl with gappy teeth and witless eyes chewing her underlip at the counter. 'Tracy Sutton,' Mrs Nokes whispered pityingly, and I turned away, finally aware of having taken a step too far, like some startled explorer descending into that lost world beyond the mountain who glimpses a pterodactyl taking wing into the gloomy sky.

THE SURVIVOR

Long steel grass –
The white soldiers pass –
The light is
braying like an ass.
See

DEAR EDITH, I have a lot to thank her for. It was she, you see, who came the closest anyone ever got to unmasking this lifetime of deceit, she who wandered most nearly into the eternity of dissimulation that has been my career. Of course, there had been near misses before – a worrying moment with Fielding back in the 1740s, born of over-confidence; a slight *contretemps* in 1873 ('Sir!' 'Sir?' 'Sir. Your knowledge of Mr Dickens' antecedents seems positively indecent. Perhaps you could explain how you came by it?') – there was a lot of stuff about the early days that didn't make it into Forster's *Life*, but nothing like this nothing, with such potential for damage. Looking back, with that uncanny, supernal memory I have for scene and incident, I can remember it all: Edith's tiny sitting-room in Pembridge Mansions, the usual watery tea in chipped china mugs, the customary sprinkling of young, literary sprigs – Brian Howard, my dears, up from Eton for the day. I was recounting one or two of my choicer anecdotes about Oscar to a corps of deferential listeners when our hostess gave me a shrewd look and remarked: 'Mr Saffery. Your account of Mr Wilde's indiscretions is extraordinarily vivid. It is almost *as if you yourself were there*.' There was some laughter at this, which picked up when Ronald uncoiled

41

himself langorously from the sofa and said in that shy, stammering way of his: 'We all know that Mr S-s-saffery is p-p-positively *protean*. A real *eminence grise* my dears.' It passed as a joke, of course – such was Firbank's paroxysm of nervous laughter that he shattered a teacup – but for once I had the ghostly feeling, like knocking heard a long way off, that exposure with all its unhappy consequences wasn't far away.

Dear Edie (I think I may call her that), Dear Ronald. They were only two stars amid a galaxy of serried acquaintance. Household names my dear, as Brian would say. Arnold and Max and Morgan. At the time – this was the early twenties – I was an aspiring man of letters going by the name of Henry Saffery (a little devilling in the *London Mercury*, a poem or two in the *Bystander* – small blooms, patiently nurtured, in any case I was winding down) and what with my war service – DSO and gammy leg – and my private income – White's, MCC, you name it I was a member – I think I can say that I didn't want for invitations. They were great days: sniffing the early morning roses at Garsington, those afternoon teas at Max Gate – one tried to draw Tom out but it never worked. Motoring down to Eton to see Aldous. I still have the correspondence: Mr Eliot's compliments, Mrs Woolf's regrets, and that bizarre epistle, signed 'D.H.L.', entreating me to 'look into your heart of innermost hearts, Henry, burn briefly for a moment and confess that you have always loved me'. A hundred years old maybe, and the ink is beginning to fade, yet on my timescale as recent as yesterday.

I don't know when it all started – let's be honest, the really early stuff leaves me cold these days, it doesn't have the immediacy it used to, doesn't have the *glamour*. There were those first inscriptions, hasty scrawls you understand, filled in next to the chalked parodies of bison and tiger. In any case, nobody at the time knew what I was doing. Hour upon hour I'd watch as some benighted fellow-troglodyte ran his paw along the line of hieroglyphics, trying vainly to decipher them, but there was never any true meeting of minds. 'This is literature dummy,' I'd shout at him. 'This is the *future*' – but no, never a flicker of interest. They were so stupid, those cavemen, so numbingly dumb: intellectual discovery had no allure. What with the bison hunts and the shindies with rival tribes it was just one long party. But I kept my head down through those grim, pre-literate years, as Stone Age gave way to Iron Age, as Iron Age gave way to Bronze – I learned all the latest tricks when the opportunity presented itself. I was a dab hand at Runic and I have slight claims – together with a druid whose name I now forget – to having invented Ogham Script. And though it was good to be in at the dawn of civilisation, these, it had to be acknowledged, were limited skills: they didn't impress anyone. Bent over your piece of granite, out over the windy heath, file in hand, you were unhappily conscious that the real action was going on elsewhere, that Ogham Script was nothing compared with the wheel or the latest hi-tech battle axe. Later on, sitting round the camp-fire as the boys toasted their victories or sang those Iron Age drinking songs, you could be pretty certain that someone would murmer 'You writer fairies' in the direction of our corner. We weren't popular, even then.

Things were better a few millennia later when I hit ancient Greece. For one thing, literacy was actually a point in your favour – being introduced to someone at a party as a scribe no longer provoked skirls of philistine laughter. Why, there were even jobs going in it. Plus, the materials had improved: no more hammering away on the walls, they had goatskin parchment by then. Better still, for the first time in history literature had a social scene, a *salon*. Poetry readings, drama clubs – we partied with the best of them. Naturally I hung around with everybody who was anybody: Homer, Aristophanes, Aesop. Homer . . . I don't want to damage any illusions, but in fact there were three Homers – you don't seriously imagine anyone could have written all that stuff on their own? – and they weren't called Homer when I knew them. Plus, the blindness thing was a gimmick – what Homer I, who was up on this sort of trick, called a sales promotion aid – and far from original. I don't want to make any apologies.

43

It was something everybody did at the time: there was Aristophanes with his limp, Menander's string of race horses. You had to give those boys credit, they could manage their careers, even to the extent of impeding other people's. Modesty forbids me to dilate, but that scene in the *Odyssey*, the big scene where Nausicca and her handmaidens discover Odysseus washed up on the beach . . . It broke my heart when Homer II put it in without telling me, without so much a credit or a by-your-leave. 'Business pal', he shrugged – all the Athenian literary editors were familiar with that shrug – when I reproached him with this oversight, 'just business'.

I was writing myself, you see. The habit goes back a long way. Even at this early stage I cultivated a varied output: a few verse fragments, epigrams, a play or two. But they were an unprincipled crowd in those days, people got wind of what you were working on and bang went your intellectual property rights. And not just the Homers. I can remember one evening about two and a half thousand years ago, putting the finishing touches to a slick little comedy, a proto-feminist farce in which the housewives of Athens tell their old men: no more sex until the war stops, when some drinking buddy arrived to drag me out to an Aristophanes first night. You guessed it, *Lysistrata*. I still have the letter I wrote him somewhere. It didn't do any good. These things never do.

Temporarily disillusioned, momentarily undone, I lay low for a while after that. I needed a change of scene, I needed *diversion* after a thousand years or so of resolute hackwork. Even then, you see, the writer found himself up against those eternal social pressures – parties, women, networking. So I took time out. I spent the best part of a century in Macedonia collecting material for a travel book – that sort of thing was very much in vogue just then, what with the *Odyssey*, what with all the talk about new horizons and the quest motive. I cultivated the critics – time spent with the critics is never wasted, let me tell you. I went on a fifty-year drinking jag with a succession of Greek poets, and then spent a couple of decades drying out in a shepherd's hut on Knossos. Idleness you reckon, that typical writerly inertia, that demure, doe-eyed inability to get things done? You'd be wrong. I'd prefer to call it an awareness of possibilities. Naturally, I was aware that the great masterpieces of early civilisation weren't getting written but it wasn't a problem, I could wait. After all, I had all the time in the world.

For all that, it was a bad time for writers. Has there ever been a good time for writers? This one was specially bad. Too many wars, too much dislocation, distraction, call it what you will. Too much heavy shit. It hit the writing community – we were calling ourselves that even then – particularly hard. All those Greek city states, all those benign dictatorships we'd thought would be good for aeons were going down like ninepins. Plus, we couldn't look to their successors. Everyone knew the Romans didn't appreciate the finer things in life. Still, I hung in there. What with the invasions and the politics there was a run on war poets, military correspondents, that sort of thing. I did my best. I covered one of the Punic wars (in which nothing ever happened, just marches and rain, nothing you could write home about); wrote an eye-witness account of the fall of Troy in heroic stanzas: no use asking, they didn't survive. Such reverses had a predictable affect on a sensitive temperament. Back from the Peloponnesian wars – Thucydides had got there first in any case – I had a writer's block lasting two hundred and fifty years.

Obviously it was time for a rethink, it was time for a re-evaluation of strategy. Fundamentally, this meant asking myself just exactly what I wanted to achieve as a writer. What were my goals, my aims, ambitions? After all, these things vary. I got super-reflective around this time, while Carthage blazed and Hannibal forged westward over the Alps (I could have covered them both – I had offers), I even thought about writing philosophy at one point. But the circumstances weren't favourable. It was all military history in those days – Livy, Tacitus, Plutarch – you know the names: serious stuff and not a smile among them. I scraped a living for a while as a publisher's reader, but it was obvious that my suggestions, my proud experience, went unheeded. I can remember arguing for hours with Caesar about that first

45

sentence, which seemed to me to lack impact, to impart an irretrievable dryness, but it was no good, he wouldn't listen, and *Omnia Gallia in tres partes divisi sunt* it was. Of course I made mistakes: telling Pliny that those nature notes wouldn't sell was one, and telling Catullus that his poems wouldn't get past the censor was another, but I made them in good faith. Meantime, I gave myself a good three hundred years to finish my next – OK my first – major project, a verse drama on the Roman conquest of Britain. I wrote closing lines early in 410, as the wind fanned the flames on Capitol Hill and Alaric's boys used the contents of the Municipal Library as fire-lighters. Once again I was a victim of circumstances, once again I was that fatal literary casualty, a man out of time.

Looking back, viewing it all with the hindsight of eternity, you can't imagine the effect that the sack of Rome had on literature. For a start, it destroyed some promising careers: Scrotus, Alba, Plauditus – I don't suppose you've ever heard of them (let's face it, nobody *has* ever heard of them) but they were very big in their day. At the same time, in the case of the major reputations it gave posterity an entirely lop-sided view. You might remember Martial for those steely epigrams, but what really sold were the smutty limericks and the poems about his ex-wife. All gone. All gone the same way as Q. Horatius Flaccus's *Tales of the Sensual Life* and Marcus Aurelius's harem memoirs.

Seldom has a profession come so near to extinction. Seldom has a profession stared so transfixedly at the brink and then shakily retreated. For a thousand years or so writers had been going around producing searing analyses of social problems, hymning martial accomplishments and taking money off indulgent patrons, and suddenly all of it – the social problems, the martial accomplishments and especially the indulgent patrons – had ceased to exist. We did what we could. We took off for Egypt, Gaul, Asia Minor, Morocco – anywhere in the Empire where the social order hadn't broken down and there was still a spare desk. I spent twenty years in a field in what has since become Norfolk with a gang of terrified Anglo-Roman *bourgeoisie*, waiting for the Saxons to arrive. When they did turn up, when the great clinker boats came nosing into the deep-water creeks, the sense of *déjà vu* was almost tangible: that primitive, penumbral murk, those drinking songs around the camp-fire, and mass illiteracy. For one who had been around at the dawn of civilisation, it was all very much like old times. I suppose you'd say, with that usual indulgent nod in the direction of the creative intelligence, that it was a Godsent opportunity, that it was history being made, and to be sure I couldn't resist keeping a diary of those meagre, intense years, but it was less about Celt and Saxon, rack and ruin, the birds making their nests in the tumbledown churches, and more about lice, scurvy and not having enough to eat. All this was compounded, naturally enough, by a shortage of materials. The ink ran out around 450 – I tried making my own out of dye, but you really need a professional – and the books started disappearing. No one quite knew where – I suspected the locals of eating them – but by the end of the century my travelling library, all those first editions of Seneca and Sallust, was down to a handful. By the dawn of the sixth century I was reading the same bedside book – a copy of Plutarch's *Lives* it was then – for ten years at a stretch.

What do I remember of those fugitive, eerie Dark Age days? Not much, except that an Anglo-Saxon cow byre is not the most congenial of literary milieux. (I know Faulkner wrote his first novel lying on a coke heap but then he didn't have to share it with Snorri the goat-herd, whose idea of a pleasant evening in was to get paralytic on turnip wine and talk about his mother back in Frisia.) For a time I considered alternatives – at one point I nearly lit out for Merovingia where something like a literary scene was supposed to be happening, and there was a time when I seriously thought about becoming a monk in Ireland – but gradually as time passed these drawbacks mattered less. They mattered less because by now I had made an important decision about my career. Naturally, in a trajectory that had already lasted several thousand years. I had made important decisions about my career before. There was the decision to get involved in

47

this whole business in the first place (that was back in the days of Cuneiform, which everybody thought was a dangerous innovation that wouldn't last); there was the decision, made about the end of the first millenium B.C. that tragedy was pretty much played out as an art-form, and there had been various other minor shifts and adjustments in perspective. But this was something different. It involved – let us be frank about this – re-evaluating my whole status, eyeing up the entire rag-bag of writerly aspirations. It happens to us all, no doubt: you look back at what you've written in the past, you sift through the unpublished stuff, argue with yourself over its merits. I spent a year or two doing that, out on the Norfolk flats with the wind sweeping in from Jutland, and it was the most depressing period of my life to date. At its close I took the contents of the goatskin bag which had accompanied me thus far on my travels – everything, the poems, the plays, the letters from Horace and Propertius, and threw them in the river. Then I went back to the byre, found Snorri and got stupendously drunk.

After that, nothing. Silence. A void. Five hundred years and not a paragraph, not a sentence. Nothing at all. Even now, gazing backwards, I stumble for an explanation. It wasn't that I lacked offers. All the big names of the period sidled up at some point to enquire if I'd collaborate: Bede, Guthlac . . . It wasn't that one lacked suitable material: after all, what with Offa, the Danes, rape, pillage and the beginnings of English nationhood (which was what Alfred liked to call the handful of third-world villages he bullied into paying him taxes) there was plenty going on. You weren't stuck for things to write about in those days. Fundamentally I suppose – and I don't want to sound pretentious about this – I was out of sympathy with the *zeitgeist*. For one who had known Petronius and partied with Plautus all this was pretty small beer. The Homers were showmen, who might have been overly concerned with where the next flagon was coming from, but at least they were artists. By contrast, Anglo-Saxon literature, if you could call it that, was painful in its ineptitude, its meagre scale; all dumb riddles and battle

48

tactics. Later on I would watch knowingly as scholarly acquaintances – Skeat, Tolkien – puzzled themselves over the Finnsburh fragment, always wanting to whisper: 'Boy, you should have seen the bits which *didn't* survive.' I had hopes of Bede for a while – I wintered out in Jarrow a couple of times – but the guy had no artistry, no sense of what was a legitimate literary device and what was a ham effect. I can remember arguing with him for hours about the scene where the sparrow flies in through the banqueting hall, but no, Bede wanted metaphor, he wanted *symbolism*. The scene stayed: I quit.

Naturally there were compensations. There were a few public commissions up for grabs – name that church, write this poem about my father – and a fair amount of royal patronage, but it was difficult to get worked up about the subject matter. Alfred versus the Danes? I'd seen the sack of Troy, and this was the equivalent of two shepherds waving sling shots at one another. A paean to Offa's Dyke? I'd been around when they built Ephesus: this was nothing to crow over, nothing to guide the quill excitedly over the parchment. Looking back at what remains from those grim, poverty-stricken times (and, needless to relate, writing didn't *pay* in those days – the man who wrote *The Battle of Maldon* got a couple of bear-skins), I can occasionally wax regretful over my non-existent output, but then I wasn't appreciated, I just wasn't appreciated. I can remember once, around the end of the tenth century, stirring myself from a decade or so of torpor to execute some piece of royal fawning for Ethelred the Unready, something to do with his martial accomplishments, his wise counsels – the exact theme escapes me. It was a sell-out, of course, but I needed the money and for once I took pains, hunkered down in the hut, barred the door to drinking buddies and laboured to produce two dozen sweetly rhymed hexameters in the grand style. The response? The usual thanks-but-no-thanks. Eventually they gave the job to some hoary-headed patriach named Egbert the Bard, whose fractured scrawls and risible punning can still be chortled over in the British Museum by such as care to examine them. It was my last public commission.

So what did I do as the years ground relentlessly on, as Old English gave way to Middle, as dynasties rose and fell, as Jute, Angle, Saxon and Dane gelled themselves up into some sort of recognisable social order? The answer is: I sat there. It's what writers do, they sit there. There were beckoning noises from afar – I could have gone for a safe court poet's job at Aachen (that Carolingian Renaissance, *so* tempting), I could have written *sagas* – but for some reason the thought of relocation scarcely appealed. You get tired of moving on, of packing and unpacking the quill, the parchment, the type-writer. Several thousand years and a dozen removals into a less than promising career I felt a hankering for permanency, for roots, even if the immediate prospects were far from enticing. So what did I do? The usual marginal, subsistence-level activities: copying for the monks, a spell on the Anglo-Saxon Chronicle, the most ball-breaking hackwork of char-ters and land agreements. The great outlines, those splendid synopses of work that would change the face of Anglo-Saxon literature lay gathering dust.

Besides, there was that decision, made a few hundred years ago now but still germane, about the future trajectory of my career. Briefly, it consisted of an acknowledgment – painful yet undeniably accurate – that hitherto my energies had been misdirected. In retrospect it was odd that realisation had come so late. For years, it seemed, I had sat around watching people misapply themselves, chase the wrong ends: I mean, we all knew at the time that Gregory of Tours wasn't cut out to be a travel writer, he was merely constrained by the predominant form. In my own case, it seemed to me that I was less a creator than a collaborator, an enlivening spark, the bright boy who strolls in to impart polish to the great man's leaden original. Reviewing my successes in this line the evidence seemed conclusive. The Homers, Horace, Bede: I had the credits. All I had to do was wait, wait until some half-decent literature came along.

I had to wait a long time. I yawned my way through

another Danish invasion, through the Normans – more military history and if you couldn't speak French, which I had some trouble picking up, the chips were stacked against you. For a time I hung out with Anselm, but he always cut out my jokes and in the end I simply gave up. *Sir Gawain and the Green Knight*, which everybody got very excited about at the time, just left me rigid. It took Gower and Chaucer – a touch vulgar for my taste, but there you are, this was the fourteenth century, they used to crease themselves laughing at cripples in those days – to convince me that something was happening again, that after a millennium and a half of amateurish incompetence I still had a rôle to play. It was a busy five hundred years all right – gone in a flash, as it always does when you're working hard. At first I concentrated on poetry: Wyatt, Herrick, Spenser – not many a line by those three got by without first being inched under my scrupulous lenses (I was wearing glasses by then, inevitably), but my chief contribution lay in titles, proper names (I can still see the look on Herrick's face when I advised him that 'Marigold flouts me' wouldn't do, that the readers were looking for aristo-cratic stuff: 'Phyllida' it was). *Anthony and Cleopatra* was called *Hot Nights in Cairo* before I got hold of it. My tornado years. Creative breakfasts with Willie – there was only one of him, you'll be relieved to know – boozy lunchtime sessions with Johnnie Kyd, the odd nighttime jaunt with Chris Marlowe down Bermondsey way and some very queer company indeed. I relished it. A whole new way of life was opening up; a whole new audience gaped and luxuriated before us, and for once we felt wanted. The boys' expressions of gratitude were quite touching when you paused to think about it – all those sonnets from Willie, Spenser's acrostic name-checks in *The Faerie Queen*, 'onlie begetter' wasn't the half of it.

I started writing my memoirs around 1600, updating them every twenty years or so. It's all in there, all the clotted detail and debris of the succeeding centuries: cruising with Roches-ter, that interminable pony-ride with Defoe (travel-writing again – you get a vogue every decade or so and there's nothing the critic can do). The time De Quincey went out of his head and tried to off me with a meat-cleaver, the time I went out of my head somewhere in Greece and nearly got raped by Byron. All the stories that never got told, all the sides to people's character that somehow eluded contemporary chroniclers, all the flotsam and jetsam of the vagrant literary life. Vagrant, elusive, yet all-seeing. Picture me, if you will, snug around the Strand coffee house fire with Sammy Johnson and that dismal Scots attourney we could never shake off, speeding through Hell Passage with William Makepeace Thackeray bent on some youthful prank. Sombre times too: watching Gissing die in St Jean Pied de Port, coughing out his life by centimetres as H.G. wrangled with the nurse in the next room; attending Firbank's last illness at Rome (Lord Berners was there as well and a sorry figure he cut, I can tell you). Without going in for anything morbid I did become something of a death-bed frequenter in those days: Coleridge, Leigh Hunt, Carlyle – all drew their final breath in my company. As the clergymen intoned and the nurses scurried, I alone remained imperturbable. Death found me at my most philosophical, ever ready to console a grieving widow, compose a respectful obit, recite some judicious *éloge* in which listeners were invited to consider the subject's demise *sub specie aeternitatis*.

It was a restless, rackety existence and I knew it couldn't last, that the role of literary confidant is not indefinitely sustainable, all too prone to irritations, nervous disagreements and vented spleen. I quarrelled quite badly with Meredith and my spat with Herbert Spencer even got into the papers. The early 1900s found me fretful and ill at ease, conscious of waning powers and deep, unconscionable tiredness. I still had sufficient nous to know where the right places to go were, the correct literary hot-spots: Edie's drawing room, the Left Bank in the twenties with Jim and Ernest and Gertrude; Hollywood a bit later with Scott, Zelda and Bill; Spain a bit later still with Eric and Cyril (who only turned up at the end). They were good times, naturally – taking dictation from Joyce and putting in *everything* (have you ever noticed how often the words 'Answer that door will you?' appear in *Finnegan's Wake*?) Taking tea with Gertrude and Alice B – boy, were *they* ever weird. But I was tired by now, oh so very tired. Ten thousand years is a long time in the same job and the language problem had irked me ever since Babel. So around 1940 I decided to downgrade my commitments to the odd prestige commission, the odd celebrity collaboration. (I managed to turn down Uncle Ez at about this time which did wonders for my subsequent reputation.) For a time all went smoothly: I look back on the fifties as a pleasant siesta, interspersed with a few flamboyant stirrings: I tinkered around with the dialogue on *Dr Zhivago*, I persuaded Golding to change the setting of *Lord of The Flies* (a boys' prep school lacked plausibility, I told him sternly). For a while – this was the fifties in England and it was all kitchens and sinks – I even hung out in America, where the atmosphere seemed briefly comfortable. Little Truman. Big Norm. Camp Gore. They were my kind of guys, and we had some good times back there sitting in our rumpus-room at the Rockefeller Institute, alternatively slipping out to sign a new petition against LBJ or buy asthmatic Truman a new inhaler. Good times. It was a shame they had to come to an end, which they did sometime around 1968 when Norman ('Jeez,' I can hear him saying as Gore sashayed out for a hank of tissues, 'what a *fag* the guy is') looked me squarely in the face and told me he didn't like the shape of my nose.

Looking back on the situation, I don't blame Norman – it was '68 and he was in one of his all-American moods, so virulently as to ignore all thoughts of his own ancestry – but it was enough. I quit. Forever. I threw all of Norman's buddy-buddy letters – alternately suggesting that we should arm-wrestle each other or find sailors to fight by way of cementing a renewed comradeship – into the Hudson, following them with my typewriter and my Author's Club ID. I refused all of Truman's invitations to tea ('but *honey*' he would murmer outrageously down the wire, 'we could have such a *fahn tahm*'), declined to attend the farewell dinner held in my honour at the Algonquin and set off for home and the fine-tuning of my memoirs. Those memoirs! By now I'd been working on them for nearly four hundred years – the early drafts done in fat Gothic script with the 'S's all 'F's – and they were shit-hot. I knew they'd cause a sensation – I even had a title, *The Writer in Time* – but still I hesitated. There had been so many near misses before, so many last-second failures to hitch a seat on the bus-ride to immortality and somewhere, deep within me, I knew this was the last chance, the big one, the make or break. I didn't know what fate had in store for me. (How could I? That's the thing about writers, they never know what fate has in store for them.) I just burned on, polishing that phrase, qualifying that character judgment, giving the Homers their collective due, waxing winningly charitable over Aesop's drug problem. For thirty years I burned on, sequestered in a tiny cottage in Hampshire, resisting the occasional blandishment (Iris, Kingsley, Martin, Julian – they all tried me at some point), pruning, shaping, discarding, revising, until finally when it was ready – when those thousands of pages were all conflated into a single mighty manuscript – I emerged blinking into the sunlight (very strong sunlight it was too) to find that fate had played its cruellest trick.

For once it wasn't another writer who was to blame. We, first started hearing about *Cryptosporidium botrytis* sometime in the early 2000s – faint noises that nobody paid much attention to – after all, we had global warming, drought and most of Norfolk was a duck-pond by this time. Nobody could get especially exercised by an obscure leaf-fungus originating somewhere in the Finnish timber forests. Looking at it a few months ago in one of those interminable drama docs they do, I was taken aback by how innocent it seemed: just a few square centimetres of rusty mould, in its preliminary form, barely discernible among the russet tints and hues of autumn. This deceptive air predictably fooled the forest scientists, most of whom assumed that it was a local variant of Dutch Elm which would go away. It wasn't. It didn't. Six months later the Finnish timber industry ceased to exist.

What happened? We don't know. The first scientific reports identified it as a tree virus, a sort of mega-compound of all the moulds, rots and algaes with which trees had been infested since the dawn of time, but with one salient difference: the incubation period. Dutch Elm can leave a tree standing for twenty years. *Cryptosporidum botrytis*, having killed off the foliage in a week, went to work like a flurry of termites, hollowing out the trunk and reducing the boughs to sawdust. Scientifically monitored for the first time in a national park near Malmo it was seen to account for two thousand hectares of prime larch in a little over three weeks. They did what they could, of course. They stopped all timber exports from Finland. They tried a fire-break – a procedure that meant torching five hundred square miles of forest near the border (you could see the flames in Moscow) and they tried blaming someone, in this case the Iranians who were accused of concocting the virus in the first place. None of these things worked. A month later *Cryptosporidum botrytis* was in Sweden. A month after that – about the time I put the finishing touches to *The Writer In Time* – the Russian pine forests went down.

After that the panic set in. The price of wood pulp on the international exchanges went up by 80 per cent, by 150 per cent, by 300 per cent. Paper supplies halved, then quartered. The big mills started revising their estimated outputs on a weekly basis. Publishers started doubling and then quadrupling their prices and reducing their print runs to a fraction. It was all very serious, all very frightening. And there wasn't anything anybody could do. They tried various expedients, of course. They tried recycling – whole warehouses of old stock, vast libraries of antiquated fiction went to the pulp – and they started using fanciful breeds of wood, previously thought unsuitable for paper production. They imported eucalyptus from the rain forests, spongy swamp saplings from the Far East. At one stage they started experimenting with man-made fibres and there were mad plans to print books on tiny sheets of plastic or strengthened cellophane. I had a contract by this time with one of the big London firms and each week I was called in for a request to cut, to prune, to hack away another chunk of manuscript (in the meantime the books were getting slimmer – novels became novellas, fat biographies became slim monographs, poems became haikus). It broke my heart but I played along. I did everything they told me to do, prised out all the stuff about the Homers, the extended recreation of dining with Dante (who made gurgling noises with his soup, but then we're none of us perfect). Even then I wasn't giving too much away – *The Writer In Time* was billed in the catalogue as 'an elaborate fantasia' would you believe. But it was no good, it just wasn't any good. Three months before publication, the vast 300,000 word chronicle reduced to forty pages, the government announced a moratorium on UK book production.

And for twenty years, that's been it. *Cryptosporidum botrytis* has slowed down a bit by now – Scandinavia is a wasted, treeless desert, there aren't a lot of places it can go to. There are hopes too that the virus will work itself out, grow weakened – in fact they did some resowing in Sweden last year and it seems to be holding up pretty much OK. In the meantime we sit and read what we always read. I've gone through *A La Recherche* a dozen times now (how pleased Marcel would be). Several times I've pondered some new career – chartered accountancy, pensions, that sort of thing – but inevitably I return to this matter-of-fact brooding, these musings over might-have-beens, this subjunctive life. Inevitably, too, I have my consolations. I go on the radio sometimes and tell them about Aristophanes, Milton, Joyce and Big Norm. (They love it – they think I'm making it up. They bill me as 'one of our leading humourists' – they don't know I was really there.) And sometimes the voices come echoing down the thin, aimless years: dead, billowing voices, and my head is a sound library where Willie tries out a couplet or two and Jim mints another eyebrow-lofting polysyllable. It's from these moments, perhaps, that I derive my greatest consolation: that, in a world without books, I am the survivor.

FINAL PAYMENTS

ANYONE WHO'S BEEN involved in the game, they'll have a story of how they got started. About how some teacher noticed them in a kickabout at school, some scout picked them out of a youth team game. Some old ex-pro their dad knew; some TV programme about George Best. Even the legends – Charlton, Moore, Hurst – they'll all have their stories. With me it was my dad, which isn't as straightforward as it sounds, really, because my dad wasn't around much when we were kids – he was a traveller in fancy goods, lighters, cigarettes, that sort of thing – and when he was there he was the kind of bloke who goes down the pub instead of sitting in the front room. Still, he saw it, and you have to give him credit for that.

What was even weirder was that at the time – I was thirteen or fourteen maybe – I didn't even like football that much, certainly not with other kids, and if anyone suggested a pick-up game I'd be the first to scoot. But I used to go out to the park sometimes – the old park near the Scrubs that isn't there any more – and kick around, always on my own, with one eye on the path to make sure I could pick up the ball and scarper if anyone else looked as if they wanted to join in. Anyway, I was doing this one time, back in 1975 it would have been, the year Fulham had their Cup-run, when I looked up and saw my dad walking towards me over the grass, coming on slowly in that vague way he had, as if he didn't quite know who he was or where he was going. I had the ball on the ground and was sitting on it before you could whistle, but my dad just sort of smiled a bit and carried straight on –

57

he had a way of making you think that whatever you were doing wasn't really important compared to him. But when I got back home that evening he walked into the kitchen where I was having my tea and said, 'Saw you playing down on the park this afternoon didn't I?' Even then, you see, my dad and me didn't get on, so I just nodded, casual like, but waiting to see what would happen next. Then he said, 'You ever play in a team or anything?' It was stupid, when you came to think about it. All those years I'd been doing swimming at school or going on at him to teach me snooker, and now all of a sudden just because he'd seen me playing football he'd come sniffing round to see if there was anything in it for him. I shook my head, but that didn't worry my dad – he knew what I thought about him by this stage – and he just nodded again. But all that week I caught him giving me a glance or two, the sort of glance he'd give women in shops if he thought my mum wasn't looking, and I knew something was up. The thing about my dad was that he had connections – always knew which horse to back, who to go and see if you wanted a car or a sofa on the never-never – so I wasn't surprised when he got me the trial at Rangers. One Friday night after school it was. And I can remember the coach saying when I went up for a high cross and missed it, 'Jesus, I don't suppose he's ever headed a ball in his life.' But I passed it all the same. Typically, my dad didn't turn up – it was fixing he liked, and getting me the trial meant he'd finished his side of the bargain.

Fulham got to the final that year: I watched every game. They had Bobby Moore playing for them – he was getting ready to retire, but he was still good even then – but somehow when they came out of the Wembley tunnel you knew they were never going to beat West Ham.

I'd already played a couple of games in the youth team by then. They'd started me out in defence, but then moved me into midfield on account of my height – I'm five feet seven, which is small for a footballer – but the youth team coach said there'd be no problem about signing schoolboy forms in a year or so. Curiously enough, I wasn't really thinking about it. Plenty of kids down our way fancied themselves as footballers, and you were always hearing about lads who'd signed for Brentford or Chelsea, or turned out for Millwall juniors, but somehow it never came to anything, and a year or so later you'd come across them stacking trolleys in Sainsbury's or looking lost in some Sunday League game. The other Rangers apprentices used to talk big sometimes about how they'd make the first team at seventeen, about how there were scouts from the big clubs already looking them over. But I kept my head down, and by '77 or '78 old Lennie the reserve team manager reckoned I was well on my way to making it. You might not be able to do anything about your height, but you can make it work to your advantage, and anywhere around the centre spot the small guy always has it over the six-footer with no pace. I had this trick of shielding the ball as I turned: you had to be a clever centre back to do anything about it.

I can remember the first time I played for the first team: it was the day after my dad finally walked out on us. To be fair it wasn't any big surprise. There'd been women before, all during the time I was a kid – though it always suited my mum not to notice – and then when I was fifteen he'd got this new travelling job with a big confectionery firm in the Midlands, which meant being away from home even more. All the same, I could have done without being told about Carole or Denise or whatever her name was – they'd got a house by this time, somewhere up Wolverhampton way – and my mum in floods of tears the morning before the Leicester game. We won, as it happened, but I didn't remember much about it. I was too busy thinking about my dad standing there in the front room – he was wearing this new suit, and you could see that he really fancied himself in it – and wondering what we were going to do about money. Looking back, I suppose I don't blame my dad that much – he was a good-looking bloke, even in his fifties, and he liked a drink and a talk, which was something my mum was never much interested in – but at the time it was as if he'd stuck two fingers up to the first eighteen years of my life. If I could have got hold of him, I'd have said something like 'All that time when we were kids, if it was so bad why didn't you say so instead of pretending?' If one of your parents makes it clear that they'd sooner not be there, then you start blaming yourself; or them, which is the same thing in a way.

It was November when he left: three months into the season. I was brilliant the rest of that year. Dave Marshall, the old centre half who I'd been brought in to cover for, spent a couple of months in the reserves and then got sold to some non-league outfit because of me. Come April we were in the top six, and we would have got promoted to the Second if we hadn't drawn the last three games. I suppose it was my dad driving me on. There were times, standing by the touchline waiting for a throw-in, mostly, or drifting up through the midfield, when I'd think I saw him in the crowd, turning away, say, behind an advertising hoarding, hidden in the shadow under the roof of the big stand. It's not true that footballers don't see the people watching: I used to think I was stuck in the middle of an enormous room crowded with screaming faces.

We didn't see him again for a while after that. He'd send my mum a postcard – some town in the North where he was stopping overnight – or there'd be a phone call sometimes late at night, but that was all. As far as us kids were concerned, it was as if we didn't exist. When she was fifteen Angie won a dance competition at the Hammersmith Apollo, and we sent him the photograph in the paper and everything, but he never wrote back. After a time, though, I stopped worrying about it. I was nineteen, twenty, playing in the first team every week, there was the odd piece in the *Recorder* about how Spurs were interested in me, and I didn't have to look for company. I'd wonder about the old man sometimes, what it was like in Wolverhampton with Louise or Kay – Carole or Denise was long gone by this time – but it never hit me, like the day it did when he walked out. Meanwhile the family settled down. Angie was doing her nurse's training at the Charing Cross; I was in digs near the ground – I always liked it that you could just see the floodlights out of the upstairs window; the old lady got a council flat Harlesden way. I used to stay over there at weekends, if it wasn't an away game. She had this framed photo of me in that classic footballer's pose – down on one knee, hands crossed over the other one – taken the day I signed on as a pro – on top of the TV, along with the picture of Angie in her dancing gear, old holiday snaps taken in Southend and Clacton.

It was the early eighties by then, and Rangers were still in the Third. Every so often they'd have a run, win half a dozen games in a row, say, and the *Recorder* would run 'Rangers for the top flight?' headlines, but they never fooled me. I knew there wasn't the money, or the interest. The chairman used to go on sometimes about redeveloping the ground and buying in big players, but in the meantime the old wooden stand was falling apart and you could have unloaded the whole defence for a hundred thousand. There were some other bad signs as well. We went through three managers in '82–3, and Jimmy Wood, the only centre forward we'd had who was any good, got sold to Man United for half a million, which was big money in those days.

What with Jimmy going, and the rest of the players not liking it, the Cup run took us by surprise. We nearly went out in the first round to a bunch of non-league amateurs from the West Country, and it took a fluky penalty to get us through. But we beat another Third Division side in the second, and then went to Coventry and won 2–1 on an ice-rink in the third. People started looking up after that, and there were a couple of giant-killer pieces in the papers, but even so nobody expected us to make it through the fourth, which was a home tie against Newcastle. Newcastle! It had been Carlisle away the week before. We packed in 17,000 people that day, and scraped home 1–0, with three of ours booked and the Newcastle skipper stretchered off with a broken leg – you could have heard the bone crack south of the river – and the chairman was supposed to have made five grand out of the bookies.

The rest of it was a blur. We played Everton at Goodison in the fifth, and it went to a second replay, but we shaded it 3–2 and I had that kind of warm feeling you get when you know your career's on a roll. I'd been a bit bogged down the last couple of seasons – there'd been a month on loan to Arsenal, but in the end they hadn't wanted me, and a try-out for the Under-21s – but now there were serious blokes in the *Telegraph* and the *Mail* going on about the Rangers midfield powerhouse and its talented playmaker, and the whole team, right down to Vinnie Cousins the reserve team goalkeeper, knew that once it was all over the big clubs would come diving in and nothing old Samuels the chairman could do would stop them.

Funnily enough, the rest of it was a doddle. Some Second Division lot – it might have been Oldham or Port Vale – in the sixth round; 2–0 against Villa in the semi. It was mayhem by then. The papers were full of celebrities going on about how they'd always been Rangers fans – I'd never seen any of them down the ground, and neither had anyone else, and the manager got invited on all the TV sports programmes. But the final looked dodgy: Liverpool. They were ten points clear of the First that year, and they hadn't lost a game in three months. He rang up the day after the semi-final. 'It's your dad here' – just like that, as if we'd spoken to each other every week for the last five years. 'Wondered if you could do me a couple of tickets for the final?' Of course I said yes – he was my dad, after all, and I felt I owed it to him – but all the same I wasn't going to make a fuss about it. I just put the tickets in an envelope and sent them off, second class, and forgot about it. But then a week before the final, when it was really just a question of keeping your mind off everything, I went round to see the old lady in Harlesden. I could tell by the way she looked at me when I came through the door that something was up, and sure enough the first thing she said was 'Your dad's been round'. 'Oh yes, and what did he want?' I asked, fairly cold, because I know the old lady can be a soft touch, but she just went on about old times and keeping in contact. He'd come in an Audi Quattro, apparently, so business must have been looking up. It was only when I got up to go that I realised the photo was missing from the top of the TV.

According to the old lady – she started crying when I asked her about it – he'd said he wanted 'something to remember me by'.

I was so angry I had to wait until the evening to ring him up. 'Those tickets,' I said, before he could get a word in, 'I want them back. Now.' I think he must have worked out what I was on about, because he tried to make a joke out of it. 'What's that?' he said. 'Not allowed to come and see my own son playing in the Cup Final?' 'The tickets,' I said. 'I want them back.' After that it got nasty. 'You can whistle for them,' he said. 'Mandy's looking forward to this, and I promised her we'd go.' I nearly broke the receiver when I put it down.

You'll remember from the papers what happened. We lost 5–1, and never had a chance. All down to the weak midfield, the commentators said, but I wouldn't know. I went down on the bus and stayed in the hotel all right, but I was gone before breakfast. I can remember ending up in a pub in Oxford Street and coming out and hearing someone say that Liverpool had won, but not much else. The queer thing was that I could remember it all: that day knocking the ball about on the old park, my dad walking towards me over the wet grass. But I knew then, knew already, that it was all over. And that I never wanted to kick a ball again.

THREE STORIES FROM COOK COUNTY

I

At Brackus's

HIS FATHER, OLD Joe Brackus, had opened the first gas station up on Choctaw the summer after they had built the freeway extension and turned the stony plateau with its view out over Tennessee and the river into a tourist site. He had put in an ice-cream parlour and a kiosk which sold cigarettes and Seven-Up, and for a time the teenagers who drove their girlfriends up there at the weekends and the aged joyriding couples who strayed over the state border by accident would stop and ask him directions or buy guttering tubs of Dixiecup ice-cream which was the parlour's stock-in-trade. But then the ridge had been bought by a real estate company from Memphis who wanted to build a block of timeshare apartments, the teenagers started heading West to Dyersburg where there was a marina complex, and Brackus found himself with an empty forecourt and a ten thousand dollar compensation fee: so he put the money into Brackus's.

It was the sort of place you find occasionally in the South, which is emulative of so many other places in the South that the effect borders on parody. There was a neon sign that said *Brackus's Bar and Diner*, there were menu cards printed in the shape of opening saloon doors and bowls of sawdust for cigarette ends. And because old Brackus was a bluegrass boy whose family had originally come out of Kentucky during the Depression, there was a squat, rickety stage where country bands used to play on Saturday nights, and a set of buckskin gear which the waitresses sometimes wore to serve drinks at the bar. 'Pure Annie Oakley,' Barrett the journalist used to say, but on the strength of it Joe Brackus got himself profiled in *Dixie* magazine standing under a Confederate flag on which was printed the slogan 'The South Will Rise'.

The *Dixie* profile was a portent. Unexpectedly, Brackus's had paid its way right from the start. Saturday nights would find a restive, cosmopolitan crowd packed together on the narrow benches or seated raucously around the big pine tables which Joe had got out of an L.L. Bean catalogue. Denimed wiseacres from the farming end of Cook County, seventy miles away, moneyed Nashville brats with their daddies' credit cards, the local lumpenproletariat from the Choctaw sawmills. In its second year of existence Brackus's got a mention in one of the Nashville listings magazines. Not long afterwards the Dixie Dance-Kings played there at the end of their first Southern tour and Joe Brackus added on a children's parlour extension, bought his wife some cosmetic surgery and wondered about sending his kids to college.

There were two children: Scott and an older girl called Elaine. 'Snipped right off the Southern vine,' Barrett sometimes said, in the days when he wrote reviews of the house bands in the local paper and occasionally had dinner at the Brackus bungalow on Sunday nights, but the precision masked an uncharacteristic lack of certainty. Joe Brackus was an easy-going, two hundred pound small-towner who, even after Brackus's got put into all the regional guidebooks and Waylon Jennings turned up unannounced to play at a charity benefit, would still walk into the local drugstore on a Saturday afternoon and treat himself to a family pack of See's chocolates. The kids were different. For a start they were brighter. They were sharper. They weren't your couple of average Southern kids who wonder maybe about going to Nashville and working in real estate but end up settling for a third share each in the old man's timber yard. All through the early years you could see old Joe figuratively scratching his head about Scott and Elaine. They dug around the local schools for a while – finishing up at high school in Jackson, which pleased Brackus – but you could tell that it was all temporary, that they viewed the old man as an embarrassment who happened to be their father. Eventually Elaine married a Florida lawyer she met at a rock concert one Fall in Miami and went to live down in Tampa Bay. She had a job in an architect's office and came home at Christmas, although Barrett used to say that the architect's office was a front and he had seen her once in an X-movie he had got from a video store. Yeah.

That left Scott. Cook County wasn't the easiest place in the world to be Scott Brackus, but he managed it somehow. He played baseball for the local team, the Cook County Pirates, and you saw him occasionally with the busty cheerleaders in the back parlour of Brackus's. When he was nineteen he won a talent contest hosted by the Nashville country station, and the picture of him dressed in his denim cowpoke's outfit shaking hands with some tubby little WA 125 announcer was taped to the wall of Brackus's. Old Joe had hopes for Scott, in that shy, puzzled way which substitutes ambition for understanding. When a second division country band played Brackus's Scott would be there backslapping with the musicians, helping to tune the steel guitars, sometimes bobbing up on stage to take part in an encore or emcee some starry-eyed pack of Louisiana grizzlies who thought Brackus's was the big time. Sometimes he did session work, away in Memphis, with the Dixie Stealers, the Cottonpickers, bands you had heard of. They had a habit of never putting the session players' names on the record sleeves. But he looked the part. He played a big, unwieldy Hofner Les Paul in a laboured style which the oldtimers said reminded them of Roy Orbison. And though the drinks at Brackus's were more expensive than anywhere else in the county, and old Joe wouldn't let him run up a tab, Scott was there drinking most nights of the week.

One Tuesday night when trade was slack and the jukebox was blaring out Allman Brothers records over the empty tables, I met him in the parlour. He looked ghostly, a little out of place amid the solidity of Brackus's cattleprod decor, the steerhorn wall fixtures and the giant bottles of Southern

Comfort. There was a rumour going round, I later discovered, that one of the Pirates' cheerleaders had spent the weekend in an abortion clinic at La Grange. But we talked about my job – I had just got Photomax, the big repro business, to give me their local franchise which meant driving round the country with a mobile photolab – and after a while I suggested that he ought to be playing more, go into a studio maybe and cut a record.

'I could do worse.' He didn't seem offended at this piece of simpleton's advice, which every bar-propper in Brackus's had been offering him for the last year-and-a-half. 'The old man wants me to get a job.'

'What sort of a job?'

'That depends. If I wrote down my qualifications you'd piss yourself. I was an English major. Subsidiaries in economics and art and design. Round here they want you to chop wood or work at the gas station carwash.'

The way he said *gas station* made me think that old Brackus must have had a few words. 'Maybe it doesn't have to be chopping wood,' I told him. 'What did you specialise in on the art and design course?'

'Christ. Ceramics. Expressionism. A little photography.'

I offered him an assistant's job in the lab there and then, which seemed to please him, and said I'd be in touch again after I'd spoken to the Photomax people. 'Here's hoping,' he said, all lazy and wide-eyed, but as if he meant it.

It took a week to get a decision out of Photomax about funding an assistant. In the meantime Barrett filled me in on the pool-table gossip from Brackus's. 'Let me tell you something, my man' – Barrett always talked as if he were some wisecracking negro from an NBC cop serial – 'the word on Scott Brackus isn't good. Sure, Ruthie – the one with the tits and the snaggle teeth – had a hoover job over the weekend. Her pa was down to see me on Monday. Plus the old man finally got to lose his temper.'

'The old man lost his temper with Scott?'

'You got it' – and here Barrett positively bridled, as if he were Huggy Bear sashaying around the set of *Starsky and*

Hutch. 'Happened in here, a couple of days ago. Rockin' Dopsie was playing, you know, those zydeco boys from the bayou. The Cajun Twisters. Scott was hanging around with his guitar, the way he does for an encore, when old Joe jumps out from behind the bar and tells him to shift his ass away from the stage. Right there in front of the Twisters' manager. You never saw anything like it.'

'So what did Scott do?'

'What would you do, my man?'

I told Barrett about the job with the mobile photolab. 'The South will rise,' he said tolerantly (Barrett had tried and failed to get a job on *Dixie* magazine). 'It's a nice idea.'

I was busy that week, ordering up film from the suppliers in Nashville and checking the insurance for the lab, but it wasn't difficult to go on hearing about Scott. The local Kodak rep had been at Brackus's the night old Joe delivered his grand remonstrance. Ruthie with the tits and the snaggle teeth made a brief, etiolated appearance at the Pirates' midweek game. People in bars and at supermarket checkouts started to talk about 'that mother', and Scott became suddenly that most typical of Southern whipping boys, the privileged kid who goes wrong, the strapping six-footer with the wide smile who breaks his daddy's heart. I saw him a couple of times down at the Stonewall, the gentlemen's club where old Brackus had bought him life membership on his eighteenth birthday, and he had that sullen, companionless look of the person who can't find anybody to accept his offers of drinks. Ruthie's father was on the committee of the Stonewall.

Then, when the letter of acceptance came from Photomax, he disappeared. Out East, people said, to see his sister, but Joe Brackus didn't know and none of the bar-proppers at the Stonewall had heard. The Pirates played their Saturday night game against the Johnson City Rednecks, but there was no sign of him down by the coaches' dug-out or swapping backchat with the Redneck supporters along by the burger stands. Midweek, the Atlanta Express were headlining at Brackus's but you looked in vain across the smoky cavern to

68

the bar, past the rows of Choctaw saw boys in their black donkey jackets, for the sight of Scott shouldering his way towards the stage with the Hofner clasped under his arm.

As usual Barrett had the details. At the close of a discussion of the feature which he figured writing about the photolab he said shyly: 'Looks as if Scott finally hit the big time, my man. Tuesday last week, down at the Winnebag. You never saw anything like it.'

I shrugged. The Winnebag was a blues bar on the west side of Cook County which might have held thirty people. Barrett went on in that half sassy, half respectful way he had: 'Sure, I was there, my man. You know the score at the Winnebag. Some Memphis brats down to get a taste of country living, half a dozen niggers hollering for "Dust My Broom", and Scott gets up and does a couple of standards – "D-I-V-O-R-C-E", "Tennessee Slide" – you get the idea? And it's not the blues, but it's kinda tuneful and since he's a local boy and everybody remembers old Joe from way back people start clapping their asses off. Which could have been just fine, just fine, my man. A little novelty. A little *colour*. Yes sir. And it happens, it just so happens that there was a guy from Cherry Red' – Cherry Red was the big Nashville country station – 'up at the bar. Seersucker suit, fancy cane, you know the sort of stuff those candyasses wear when they're out to impress the hicks. Looking at Scott with his tongue hanging down to his chin.'

Barrett flicked me an inscrutable look – the sort of look he gave when the paper sent him to cover an Odd Fellows convention at Lafayette.

'And after that he lit out?'

'And after that he lit out. Nashville. Memphis. One of the Cherry Red studios someplace. But take it from me, my man, you can kiss goodbye to your photolab assistant.'

The crises of Joe Brackus's commercial career had been flagposted by his ability to bury the hatchet. Even when the real estate company had bought him out from the gas station the old man hitched up his trousers, marched into the Stonewall and stood the company lawyers a four-course

69

dinner. So a week later when Scott got back from Nashville there was a tab at the bar at Brackus's and anyone who could claim the slightest acquaintance with the family was swarming after free beer. I saw him there one evening in the middle of a cloud of hangers-on: local guitarists who figured he might put a word in at Nashville, a flaxen-haired grandmother who had appeared at the Opry in 1957, a couple of the Pirates' cheerleaders. He looked tired and flustered, but when he saw me he prised himself free from the grasp of Ruthie with the tits and the snaggle teeth and came loping over. I told him I'd heard the news.

'It's a break,' he said, a touch sheepishly. 'Too bad about the photolab, huh?'

'It doesn't matter,' I told him. 'Congratulations. What's the deal with Cherry Red?'

'The usual thing. A couple of weeks demoing. Some radio work – they got a majority stake in the two Nashville country stations. Maybe a billing at the Opry if I shape up.'

'What does the old man think?'

Scott grinned. 'He's on cloud nine. You know he used to play himself? Bluegrass. Kentucky stomp. I reckon I owed him this. You know,' he went on, 'I've had so many people tell me I've arrived that I might just start believing it.'

The way he said *arrived* made me wish I hadn't written the polite letter to Photomax.

After that you couldn't walk into a bar or diner without hearing about Scott. It wasn't that there hadn't been people like him before – after all, you could hardly throw a stone in Cook County without hitting a pedal steel guitarist or a guy who figured he could write lyrics for Willie Nelson – but somehow they had all faded away, to playing hotel residencies or copier salesmen's conventions. Barrett's favourite story was of a faded family act called the Country Cousins ('Cook County's Finest') whom he had discovered playing in a motel outside Atlanta. The irony, according to Barrett, was that the Country Cousins had actually *improved*. Set against this catalogue of blighted hopes and thwarted ambition, Scott looked a success. There was the letter from Cherry Red.

70

People remembered the talent contest, and the youthful Scott singing at kids' parties and the boy scout barbecues of long ago. Even Barrett unbent sufficiently to write it up for the *Cook County Sentinel* and a second photograph of him, square-jawed and resolute, got taped to the wall of Brackus's.

Not long after the story appeared he was gone again, to Nashville, people said. Taking the photolab out round the county I used to look for mentions of him in the trade papers you found lying around the barbers' shops or pinned to the walls of roadside diners. There was a paragraph or two, early on, listing him among the 'New signings to Cherry Red' but that was all. Somebody came back from Nashville and said they'd seen him on stage at one of the small talent clubs, along with some harmonica players and the Tallahassee Country Gospel Choir. Third on the bill. Old Joe Brackus stopped answering enquiries. People stopped asking.

Maybe six months later I bumped into Barrett at the Stonewall, where he'd been taking the committee's views on the new freeway. 'Scott's back,' he said.

'At Brackus's?'

'You got it, my man.' And Barrett smiled that lazy, mischievous smile that made me think again of Antonio Fargas. 'Prodigal son,' he said.

I stopped off at the bar a couple of nights later when the Dixie Stealers were headlining. It was one of those tense, sultry evenings you got occasionally at the end of summer when the crowd at Brackus's got surly and the sawmill boys threw beer glasses at the microphones. I got there just as the Stealers were finishing their set ('Sweet home Alabama' sung to the accompaniment of lofted Confederate flags) but there was no sign of Scott on the stage or waiting, guitar slung under his arm, over by the PA stacks. At the bar I brushed past Barrett, who had his arm round a cheerleader and his tie yanked down into a low, pendulous knot on his chest.

'You seen Scott?'

Barrett jerked his finger back over the bar, pointing hard at the giant bottles of Southern Comfort and the henge of beer cans. When I saw Scott bending down over the beer pump,

71

straightening up as old Joe snapped an order from the cash register, I realised that none of the carefully chosen phrases of welcome I'd rehearsed would do. 'The South will *rise*,' Barrett said gleefully, loud enough for the bar to hear, and I stayed just long enough for Scott to catch sight of me, sidling off with that sad, resolute feeling you get head on with somebody else's tragedy.

II

La Grange

SUMMER '83 WASN'T a good time for the repro business. Kodak had a three-month strike at their warehouse at Dyersburg, there was a run on the world silver market that sent up the price of film, and what with the expense and the flaring heat which hung over the cornfields from dawn till sunset people stopped using their cameras so much. For a time I tried to ignore the disappearing orders and the shaking heads at the roadside pharmacies – I headed north Kentucky, went to trade fairs in Lafayette offering bargain rates, thought about going into partnership with one of the local chemists, but then the drought set in, the dust swarmed up over the bumpy Cook County backroads, the drug-store windows were full of second-hand Leicas and Hasselblads and it was suddenly cheaper to stay at home. 'When the punch comes, ride it,' Barrett the journalist used to say, so I made the call to Photomax, put the mobile lab in storage and took the job at La Grange.

It was one of those places you see very often in the South, which has outgrown its origins without ever letting go of them. The dirt farmer with a thousand acres and a contract with three flour mills who still has trouble signing his name; the small-town newscaster who makes it on to network TV and still says 'y'all' and 'I guess' when she comes home to visit her folks: such sights were common in Cook County. La Grange was the biggest track complex for a hundred miles, but they still kept on the old, slow-witted announcer who had been with them twenty years back when the site was opened and Howie Jasper, the owner, still took two days a week off

73

to dodge the phone calls from the West Coast agents and the Ivy League track clubs and go duck-shooting in Johnson City marshes. 'Just your average hillbilly with a wallet,' Barrett used to say disparagingly, but the local TV station covered two meetings a month in the summer and the results got printed in the East Coast sports papers. In the early eighties Calvin Smith ran there at a charity meet and two reporters and a photographer arrived from Houston to write Howie Jasper up for *Track and Field*.

After that things began to take off. He had plans for La Grange, Howie Jasper told us, in that shy, puzzled way that redeems its guile with transparency. Pretty soon he had the stadium turned into a limited company with investors in Jackson loaning him money for redevelopment. He took out the old cinder track and had a sports contractor from Memphis come and lay an all-weather surface. He put a roof on the rickety grandstand and sold concessions to the local burger salesmen and the McDonald's franchises, finessed his way into sports sponsorship schemes that would bring in the big names from UCLA and the Santa Monica track club. And, most important of all, he signed the deal that made him Clyde Hopkins's manager.

I was busy the first couple of weeks at La Grange, sending out franchise forms to the Coke and Burger King reps, dealing with the contractors who were putting in the new electronic scoreboard, but it wasn't difficult to find out about Clyde Hopkins. The bar-hall idlers and the local talent spotters who hung around the stadium of an evening taking drinks off Howie were already talking about him, this kid who still ran barefoot but could whip any college boy the West Coast cared to send down. Barrett, who turned up halfway through the third week to write him up for the Cook County *Sentinel*, filled me in on the details.

'Sure, my man. All happened a month ago, down near Atalanta' – Atalanta was the farming end of Cook County, seventy miles away – 'when Howie decides he'll checkout some of the local talent, you know, turn up at one of the high school meets with a stop-watch and see if anything takes his fancy. And it's the usual thing – a few bullet-heads throwing the shot around, teenage high-jumpers thinking they're Dwight Stones – and Howie's on his way back to the car when up steps this kid in a windcheater and runs the hurdles in fourteen dead.'

'That's a state record.'

'You got it, my man,' Barrett said tolerantly. 'Or would have been if they hadn't been using a hand-timer. So Howie makes enquiries and finds out the kid's seventeen years old, never run outside the county before. Real country bumpkin stuff. Howie asked him where his track shoes were and he says, he'd never gotten used to them: did all his running on grass.' Barrett flicked his head towards the window, where his track-suited joggers laboured through the shimmering after-noon heat. 'Lick anyone in *this* stadium, that's for sure.

'And another thing,' Barrett said. 'There's a little part-time photography job going down at the *Sentinel*. Weddings, mayoral clam-bakes – you know the score. I put in a word.'

There was a fortnight until the *Sentinel* started interview-ing. In the mean time, repairing the stadium advertising hoardings from the top of a twenty-foot ladder or sitting in the office typing up CVs, I saw quite a lot of Clyde Hopkins. He came and sat in the admin block, while the secretaries made long-distance phone calls to Miami and Tampa Bay or talked about driving to Nashville for the weekend to see the Atlanta Dance Kings, and flicked through the back numbers of *Dixie* magazine. Other times he stayed out on the track running circuits or lining up the hurdles in files of six or eight and doing stepping exercises. The other runners, the lanky PT students who reckoned on making the state championships in Jackson, the burly National Guardsmen sweating to pass army medicals, offered him handshakes, tried to buy him beers in the stadium bar, but he kept out of their reach. He seemed remote, preoccupied, embarrassed by the way people called him 'Lightnin' ' after the old blues singer, by Howie's back-slapping and the posters billing him as the 'Cook County Express' which appeared in the barbers' shops and on the motel display boards. But in early July he walked away

75

from a field that included the state champion and a sweating two-hundred-pounder who had once come seventh in the US junior trials, and Howie talked about entering him for some of the West Coast college meets or getting him a track scholarship somewhere out East.

Barrett got interested then, in his sideways-on, reporter's way. At the close of a discussion of the photographer's job, which it turned out was going on ice until the end of the summer, he said, 'Hear Howie's been talking big about the Cook County Express. Track scholarships. The West Coast. Isn't that right?'

I nodded. 'A pile of forms came in the office this morning.'

'Uh huh. I heard.' Barrett smiled in that mischievous way that lifted him a thousand miles north of Cook County and put him on a TV screen opposite Paul Michael Glaser. 'Well, you can kiss your ass goodbye to that, my man. Sure, there's plenty of track scholarships going for meathead hurdlers, and nobody's going to mind an awful lot about your grade point average, but you have to be able to read and write. I talked to one of the Grange lawyers who stopped by the other day. Seems like the kid had to have that contract Howie made him sign explained to him clause by clause. You never saw anything like it.'

But there were other reasons, I discovered, why it would be difficult to get Howie's prodigy up there on the national circuit with Greg Foster and Skeats Nehemiah. Two nights later at the big La Grange invitation meet he came second to a fading thirty-year-old from Mississippi who had hung around the fringes of the '76 Olympic squad, but he did it in thirteen seven zero. I skipped the post-race celebrations – there were letters I needed to write to the other big repro houses in the East – and was heading out through the empty foyer when a girl's voice pulled me up.

'You know where I can find Clyde Hopkins, mister?'

She couldn't have been more than sixteen. There was a dirt bike propped up against the foyer's glass exit gate with a Snoopy pennant fixed to its handlebars. I explained about the party.

76

'You want to come along? I can take you up.'

The girl twisted her fingers uncertainly for a while. She had very pale blonde hair that reminded you of Cissy Spacek. 'I guess not,' she said finally. 'Listen,' she went on. 'Next time you see him you could tell him that Terry was waiting.'

I watched her riding off through the rows of Lincolns and Pontiacs in the stadium forecourt and out on to the highway. Next day I gave the message to Clyde but I needn't have bothered. She was round at the stadium in the morning and the two of them stood there arguing while the hurdles Howie Jasper had lined up for a demonstration race in front of cable TV got taken down and the local reporters kicked their heels and drank whiskey sours in the hospitality suite.

Summer dragged. The heat rose up over the parched grass and the cotton died in the fields, so that there were rumours of hardship funds and the insurance company travellers sat in the roadside diners selling fifty-dollar policies against drought. I had cool, non-committal letters from the East, from Philadelphia, Boston, Pittsburgh, from big repro houses who said they wanted college graduates or ten years' experience and told me to write again in the Fall. Then a week into August Barrett wrapped his car round a fire hydrant over near the Tennessee border and broke his thigh-bone, so I took a day's holiday, borrowed Howie Jasper's pick-up and drove over to the hospital at Union City to see him.

'One of those things, my man, just one of those things,' Barrett said. He was grim and irritable because the nurses wouldn't let him smoke and there was a rumour that his mother was arriving that afternoon from Memphis. There was a copy of the *Tennessee Sports Illustrated* lying on the bed with a picture of Clyde rising up effortlessly over a hurdle, the bunch of perspiring also-rans seen dimly in the distance behind him. 'You heard the latest about Lightnin'? Looks like Howie's sending him West for a couple of months. Catching the big LA meets and the Prairie Games. Plus a five-thousand-dollar sponsorship deal from some sportswear manufacturer Howie reckons owes him a favour.'

I told him about Terry. Barrett laughed. 'Uh huh. I heard. You know he ran thirteen five eight midweek over at Lafayette? Beat Missouri Joe Constantine into third. And another thing, old man Hopkins comes up for trial at Jackson tomorrow on a repossession order. Put those two together and see what they come to.'

After that I didn't stop hearing about Clyde Hopkins. About how his pa was a dirt farmer ruined by the drought, about how his mother had to wash dishes at the diner in Degville. You couldn't stop at a gas station without some wisecracking ancient hawking his gum in the dust to tell you that he'd known Grandpa Hopkins way back in the Depression when he'd gone out West to pick oranges in California. Howie Jasper was very great around this time, bustling about in a new Fox Brothers suit, though the temperature hit 92 that week, and hosting afternoon-long lunches for the company shareholders. There were other signs, too, of this new-found confidence. Come mid-August a couple of NBC lawyers showed up for a meeting and anyone who worked full-time at the stadium had to wear a scarlet and blue uniform mocked up to look like a track-suit with the La Grange jack-rabbit logo on the back. Then, when Clyde got accepted for the September meets at UCLA and Frisco, he bought airtime on the Memphis radio stations to advertise it. And though the kid hated drinking and the air conditioning had stopped working in the heat, Howie made him put on a suit and sit in the stadium bar three nights a week talking to the fans.

I saw him there one Sunday night when it was getting late and the barman was already putting the towels over the Seven-Up dispensers and corking up the barrels of root beer which Howie bought at a discount from a supplier in Nashville and which nobody would drink. He looked a little uncertain amid the fading light, mightily uncomfortable in the suit Howie had bought for him, tie yanked up against his throat. There was a cup of coffee on the table in front of him with the surface stretched into a skin and a packet of the Bluegrass cigarettes which the farmers used to smoke.

I said, 'You don't want to let Howie see you with those things.'

He shrugged. 'Howie went off to Degville, a while back. Said he had to talk to my daddy.' When I didn't answer he went on, 'You know, I ain't ever been out of Cook County before. Never did leave it, 'cept to go to some fancy farm convention once away in Kansas, time the old man thought about buying a new seed drill. What do you reckon it's like in California?'

'Some people seem to like it.'

'Uh huh. My grand-daddy went there, picking oranges in the Depression. Seems a funny thing to do in the Depression, don't it? Picking oranges.' He shrugged again. 'You know, I don't even want to see that five thousand dollars. Don't care if Pa gets it or it goes straight to the bank. Just don't want to see it, that's all.'

And after that he disappeared: driven out to the airport first thing in Howie Jasper's pick-up, people said, off on the charter flight to San Francisco. There was a charity meet two nights later at La Grange, with a one-lap wheelchair race and a thousand-dollar invitation steeplechase, but there was no sign of him amongst the crowd of kids in their red track-suits by the electronic scoreboard or standing with Howie's guest stars in the celebrity enclosure. Old man Hopkins came into the office a couple of times but he had that furtive, hang-dog look of the man who can't understand why people are doing him favours and he didn't want to talk. No one had seen Terry in a month.

I was keeping my head down around that time, writing letters and buying air tickets – Pictureworld in Philadelphia were finally giving me an interview – and I had to wait a few days to catch up with the sports papers. The news was mixed. He won a couple of inter-state meets in thirteen eight, thirteen nine five, then he bombed out in the West Coast games against a row of Olympic trialists and there was a story that he'd injured himself, torn a hamstring, that sort of thing. September came, but the drought lasted through: the roadside verges were white-coloured now and all along the horizon you could see the dust from the army lorries bringing water in from the big reservoirs across the state border, and Howie Jasper worried that the tarmac would crack before his big end-of-season meet. The day I got the acceptance letter from Pictureworld they let Barrett out of the hospital and he limped into the office to catch up.

'Guess what, my man? Terry got married last week. Over at Choctaw.'

'Who to?'

Barrett smiled that lazy, insouciant smile. 'Oh, just some hillbilly with a wallet. Some *farmer*.'

'How'd Clyde take it?'

'How would you take it, my man? Leastways, he's advertised in Howie's end-of-season special. The ads came in at the *Sentinel* this morning. "Local boy comes home", that sort of thing. Plus two national record-holders and an NBC camera team. They reckon Howie gets a network contract if it goes OK.'

The evening before the meet I stood on the pine-ridge two miles outside the stadium and watched the grey clouds roll in from Baton Rouge and the Gulf: the drought broke early next morning and covered the La Grange track in three inches of water. The athletes shivered and fretted but they went ahead anyhow, with Howie Jasper cursing and shouting and the NBC team filming from behind polythene shelters. By the time the hurdles came on most of the crowd had gone and there was an inevitability about the way Clyde sauntered out of the blocks with an odd, sick smile on his face, battered his way through half a dozen hurdles or so and then stopped dead to head off on to the trackside where Howie was yelling and hit him in the mouth. I watched them for a while as the rain fell and the cameramen drifted away and a couple of the La Grange investors stood around with disappointed faces, while Clyde squatted absently on his hunkers and Howie raged at him with the blood and the water gumming up the collar of his shirt. Barrett was saying something and the old announcer's voice cracked through the tannoy but I headed off thinking, of all things, about Terry, about the dirt bike

80

propped against the foyer door and what it must have been like to pick oranges, in the Depression, in California.

III

Disturbance at the Heron House

HIS MOTHER, OLD Lila-Mae Fuller, had been the great
grand-daughter of a Confederate general killed outside
Vicksburg in 1863, and it was this that gave the family its
status. Twenty years ago busloads of Yankee tourists had
arrived to loiter round the Fuller mansion at Choctaw Ridge
and peer at the sepia portrait of the old gentleman surrounded by his Louisiana 7th Company Militia, the Tennessee Civil War Re-enactment Society had staged a mock
skirmish in the big pinewood at the west end of the family
estate, and Lila-Mae had wondered about getting a grant
from the State Heritage Commission and putting in a coffee
room and an amusement parlour. But then the old lady had
got Alzheimer's disease, the State Heritage Commission had
decided to fund a battle site near Nashville instead, and
though the occasional researcher in a pick-up still drove
purposefully over the dirt-track roads to the Fuller estate the
grass grew up six feet high outside the tall windows and there
was no one to cut it. 'Kind of sad,' people said in the tones
they used whenever a State congressman went down under an
embezzlement charge, 'and kind of unnecessary'.

The gloss was significant, for there was a symbolism about
the Fullers' decline. Thirty years ago you couldn't travel a
mile in Cook County without coming across some vagrant
memento of the war, a roadside diner, say, with a Confederate flag hanging listlessly on the pole outside, called the
Robert E. Lee, or a granite memorial stone fenced off from
the fields by picketwire and hung round with flowers. The last
registered state veteran didn't die until as late as 1957: they

had a funeral service in Johnson City lasting three hours and two thousand people turned up to stare at the old dirt farmer's grizzled corpse – he'd been a bugler boy who joined up under age – and run their fingers over the faded calico fatigue jacket they buried him in. But after that people forgot. The woodcut illustrations of the Battle of Gettysburg that used to hang round the walls of the Stonewall gentlemen's drinking club cracked in their frames and got taken away. The *Cook County Sentinel* stopped printing its April 9 memorial edition. Driving round the county with the mobile photolab I used to pull up sometimes at the sight of an abandoned screw-gun rusting in a field, a flock of crows rising up off ancient, tarnished metal, think for a moment how frail the present was in the face of past solidity. But it didn't last. The fields got cleared, the county war museum closed down through lack of funds, and people started saying that the Fuller children were thinking of selling up to a real estate company in Memphis.

There was only a handful of Fuller kids by this time. Since old Miz Fuller had taken sick they had all fallen away, in the way that ancient Southern families sometimes have when the old man dies and there isn't anyone left to hire the farmhands or tell you to button your shirt properly, gone off to Canada or out West to take jobs in motel management or fire insurance. By the early eighties when the shutters went up over the windows of the big house there was only a single daughter left and then even she disappeared, lit out East somewhere, propping up a bar-stool in Florida, people said: the Fullers were famous drinkers. That left Travis. Even to the tolerant Choctaw neighbours Travis seemed an unlikely custodian of the the Fuller heritage. 'Looks like a farmer,' Barrett the journalist had pronounced, and it wasn't meant as a compliment. Taking the photolab out over the ridge towards the state border I used to see him sometimes, ambling along the backroads with a dog at his heels, head down against the sun, wearing an old wide-brimmed straw hat to keep the flies off. He never returned a wave. Once a month maybe he drove into town in an old Dodge convertible with the number plates dragging in the dust and stood silently in the grocery store queues and the line at the bank with his head tilted awkwardly to one side. 'A real meat-head,' people said, and eventually in that quiet, gradual way, the Fullers became a talking point, something to be taken out, argued over and eventually disparaged over the long tables at Brackus's bar and diner or in the card room at the Stonewall. People said that the old lady was still alive somewhere in the big house with the shuttered windows and they wondered what had happened to the money old man Fuller had made selling timber to the government back in the fifties. Barrett sometimes talked big about finessing his way onto the Fuller estate, writing the place up for the *Sentinel*, but no one ever answered the letters he wrote and the Fullers had never got round to putting the phone in. Meanwhile the real estate company surveyors came over from Memphis, stuck a few posts in the ground alongside Choctaw Ridge, and then went away again. Travis had decided not to sell, they said.

I was away out of the country that summer, running the picture desk for a Nashville sports paper, but Travis turned up occasionally in the bulletins of local gossip Barrett communicated late at night over the phone from the *Sentinel* office. In town two or three times a week now, Barrett said, buying corn at the agricultural suppliers, and there had been delivery trucks with New Jersey numberplates calling at the Fuller estate. But then Barrett got sent out on tour with the Cook County Pirates baseball team and the news died away, so that coming back into Brackus's one night in Thanksgiving week I had to think for a while to register the identity of the tall man sitting on his own at a corner table drinking his way steadily through a jug of Joe Brackus's Tennessee whiskey. But it was Travis all right. He had that faraway long-sighted look in his eyes, characteristic of all the Fullers, that suggested he didn't quite see you, that he was looking at something else away on the horizon. We talked for a while about the weather – it had been a wet summer in Cook County and all the farmers were putting in crop failure claims with the local insurance offices – and how there had been a D.A.'s investigation at the County Treasurer's office, but it was obvious that his mind wasn't on it. Finally he said:

'I'm wearing this badge on account of my great-great grand-daddy.'

I hadn't taken any notice of the medallion he had pinned onto the strap of his farmer's dungarees, but now out of politeness I took a look. It was a design you saw quite a lot in Cook County, that the country bands who played at the local beer festivals wore or state politicians fixed onto their suit lapels when they were going all out for the agricultural vote, the stars and bars of the Confederacy and a pair of crossed cavalry swords above the motto 'The South Will Rise'. Travis nodded.

'I guess you heard about my great-great grand-daddy. Guess you knew he was a real Johnny Reb.' Then he said unexpectedly: 'Heard you take photographs?'

I started explaining about the photolab and the job in the Nashville picture desk, but he cut me off with a wave of his fist.

'Uh huh. I heard. You ever take photographs of birds?'

'What kinds of birds?'

'Let's see now. Cranes. Herons. Couple of Kentucky Orioles.' He made a gesture with his hand, a movement that was almost poetic in its suggestion of billowing, lofted feathers. 'You reckon you could take photographs of them?'

I nodded, not sure whether he was stark crazy or whether this was some piece of wiseacre's practical joking, like the way Barrett used to call up the local radio station phone-ins sometimes and pretend that he was a big Nashville producer looking for talent. Travis guffawed. 'Catch you later, boy,' he grinned as he got up and slid past the big pinewood table to the door, and the way he said *boy* convinced me that he was administering some sort of rebuke.

As usual Barrett had the details. 'Seems Travis been making a name for himself,' he said when I called at his office a couple of days later. There was an advance copy of that month's *Dixie* magazine lying on the rickety horsehair sofa where the Republican mayoral candidates sat unhappily in

85

expensive, badly-fitting suits while they gave Barrett their views on the freeway extension. Barrett jabbed at it with his finger. 'Take a look at that, my man.'

I looked at the grainy, wide-angle picture; of huddled waterfowl, Canada geese flexing their wings high up over their heads like pieces of origami, a final shot of Travis staring sheepishly out across the grey water of the lake. His eyes were hardly focussing. Barrett went on: 'Yeah, I was over there Tuesday checking it out. Artificial lake, heronry, breeding pens, the works. Biggest bird sanctuary in the state, I guess. And Travis standing there rubbing his hands like he's embarrassed, telling everybody that he's prepared to make it a county amenity provided they let him call it the General James T. Peterson Memorial Reserve out of respect to his great-great grand-daddy. You never saw anything like it.'

When I explained about the conversation I'd had with Travis, Barrett looked irritated. 'The guy's ancestor died at Vicksburg,' he said severely. 'Least you could do was to show a little respect.'

I was back in Nashville on and off for the Fall, but it was never far enough away to stop hearing about Travis. The county leisure and recreation department sent a surveyor out to the Fuller estate who sat on the back porch – he wasn't allowed in the house – drinking whisky sours with Travis for an hour or so, and pretty soon there was a licensing board up, a couple of vending machines selling Coke and Seven-Up, and a kiosk offering sepia postcards of the old general. A few families struggled out there on weekend afternoons while the autumn weather held and said that it was OK if you liked that sort of thing. In between talking about the scandal involving the County Treasurer people remembered old man Fuller the timber merchant and reckoned that it was kind of public-spirited what Travis was doing with his money. Then, when the bad weather came and the snow blanked out the approach roads over by Choctaw, he disappeared: holed up for the winter, people said, hibernating. I looked for him once or twice in town, but there was no sign of him in the grocery crowds or in the bank hunching his shoulders down as he came up level with the teller's window.

It was a bad winter in Cook County that year. Eight feet of snow fell on Choctaw. The meteorological centre at Dyersburg registered thirty degrees of frost one night in January and the cattle froze to death in the fields. Driving backwards and forwards to Nashville – the paper was talking about offering me a full-time job but nothing would happen before spring – I used to wonder about Travis, holed up in the big house on the empty estate, as the snow fell over the artificial lake, with only the birds and the picture of his great-great grand-daddy for company. But there were other people, I found out, with an interest in Travis Fuller. An associate professor from the University of Texas had called in at the *Sentinel* office, Barrett maintained, wanting to get in touch with him. 'Girl looked like Farrah Fawcett,' he explained disbelievingly when I went round. 'Reckoned she was writing some thesis on Confederate families and wanted to know about the old general.'

I looked on while Barrett, who had skidded his car into a ditch coming back from an Oddfellow's convention in Lafayette and emerged two hours later with first-degree exposure and three frost-bitten fingers, attempted to light a cigarette. 'What did you tell her?'

'What would you have said, my man? Told her to drive straight on out to the Heron House and take a look.'

The Nashville paper got in touch again after that inviting me to come back for an extra two weeks' work, so I never got to meet the girl from the University of Texas. But back in town a month or so later I caught sight of Travis buying liquor in the off-licence Joe Brackus ran as a sideline to the bar and diner. He had his head down low over the pile of cans wedged to his chest and didn't look up when I waved.

Barrett called that night: random shards of gossip floating over the wire. 'Yeah, the County Treasurer comes up in court next week ... Plus I got to speak to that girl, the one that reckoned on talking to Travis Fuller. You never heard anything like it, my man.' Barrett hadn't sounded so pleased since the time his editor had shot himself in the hand out duck-shooting in Johnson City marshes. 'Seems from what she turned up that old Lila-Mae's great grand-daddy weren't no Confederate general after all. Just an ordinary powder monkey died of a fever at Louisville years after, she told Travis, and the old picture ain't nothing to do with him.'

I remembered the medallion on Travis Fuller's dungarees. 'What did Travis say to that?'

'Didn't seem to make no difference to him, she said. Anyhow, I got a card here asking me to the grand re-opening of the General James T. Peterson Memorial Reserve.'

I got to look at Barrett's invitation card, all black borders and fancy type: a fortnight away. But two nights later the alarm bells started ringing all over the Fuller estate and the Choctaw neighbours called up the county police department on account of the noise. I hitched a ride with one of the local sergeants Barrett used to give bottles of whisky to at Christmas in return for services rendered. I remember the night for the weather, a great protuberant moon that drenched the highway with blood-red light. By the time we reached the Fuller estate the alarm bells had stopped ringing, but it wasn't difficult to work out what had happened. There were dead birds all over the driveway, cranes with their heads torn off and their carcasses cut to ribbons, and a pall of smoke hanging over the heronry. The big house was shut up, but eventually they broke in. Travis was sitting with his eyes back in his head staring at the body of an old lady. Miz Fuller, the doctors said, though it was hard to tell, she'd been dead so long.

They buried the old lady with a Confederate flag draped over her coffin, and you could tell from the way the whole town turned out that they figured it was some sort of occasion. There was a state congressman at the church and the County Treasurer came, flanked by a couple of guys from the D.A.'s office and smiling whenever anybody tried to shake his hand. Later, looking at the photograph of the old general that the *Sentinel* printed along with its obituary, I thought about the gun carriages rusting in the fields, realising that I would never see them again, however hard I looked, and that this, somehow, was the saddest feeling of all.

89

SEEING LONDON

BOBBY WALKED IN front of us, stiffly, over the wet grass. Roxeanne said (it was a Sunday lunch party at somebody's house): 'I guess you were right when you said I needed someone to show me London: with you being at the office all day. But I never thought I'd find him just like that. Can you believe it? I'm sitting outside one of those pavement cafés in South Molton Street when this guy comes up and says in the cutest English accent: "Excuse me, is this yours?" And it's that ivory comb you bought me, that time you took me round the antiques market in, where was it, Portobello. It just fell out of my bag. You ever hear anything so corny? Anyway, there's a spare seat at the table and pretty soon we're talking like old buddies and I suppose I must have said something about wanting to see the sights, because pretty soon he looks at me all serious and says: "Would *I* do? As a guide I mean" – still with that accent like Jeremy Irons. So I put on my best Manhattan voice – you know, that husky drawl you laugh at over the phone – and said: "So where are you taking me, honey?" Just like that.

'"Don't worry," he said. "I can show you London." And that was the time I thought I'd made a mistake, because usually when an English guy says he's going to show you London he means Westminster and the Tower and between you and me I don't ever want to see another Beefeater again. Anyway it was raining by then so I said, "Let's take a taxi." But he just looked at me and said, "What's wrong with your legs? It's not very far." He can be very authoritative, you know. So we started walking down through Soho looking in

90

the shops and, boy, does he know his history. Do you know they call it Soho because they used to hunt foxes there and that was what the huntsmen used to shout? I asked Bobby how he knew about this and he said he read a lot and he was interested. I like it when people are modest like that. There are some guys would have given you a reading list. A bit later I had to go – you remember I was meeting you to go to the ballet? – but I gave him my address. Yeah, I know what you told me but I could see he wasn't a psycho or anything, and next morning a guy turns up on a motorbike with a dozen white roses and a note from Bobby saying can he see me again? Can you believe it? Just like in a movie with Robert Taylor.'

Bobby lingered behind us at the bar, paying for the drinks. Roxeanne said (it was at a theatre in the Strand): 'OK. I'd better be straight with you. I know I haven't been about much the last two weeks, but you see Bobby moved in a month ago and I thought I ought to stay around. Don't worry, it was my idea, well both our ideas, and anyway I was so angry with the way Bobby was treated by the guys in his house. You remember when I met him he lived in this place in Battersea? Anyway, last week somebody stole fifty pounds off the landlord and they decided it was Bobby and he had to leave. And Bobby knew it was one of the other guys but he's so straight he didn't want to say so. Can you imagine that? So when he turned up at the apartment with a couple of suitcases, of course I let him in. Not that I actually mind having him around the place. He's so considerate – not like some of your Englishmen – and boy, does he like doing it. I talked to my mother on the phone the other night and she told me I sounded tired. 'You'd be tired as well if you were doing what I've been doing,' I told her.

'Plus I finally got to find out what he does for a job. You know I always wondered why he was around in the afternoons but wouldn't phone for a couple of days? Well, it turns out he's an actor! Not in movies or anything like that, but TV ads. You know the ad where the guys are sitting there drinking coffee and the first one has to borrow the second one's fountain pen? Well, that's Bobby standing there in the background mixing a drink. I got him to tell me about it. He told me he'd been to RADA on some scholarship – but there weren't any proper jobs for actors over here so he had to do ads for coffee powder. Can you believe that? I told him he ought to come out to the States and try for the network shows and he said he'd think about it. He'd go down a bomb with that accent.

'And the joke of it is he isn't English. Not properly. It came out because I was talking a lot about Mom and Dad. I mean, I guess if your father teaches at Princeton and your mother went to Vassar you tend to talk about it. He looked serious, you know that way he has, and said did I want to hear about his family? Anyway it turns out that he's Greek Cypriot. His father came over here just after Independence and married an English girl. I guess I can relate to that, what with Mom's family coming from Athens. He's really serious about that side of his life. I mean, if he has a spare couple of weeks in the summer he goes back to Cyprus to see his cousins and stay on the farm. I said I might go with him this year – you know how I always got off on that primitive community thing – if I can square it with the faculty. Yeah, and that reminds me, I thought you said actors over here were dumb? Well, I took Bobby to this party the department had last week – the one I told you about where all the lecturers come along with their wives and it's all terribly *English* and cultured – and he really wowed them. Spent half an hour talking to the Professor about the novels of Anthony Powell. When we came out I said to him: "How come you know all that stuff?" and he just said – you know that way he has of turning his head when he looks at you? – "Oh, I have hidden depths."

'Plus I'm still seeing London. Bobby's very serious about that. Sometimes I get back to the apartment in the evening really exhausted. But Bobby just says: 'I promised I'd show you London,' and so we'll get up, go to Trafalgar Square, Piccadilly or someplace and just look at the lights going on and all the people. And he has these plans, you know, about the places I ought to see. I mean, last week he got me up at six to drive down to Greenwich Park and see the dawn come up. He says you get a light there like nowhere else in London. We just had half an hour. Bobby had to get back for a shoot. Half an hour running around in the wet grass, playing hide-and-seek behind the trees. Bobby can be a real kid when he wants to – and you know, I couldn't remember a time when I was so happy . . .'

Bobby sat in the deck chair, staring silently at the newspaper. Roxeanne said (it was at our house one evening in summer): 'Yeah I know I didn't come to the concert last night with you and Sam like I said I would. I know I didn't phone you at the office like we arranged. But Bobby had these friends round and I figured I ought to stay home. It was my fault. He was going to take them to a restaurant. But I told him: "Listen sugar, this is a partnership, right, and if you want me to stay home and cook for your friends then I'm happy to do it." I did that jambalaya you had when you came over that time and hash browns. Anyway they all seemed to like it. Just some guys Bobby knows from acting. To tell you the truth, he doesn't really like them. He just says that if you're an actor you have to hang around with people, you know, so you can find out when the jobs are coming up. Actually Bobby hates all that. He said he felt morally degraded having to sit there, smile and listen to these asshole directors. I said, listen honey, you don't have to tell me about that, you should see how things are in the faculty, the way people hang around the Professor trying to kid him he's got a sense of humour. Still I agree with him about those guys. After the meal they just sat there round the table, wouldn't help with the dishes or anything. And then when they'd gone I found someone had stubbed a cigarette out in that Sèvres vase – the one Dad gave me a couple of years back. Bobby was really furious about that – and when Bobby gets mad with someone he gets mad. He said if he could find out who did it he'd make them apologise to me personally. If I hadn't stopped him he'd have telephoned everybody right there on the spot at two o'clock in the morning. So I said, forget it hon, it's just a piece of china. No need to worry yourself about it. But do you know what he did? Next evening when I got back from the college – you know I've been working late a lot trying to finish that article on Robbe-Grillet – when I got back there is the most beautiful, not to say expensive, porcelain dish lying on the table and a note from Bobby saying he was sorry. Must have cost two hundred, three hundred dollars. And you know how broke Bobby always is . . .

'Which reminds me, I know it was all fixed and I know I said I would and everything but we can't make it to your picnic on Saturday. The fact is I said I'd get up early and drive Bobby out to this shoot someplace in the country. I mean, he has to be there at nine, and boy, don't we know all about the transport system over here. So I reckon the least I can do is to take him. Plus the really exciting thing is that Bobby thinks it's his big break, yes sir, a whole three-parter on TV. It might even get shown in the States, Bobby reckons. He told me the plot, you know, one of those mystery stories set in a country house, that Agatha Christie thing. So, no more crummy ads for a while. He's been working terribly hard, filming all week and there's another week after this one. Anyway, we've got quite a routine going. We get up at six, we have breakfast – Bobby's so *English* about breakfast, bacon, eggs, the whole caboodle – and drive down. And then in the evening I pick him up and we head back into town for supper. I don't know where Bobby gets his energy. After a day like that I'd be ready to flake out, but no sir, not Bobby. He wants to go out dancing, to the clubs, take in a movie. He's cute about that. He says to me, 'Don't think, do' – you know how introspective I can get. And, Jesus, I get so tired sometimes. Especially in the mornings. The mornings is when he likes doing it, too. But then I reckon anything that makes my Bobby happy is fine by me . . .'

Bobby wasn't there.

Roxeanne said: 'You know I never did like to bad-mouth people, and I hate talking about Bobby behind his back, but if

94

I ever meet a guy with problems like that again then I'll count myself unlucky. I mean, I didn't know there could be people that jealous. You remember Max. You met him that Fall at my folks' place. I haven't seen him in years but he sometimes calls me up in the evenings, just to talk about old times. He has this associate professor's job at Syracuse now. Well, he called one evening and Bobby picked up the phone. As soon as he heard it was a man's voice he said: "Forget it, she's out." Just like that. Anyway, I played it cool. I told him: "Honey, you might be a little upset about something but Max is one of my oldest friends and I can't have you talking to him like that," and he apologised, but it kind of pissed me off all the same . . .

'. . . But between you and me it was the dishonesty I couldn't take, because as you know I have this thing about being honest in a relationship. I mean, when Bobby moved in I said: "Look honey, I want you to treat this place as if it was your own. Don't think you have to ask permission every time you want to take a shower." But boy, did he take me at my word. Sometimes I thought we were just throwing one big party for Bobby's friends. And then I started missing things. Just little things. You know that bracelet Mom gave me when I got my doctorate accepted? It couldn't have been worth more than a few dollars. I thought I must have just lost it, you know how good I am at losing things. Same thing happened when I started losing bills out of my wallet. Nothing major, just fives and tens, and I thought: Uh huh, you must have spent more last night than you thought. But then finally I reckoned I had to confront Bobby about this: "Look, sugar, I know this is a difficult thing for me to ask but I think you're stealing from me and I have to know why." And do you know what he did? He started crying. Just lay down on that sofa there and burst into tears, said I'd been so good to him and he felt so ashamed and could I ever forgive him? So I told him: listen, it doesn't matter. You know I'd have given you the money if you'd asked me, just don't ever lie to me. And after that everything was OK for a while . . .

'. . . But it was the stuff about the job that really threw me.

95

All that business about Bobby being an actor and waiting for a break. Well, let me tell you that Bobby had as much chance of being a star as I have of teaching semiotics at Yale. Straight up. I once went to see him in this play at some theatre in, where was it, Lewisham, just in a room over some pub, and you know it was pathetic? Like some kid in a high-school prom, screwing up his lines and looking sort of helpless and upset. What beat me was how seriously he took it. I mean, he really thought he was going to be Scofield or someone. And then finding out that all the stuff about the shoot in the country was just a fake. Just hanging around with the guys in the tape room and hoping that someone was going to give him a job. How can you respect someone who behaves like that?

'. . . The sex? Well, when you get to my age, honey, you can take or leave the sex, especially when it's coming courtesy of some gorilla who can't even wait for you to get your breath back. But do you know what really blew it? Do you know what really knocked it on the head? Last week, when I was really tired – you know I had to rewrite that Robbe-Grillet piece for the *Journal of Aesthetics* – well, one night Bobby says: "We'd better get up early tomorrow. I've got something really special to show you, somewhere you have to go if you're seeing London." So we got up – four, five in the morning, I can't remember, I was so bombed – and took this cab way out through the City. Someplace called Billingsgate – guys in white coats and stinking fish lying around in piles. Bobby was really excited. He was sort of *proud* of it, if you know what I mean. He said: "Isn't this great? Right out of Dickens. I bet you never saw anything like this before." And I said: "Let's get this straight. You're making me lose four hours' sleep just to see a *fish market*? Forget it." And after that I thought, this is it, this is the end, this is where I quit . . .'

Michael sat hunched over the chessboard, his forehead creased in concentration. Roxeanne said (it was a Sunday lunch party at someone's house): 'The thing I like about Michael is that he's got a sense of humour. I mean, there I was standing in this gallery looking at some great mess of colouring when this guy comes up and says: "Of course you have to realise that what the surrealists were trying to do was to paint without any effort, and we all know what *that* leads to." Now I thought that was really funny, especially as Michael really *knows* about art. I appreciate every Englishman you come across in a gallery tells you he's done three years at the Courtauld, but Michael's stuff . . . The other day he was showing me these book illustrations he's done – it's a project he's working on and you have to give him the third degree to get him to talk about it. And let me tell you, they're as good as any of that Aubrey Beardsley thing you guys always go on about . . .

'. . . You mustn't ever tell him I told you this, but the first time I met him I thought he was gay! Something about the way he speaks. Yeah, I know when English people talk about art it's as if they were holding an egg in their mouths. Well, I won't go into details but let me tell you I was one hundred per cent wrong about that! Of course, Michael's very busy right now, finishing the book and everything. But in the evenings I go round there – he has the cutest little apartment in South Ken. We have supper. A helpmeet? This guy is a grade-A *cordon bleu* chef, honey, which makes a change from some people I could . . .

'. . . Bobby? Funny you should mention Bobby. I heard about him just the other day. Bobby's in jail someplace. You didn't know? Well, it turns out that when Bobby got together with those actor friends of his it wasn't just cigarettes they used to smoke, no sir. They reckoned when the police raided the place Bobby was staying they found enough dope to keep half of London hired for a week. Nine months for possession with intent to supply. To tell you the truth I used to wonder about it when he was with me. I can remember one time picking up his jacket and watching the papers roll out onto the carpet . . . You know, I went down to Greenwich with Michael the other day: there was this gallery he wanted to go to. And we ended up in that park, you remember, that godawful park with all the trees and the dogshit. And I suddenly thought about Bobby and, do you know, it was as if it had never happened. Believe me, sugar, it was as if it had never happened at all.'

LOOKING FOR LEWIS AND CLARK

TRUTH TO TELL, we didn't even come from Seattle. I know all the music papers used to write us up as part of the Seattle Sound, and maybe we played with Nirvana and Pearl Jam one time – I don't rightly remember – but you ever hear of a rock band out of Bozeman, Montana? Isn't nothing there but steers and cowboys in ten-gallon hats. So we figured it might as well be Seattle. Same thing with the country gear. I know they put us in buckskins for the cover of the first album, and Jimmy did that Wrangler ad a while back, but none of us ever been on a horse in our lives. Closest any of us got was Curtis when he worked for a vet one time, out on Vosper Mountain. As for the others, Jimmy now, he went in the meat-packing plant when he was sixteen. Errol was a college kid – you know, processed hair and a windcheater, kind of kid you didn't see around too often. Me, I just collected my welfare check. So no horses, or cattle neither. And from Bozeman too. Anybody back there get to hear about it and I wouldn't show up in town in a hurry, no.

Sure, the place has changed. I was back there last year in the Fall and they had a longhair record shop, and Mudhoney were supposed to be playing the local sports hall. Hollywood actors buying vacation homes out by the lake too. Wouldn't have had that fifteen years ago – now if Jane Fonda had strolled down Main Street when I was a kid and told a few ranchers she planned on reintroducing the wolf, someone would have torched that bungalow down and never thought twice about it. Same thing with fashion. Clothes I'm wearing now – you wouldn't reckon on people being pissed off by a

T-shirt and a pair of K-Mart sneakers and a ponytail: I seen a Warners executive – guy who signed us – in a ponytail. Well. you couldn't have worn that stuff in Bozeman back in '75. I was in a two-dollar diner one time when a kid came in with an afro and leathers and someone smacked a pool cue over his head. Now they got an AIDS clinic and the congressman don't know one end of a steer from another, so I reckon the kid won the deal.

The first time I saw Jimmy wasn't long after that. All on account of the only job I ever had. They were building the new freeway then out towards Livingston, and taking up the asphalt the old-timers said had been there since Lewis and Clark, and anyone who wanted to shovel tar could get eighty dollars a week for doing it. Evenings after work we used to hitch a ride back into town and fetch up at Mother McKechnie's. You ever catch the scene in *The Blues Brothers* where the band gets to play at Bob's Country Bunker? Well, Mother McKechnie's was like that, and then some. The ranchers used to drive in fifty miles on Saturday nights to check out the country bands, and if anyone tried to play up-tempo or didn't have a steel guitar they'd throw beer bottles. I seen a waitress lose an eye once on account of that. Jimmy now, he stuck out at Mother McKechnie's like a Democrat at the state farmer's convention. Tall, skinny kid in a Fresno biker's jacket with his hair quiffed like the Fonz in *Happy Days* – you could see the cowboys bristle up at him every time he walked up to the bar. But somehow no one ever laid a finger on Jimmy. You see, even then he had the reputation of being a mean kid – and that meant something in Bozeman, where if you were sixteen and hadn't seen the inside of a police truck you were looked on as some kind of degenerate – and everyone knew about the pills and the cop he was supposed to have taken out in a poolhall at Billings the Summer before. I saw him in there one night in Winter '81 when the Dixie Stealers were playing – four old boys in Roy Rodgers outfits doing close-harmony versions of 'The Old Rugged Cross' – and he winked and said, 'Beats me, but there's people come seventy miles to hear this shit' and we

100

kind of laughed, and for once I didn't feel so bad about working on the freeway or living in Sally Pasricha's boarding house out on Clearwater Street where you could never open the windows because of the smell from the tanning factory.

We started hanging out together after that, the way kids do when they got shit jobs and no family to speak of. My pa was dead by this time and my ma had gone back to her folks in Minnesota – I was supposed to visit at Thanksgiving, but somehow I never got round to it. When we got famous and the second album had been on the Billboard chart a month I went over there with a convertible and ten thousand dollars in a bank teller's envelope, but it wasn't any good – we just sat there staring at each other and watching the kids play on the patio, and then when she did start to talk it was about my aunt Abbie and how she couldn't wash her hair except on Friday nights. Anyway, we went to concerts sometimes – they had a new 5,000 seater amphitheatre over at Billings by this time – if the major-league bands stopped by on their Western tours. This was '82, '83 remember, and all anybody wanted to listen to was Southern boogie – rows of guitars and the PA playing 'Freebird' in the intervals. We hitched all the way to Denver once to catch Kiss at the Four Springs Theater, and we wouldn't have got in unless Jimmy hadn't finessed his way into the hospitality lounge claiming he was a guy from the lighting company and I was his assistant. Weird thing was that Jimmy didn't even like all that stuff. He reckoned it was too dumb, too ordinary, just songs about motorcycles and women and beer. 'Kind of music you have to get out of your head to appreciate,' he used to say.

Was '84. '85 by then. We met up with the others round that time, the way you do. Curtis wandered into a music store one day when we were trying to talk the owner into loaning us a brace of Marshall amplifiers; Errol Jimmy knew from way back. Even then, though, when there were just the four of us, and Curtis was still paying off the credit loan on his drum kit, I could see that things were changing. All of a sudden I'd stopped working for the highways department and hanging out at Sally Pasricha's, where the whores who lived in the upstairs apartments used to stop you on the stairs and ask for change, and was staying with Jimmy in some beat-up trailer in the park outside of Bozeman. The freeway was nearly finished, and most of the guys who'd built it were back in the line at the welfare office, but Jimmy and me got by somehow. Sometimes we stuck around Errol's place, where there was a swimpool and a pin-table if you didn't mind Errol's mom, who disapproved of us on account of our hair, but mostly we just stayed in the trailer and talked. He was one of those vague, dreamy kids who like lying around smoking and blowing their mouths off: stuff about the old West Coast explorers, about how his grand-daddy had been a cowboy down on the Panhandle. Later on, some music journalist asked me if I could remember any of it, but it wasn't there any more. Everything else I could tell you about – the inside of the trailer with the pictures of Robert Plant Jimmy razored out of *Rolling Stone*, Jimmy's leather jacket with the death's head pins shining out of the dark – only the words had gone.

We took off after that. I mean *took off*. One day we were hanging out in the pool hall on Bozeman Main Street, the next we were a thousand miles away in some studio Warners owned out in the Arizona desert with a hot-shit producer from Memphis and a sound engineer on five hundred dollars a day. Leastways that's how it seemed. If I look back there are great parcels of time just gone and vanished, like an old settler's map of Montana Jimmy had on his wall one time where the edges just fell away into white space. There was stuff in the music papers by now, and Bruce Springsteen turned up at a promo we did someplace out on the West Coast, but even then Jimmy didn't help. He had this trick about not showing up at business meetings or TV interviews, and then coming out with some asshole excuse about his chest hurt or he'd slept over. Other times he'd sulk round the stage like he wasn't there, mumble his lines or just stand there looking dumb and letting the crowd take the chorus. Sometimes, weekends mostly when we'd stay at his mother's place at Belmont – it wasn't more than a shack bungalow up

102

in the woods, but Jimmy kind of liked it – I'd try and figure him out, figure out the sulks and the missed cues, the way he deliberately came in a split-second off the beat, but it was never any good. 'If it wasn't for me you'd still be laying tarmac outside of Bozeman,' he'd say, as if that was an answer. I could have smacked him for that – I'd done it once, years back, for something he'd said – but somehow I didn't say anything. Not at his mother's place, with her fixing the supper out back. She was a tiny old lady with a pinafore and bi-focals, and Jimmy called her 'ma'am' like a little kid in a black and white movie.

But all this time it was falling apart. Us and Jimmy, that is. Even when we signed the record deal in a Warners suite at some fancy hotel in NYC, he wasn't there. Disappeared off to the mountains, people said, but his mom didn't know and none of the guys in the Bozeman pool halls had seen him in months. When he fetched up in Denver a week later, all he'd say was that he'd been looking for Lewis and Clark – I thought he meant Lois Lane and Clark Kent until Errol figured it was the guys who'd found the Oregon trail. They packed us off on tour after that – I had a feeling one of the record company execs had decided Jimmy was bad news – doing college gigs, East Coast theatres that took four, five thousand kids, which was shit-scaring when you remembered that six months back we'd been playing flophouses in front of thirty people. For a while Jimmy did fine. He had this bad boy image in the press, what with the leather jackets and the biker pins, he had himself photographed with Mickey Rourke like they were buddies, and he said 'Shit' on the *David Letterman Show*, which the record company reckoned was great publicity. But back there on the corner of the stage with my bass guitar – I used to hunker down next to Curtis's kit so that Jimmy and Errol could take the spotlights – I'd catch sight of him sometimes, staring at the crowd or off into space as if there was only him there, and I'd wonder. We did a live show on MTV the week they put out the first album and he was like a spoiled kid at a party, kicking over the monitors and bad-mouthing the lighting guys, and halfway through the last number he trashed a three-thousand-dollar Telefunken microphone, and that was serious, even at MTV. He'd met Marsha by then, who none of us ever liked – dark-haired girl who worked as a model on the East Coast fashion magazines and had Indian blood, Jimmy said – and Errol, who'd roomed next to them a couple of times, said you couldn't get through the door on account of the dealers.

He disappeared again in the spring, time we were cutting the second album, off to some Indian reservation in Nebraska where there was a kid drummer he wanted to record on an eight-track. We went ahead and finished all the same, and you can take it from me the voice you hear on 'Lonesome Dove' isn't Jimmy's, no way. When he got back from Nebraska he gave these interviews saying rock and roll was dead, and he just wanted to play chicken skin stuff from the prairies. No amplification, just country music like his grand-daddy had sung him. We toured Europe that Summer. Frankfurt. Paris. London. I don't remember the places too well. He waited till the last gig until he walked out on us. In style, too. Half an hour before the soundcheck, when he hadn't shown, Curtis broke into his room and there were a couple of bolsters twisted up on the mattress to look like a body, with a watermelon from the complimentary fruit selection for a head.

Back home he wrote us this letter that some of the music papers printed, about Indian music and not being on the same wavelength. Every time a band breaks up you get a letter. I hardly noticed. Curtis, Errol and me were auditioning for another singer, but it was pretty clear by then that we weren't going to find one, and that the record company wouldn't care if we did. But I still kept hearing about Jimmy. Marsha had quit by then and was dating some Hollywood actor, but he got a solo deal someplace. I even went to see him on his first tour – the hall was half-empty and he got mad every time somebody shouted for one of the old songs. Then when he disappeared the last time it didn't even register: Curtis and me were too busy picking up our careers, building the studio and guesting on that Soundgarden album. But I read the stories in the papers. They found him out on the Bozeman trail, head down in some dried-up creek with a backpack and a couple of empty water carriers: dead a month, the medical guys reckoned, and never did find Lewis and Clark. But a month or so later I was back in Bozeman, looking around the old places – Sally Pasricha was dead and the pool hall was closed down – and I hitched up to Belmont and the woods and the old bungalow. There was no one around – his mother had gone off someplace on the East Coast, people said, and the roof had fallen in over the dime store linoleum – but I stood there for a long time staring down at the freeway stretched out in the distance like an old black snake, remembering how I'd met him and the times we'd had, and thinking that it was kind of sad and kind of unnecessary, like the way the whores asked for change on Sally Pasricha's staircase or the tumble-weeds blew in over the old river bed with no one to stop them or care which way they fell.

SATURDAY NIGHT AT THE JENKS MOTEL

JOE SITS HEAVILY in front of the big oblong dressing mirror – a gift from Ella's folks, he remembers, fifteen years back – tying the tie that Ella gave him that morning. Ten dollars it cost, Ella said, out of an L. L. Bean catalogue, which Joe privately thinks is extortion, and Joe hasn't worn a tie in five, six, years, not since he gave up the insurance salesman's job and they moved up here to Missouri, but here he is, anyhow, sitting on the end of the bed fixing this weird, multi-coloured noose under the collar of his white shirt. Kind of thing that goes down well with the customers, Ella thinks, a guy wearing a tie, and Ella knows about these things, Joe reckons. He fixes it some more, flapping the end over his fingers and letting it loll down over the mound of his stomach. Beyond the mirror is a gap in the winceyette curtain where Joe can see the neon sign that says *Jenks Motel, Bar and Grill, Children Welcome* moving backwards and forwards in the wind. One of these nights, Joe knows, the sign will slam down and shatter on the forecourt, but somehow he never has time to fix it. In the distance he can hear the sound of the cars out on the freeway and the noise of the police sirens doing speed patrols over by Jackson Gap – Saturday night sounds. Saturday nights make Joe nervous, have done ever since a couple of years ago when the local Hell's Angels chapter tried to check in and hold a party. Wasn't anything you could call trouble – two extinguishers broke and a busted window – but the memory still makes Joe uneasy. He sits staring at his face in the mirror, at the tie and the listing sign, not seeing them, or anything.

In the kitchen, Ella daydreams. About the past, mostly: staying with her grandparents in Kentucky when she was a kid, but there are other flashes – wondering if they would get the motel registered in the state leisure and amenities guide, wondering what she would say if Billie-Sue, who hadn't called in six months, was there on the phone, and how the conversation would go. There is a big pile of food on the slab in front of her – steaks and gammon slices and huge Florida tomatoes – that will need cooking, and Ella gazes at it awhile before thinking that she'll get Larry to do it when he comes in, which isn't fair on Larry, who has eight rooms to clean and the kitchen floor to swab down, but then who else in Missouri is paying five an hour for the sort of work Larry wants? Remembering Larry's money sets Ella thinking about trade and she peeks through the kitchen door into the lobby where there are still six keys hanging on the wood and six empty hooks. Still, she reckons, it's a Saturday night with the summer coming and ten to one some teenage kid wanting to ball his girlfriend will feel like stopping here and paying thirty dollars to do it. And then the daydream whistles up again and Ella stops worrying about Joe and howcome he doesn't talk to her anymore and Billie-Sue and howcome she never phones and is back in Kentucky on a spring morning with her grandpa pointing out over the bluegrass and saying that you could always tell where a jackrabbit was hiding because eventually, never mind how long it took, the ears would twitch.

In Number 5 Loretta lies on her stomach in the sky-blue dressing gown Henry likes drinking from a glass of iced water. There is a bottle of bourbon on the side table in the plastic cover that the liquor store checkout girl wrapped it in, but Loretta thinks she'll save that for later, after Henry arrives. She imagines the two of them curled up on the bed late at night toasting each other in neat bourbon. Even now Loretta can't stop congratulating herself on how things have worked out, on Henry being in this part of the county for a copier salesmen's convention and wanting to get back together again, and Henry's wife being away in Maine for the weekend visiting her folks. Loretta checks her watch. 7 p.m. An hour, maybe, or an hour and a half and then Henry will be here, dusting his hands down on his knees that way he has, telling her how fine-looking she is and how much he's missed her. Loretta rolls over onto her back and lights a cigarette, like in a movie with Michelle Pfeiffer or Ellen Barkin, where the girl lies in the darkened room on the unmade bed so that when the phone rings and she starts up her breasts tumble into her hands like ripe fruit.

Joe and Ella jostle into each other in the kitchen, where Larry stands slicing tomatoes with a long-handled knife. He has a trick of throwing each tomato in the air and catching it on the blade as it falls. 'Like that tie,' Ella says, and Joe nods self-consciously. Neither of them knows how to behave in front of Larry, who is eighteen and saving up to pay his way through medical school. 'You put them extra towels in Number 3?' Ella asks. Joe shakes his head and looks at Larry. Larry smiles. Another thing about Larry is that he has this habit of quoting details from all the medical textbooks he reads, details about tapeworms and inflated livers and all the weird stuff that can kill you. Ella wishes secretly that Larry would say some of this stuff now, but Larry stays quiet and flicks another tomato effortlessly into the air. 'And the sign,' Ella tells Joe. 'You could at least have fixed the sign.' Joe shrugs, the way he has done every Saturday night these last five years, the way he did when his mother died, the way he did when Billie-Sue told them she was moving in with some longhair over at Carson Lake. The wind scrabbles at the window. Outside Ella can hear heavy car tyres – a station wagon, maybe, or a Pontiac – crunching up the dirt in the driveway.

In Number 7 the Fergusons continue the argument they began twelve hours ago over breakfast and carried on through the three-hundred mile drive east from Kansas City. On the TV screen in the corner of the room a grey-haired man in an expensive-looking suit is talking to a glamorous woman in a one-piece bathing costume, and Mrs Ferguson watches them as she argues. 'You got no right,' she says bitterly. 'Driving her home like that in broad daylight, staying out there on the patio for a coupla hours like it was a free show for the neighbourhood. No right at all.' Mr Ferguson lies sprawled over the bed counting cigarettes from out of a bent, crimson packet. There are seventeen. He flicks one up from between thumb and forefinger into his mouth, focusing only on the moment, the noise of the flints colliding beneath the chromium of the lighter. Mrs Ferguson's voice is a faint susurration, like rainfall heard a long way off.

In the kitchen Larry is frying gammon slices in a big open frypan. When each slice is done he transfers it from the pan onto the glass hotplate under the grill. Ella sits watching him from the kitchen table. There is no sign of Joe, who has gone to checkout the new arrivals in the lobby. Eventually Larry says: 'I mean, take your lungs, right? Say you cut them open and pulled all the surfaces out flat, how much of them do you reckon there'd be?' Ella frowns. 'I guess I don't know, Larry,' she says. She thinks for a moment, hard, not wanting to seem stupid. 'About the size of a blanket maybe?' Larry grins, takes another gammon slice out of the pan and puts it on the hotplate. 'Couple of baseball pitches more like,' he says. Ella listens, open-mouthed. Larry is eighteen years old and all that, but Ella thinks he is the most interesting person she has ever met.

In Number 4 Mr and Mrs McCormack rest side by side under the pink coverlet, watching the light fade in blues and greys over beyond the outhouse wall. Snowbirds, both of them, been on the road for five years with the trailer and the mobile home until Mr McCormack got sick, which is why they've been spending time in the motels and the resthouses. Their joint age is a hundred and sixty-three. The light fades some more and the cartoons on the silent TV give way to a re-run of *The Golden Girls*, which is a series Mrs McCormack likes but doesn't care to turn up for fear of waking Clyde. Mrs McCormack checks the alarm clock on the bedside table and finds that it is eight o'clock. A whole eleven hours until it goes off. Mornings are the worst times, listening while Clyde rolls over in bed, trying to figure out whether he feels good or bad. Most mornings these days he feels bad, and Mrs McCormack resigns herself to another day of TV, catnapping and watching Clyde drowse his way through the long summer afternoons. For a moment Mrs McCormack feels panicky and wants to reach out and touch Clyde under the coverlet, prod him until he's awake, but then she calms down again. She remembers seeing Clyde this way before and every time he's gotten himself right again. Always figured that he could sleep himself back to health. Mrs McCormack watches the light again and then wonders fretfully just what it is that she's going to do about Clyde, about the way Ella looks at her in the mornings, about the three-ton mobile home in the driveway which will be falling apart soon with no one to check the tyres or clean out the portable sanitary closet. She takes a hand mirror out of her bag and starts to check her make-up before thinking that this is a foolish thing to do and throwing the mirror on the floor where it lies amid the trail of used tissues, cash dispenser receipts and old copies of *Senior Citizen* magazine.

Lying on the bed, Loretta wonders what time Henry will come. He said eight or nine, but Loretta doesn't mind when it is, just so long as he gets there. She imagines him striding into the room, not even bothering to knock, and sweeping her up in a bear-hug. Loretta's glass is empty again, so she sashays over to the table by the door and pours herself some more iced water out of the pitcher. She thinks about opening the bourbon, only this would be mean on Henry, to start drinking before he's arrived. In the end she tugs off the plastic cover and measures herself a finger. After all, Loretta reflects, there isn't anything else to do, here in a motel in Missouri, listening to the cars on the freeway and waiting for Henry.

110

Joe stands uncertainly in the doorway of the diner. There are only three or four people in there eating the gammon slices and the steak and tomato platters, and Joe doesn't know whether to walk on in and say hello. Eventually he decides not to and moves off into the lobby where Ella is checking in a couple of blond-haired guys with thick moustaches and backpacks. Couple of faggots, Joe reckons, and good luck to them. He guesses that his tolerance goes with the job. Being a motel owner doesn't leave you much time for scruples. Ella now, she just hates faggots. There are five, six rooms free right now, but Joe knows, just as he knows the wind won't let up till dawn, that Ella will book the two blond guys into the worst one and then try and charge them double for room service. He wanders out onto the back porch where it is quite dark now and light shines through curtained windows. There are raised voices coming from Number 7, but Joe doesn't stop to listen. He and Ella used to go on like that sometimes, back in the old days before he gave up the insurance job. Joe wonders about Billie-Sue for a while, and whether this had anything to do with it all. He decides not, pads back inside where he can hear laughter coming from the kitchen, wondering what crap Larry is telling Ella now.

Mr Ferguson lies on his back, stripped down to his vest and undershorts, counting the cigarettes. He wonders about going out to the lobby for a fresh pack, but this will mean putting his pants back on so he forgets the idea. Mrs Ferguson is brushing her hair with short, angry strokes. 'Listen,' she says. 'You lay a finger on me and I'll holler so loud every cop in the state'll be here.' Mr Ferguson shrugs, like the guy in the cartoon whose wife buys a sofa out of the catalogue without telling him. 'Have it your own way,' he says.

Lying on her back in the darkness, Loretta wonders what she'll say to Henry when he arrives. She remembers a movie where this girl sits there waiting for her boyfriend to come back from New Jersey or Vermont or someplace, and when he gets there she simply says nothing, just folds up into him.

Loretta wonders if she'll be awake enough to do this. She reaches over and looks at her watch, which has a luminous dial, and discovers that it's 10.15. After that she switches on the light again and takes another drink, thinking maybe this is how Henry will find her, sitting up in bed sipping liquor and giggling. She thinks about the copier salesmen's convention, and that it's a pity Henry doesn't do something more glamorous – be a cop, say, or sell real estate. But then Loretta doesn't think she'd like to go out with a cop and you need qualifications for selling real estate, so perhaps it's for the best. She takes another drink and listens to the wind, which is getting up now and, she thinks, kind of scary and comforting at the same time.

In the kitchen Larry is finishing the dishes, while Ella puts the unused gammon slices back in the freezer. Joe, wandering in through the yard door, hears him say: 'And you ain't gonna believe me, Mrs Jenks, but twenty-three inches is the record for a dick. Some old negro they had in a hospital in St Louis.' Ella roars, but Joe stays quiet. He wishes Larry wouldn't say that stuff to Ella, but it hasn't ever occurred to him to ask him not to. The phone rings and Ella picks it up, turning round so that Joe can see the look on her face change from irritation to anxiety. 'Baby,' Joe hears Ella say, 'baby, where you *been*?' and Joe realises that it's Billie-Sue, Billie-Sue on the end of some phone, in some call box a thousand miles away most probably. Larry tries to catch his eye, but Joe isn't talking. He moves off again into the shadow, shoulders down, his head twisted to one side.

In Number 4 Mrs McCormack thinks that she'll try shaking Clyde just one more time and then if nothing happens she'll go for help. Making this decision gives Mrs McCormack confidence. She can see herself tugging Clyde's arm, see him roll over and say, 'What's with you then?' in that way he has. She pulls hard on Clyde's hand, pressing down on the fingers hard enough to hurt, staring all the time into Clyde's wide-open eyes, but nothing happens. For a moment Mrs McCormack wonders what to do. She cannot get the thought of the mobile home out of her head, wondering who'll drive it away, who'll pay for it and for her. Then she remembers the deal she did with herself, that it's already midnight and most likely people will be asleep and that somehow this will make it worse.

Joe, standing in the shower-room in his pyjamas, hears the crash of glass on stone and knows instinctively that the neon sign has gone down in the wind. In a way he is pleased at the interruption, as Ella went straight to bed after Billie-Sue's phone call and Joe isn't too keen on disturbing her. He moves through the empty corridors to the lobby, where the night lamp is burring and Mrs McCormack stands timidly in front of the reception desk. 'Can I help you?' Joe says politely – he is always polite to Mrs McCormack – but he knows what has happened, and Mrs McCormack knows he knows. They look at one another steadily for a while, without speaking, while the insects whirl crazily round the lamp.

At 2 a.m. Loretta wakes up in a roomful of light. Henry is standing over her waving the empty bourbon bottle in her face like it was a TV reporter's microphone. He is tired, she thinks, and the bald patch on the crown of his scalp is showing even more. 'You're paralytic, you know,' Henry is yelling. 'Just a disgrace, you know that?' And Loretta laughs uncontrollably, as if it were the funniest thing she had ever heard. Outside the blue emergency lights dart and flicker.

MCKECHNIE'S DINER, 9 A.M.

FROM THE WASHROOM window Lila watches the smoke move up from beyond the trees: thick, ochre-brown smoke that hangs over the lines of pantsuits and towels Ella McKechnie has drying on the big hickory clothes-horses. For some reason the smoke makes her think of the old days, back in Indiana, and she concentrates for a while on these distant, phantom images – a maple tree that grew over the back porch, seeing Bob coming in over the fields wearing that shirt she bought him out of a catalogue – until someone hammers on the washroom door and there is the sound of feet moving in the passage outside. Lila doesn't care too much about the hammering – the only person she defers to around here is Mr McKechnie, and it isn't his time for the washroom, not for an hour – but still she pulls herself up off the can and starts putting make-up on her face from out of an old vanity case lying on the window rest. There is a message on the bag says *Elegant Living*, and Lila can recollect buying it twenty years ago in Macey's and wondering what elegant living was and how you lived it.

The smoke is disappearing now, drifting away across the tree-tops down to the creek, and Lila figures it's that Larry Frazier over at the garage, most likely, burning car tyres again. Mr McKechnie doesn't like Larry Frazier, nor the bikers who hang around Larry Frazier's forecourt, nor the smell of the sump oil. 'Guy is a *cracker*,' Mr McKechnie will sometimes say late in the evening, getting confidential over a Coke or a whisky sour, and Lila will nod and hold her glass in the way the celebrity guests do on the Dick Cavett Show.

114

There is more knocking on the washroom door, and Lila frowns slightly so she can fix her eyes, watches as the creases run in chevrons down each side of her face. She blinks a couple of times, pushes open the door and stares out into the corridor, where there is a punk kid with yellow hair and K-Mart sneakers smoking a cigarette up against the wall. Lila shrugs, adjusts her waitress's uniform – they still have dinky bomber jackets that say *McKechnie's diner* – moves past him into the sweet, syrupy air.

In his office out behind the checkout till and the Coke dispenser Mr McKechnie sits staring at the mail. A dozen letters maybe, circulars, bills, junk from the *Reader's Digest* and the NRA, a card which Mr McKechnie can tell by the handwriting is from his brother in Tampa Bay. Above his head a fan winnows the stale air. The phone on the desk buzzes, but Mr McKechnie carries on sifting, like a kid rooting through a toy box after his favourite muppet doll, until, sure enough, right at the the bottom of the stack he finds the letter with the Tennessee Loan Bank stamp. Putting it on the desk at right-angles to the photo of Ella and the framed citation from the Guild of Kentucky Restauranteurs, he looks through the window to the diner, where there are early customers ordering breakfast fries or studying copies of the *Lafayette Sentinel* while they wait for fresh coffee to brew. A tall guy in his twenties wearing a suit sits smiling in front of a plate of hash browns, and Mr McKechnie, who is 180 pounds and five feet six, looks at him for a while, wondering what it must be like to be twenty-five and work as a lawyer or in real estate instead of being fifty with the bank talking about repossession and non-renewable loans. Was an article Ella read him the other night from one of her digests about looking on the bright side and controlling your life, but Mr McKechnie doesn't believe in that stuff, ever since the steel cable snapped above the car hoist ten years back and sent a ton of metal down onto his leg. Took three operations and a metal plate to get him to walk again, and even now a stroll across the yard leaves him out of breath. Reaching down beneath the desk, Mr McKechnie fingers the ridge of hard skin above his knee, waits for the little shiver of pain to edge along the bone, wondering all the time what Ella will say, so that in the end the thoughts merge and for ever after the letter will remind him of pain, Ella's face seen through the perspex divide, the young guy in the suit smiling over his breakfast.

Back in the diner Lila takes side orders: French fries, apple pie, milk shakes. Over the years Lila has evolved a formula to remember her customers by, stripping them down to the basics of looks and gesture. The guy in the suit is Steel Nose; the punk kid is Corn Hair; the old man who comes in every morning for a popsicle is Dentures. Never fails. Sometimes the waitresses trade shorthand gossip about the customers with her: 'Steel Nose left me a dollar tip'; 'You catch the mess Dentures left under his seat?' Lila stoops down to whip a plate off an empty table and then swerves to avoid Duane, the kid Mr McKechnie hires to swab the floors, as he moves past with his mop and pail. Lila smiles and Duane says 'Howdy Miz Lila', which though Lila thinks Duane is a weird kid, what with his rat's-tail hair and the black T-shirt, she kind of appreciates. She peeks up at the perspex divide, but Mr McKechnie is slumped down over his desk, as the fans beat above his head, and Lila knows that his leg is hurting him again. Lila feels sympathy for Mr McKechnie, has done ever since the day three years back when he picked her letter out of the pile of application forms and gave her the job, even though there were two twenty-year-olds with torpedo tits showing off their legs in the waiting area. For a moment Lila wonders what Bob would have said about Mr McKechnie, but somehow this comparison doesn't help and she concentrates instead on cleaning up a chair where someone has left two pieces of pie, an empty pack of Merits and two state lottery tickets. Above her waitress's cap the flies whirr and cluster.

Back in the bungalow Mrs McKechnie stuffs clothes into a travel bag. Pantsuits, jeans, sneakers, a pair of high heels she bought in Louisville last Fall when they were there on a day trip. Mrs McKechnie doesn't know what the weather's like this time of year in California, but she guesses it's going to be hot. Outside the window the smoke is drifting in again from across the trees, and Mrs McKechnie figures that it's typical of Larry Frazier to play a stunt like that, today of all days. She peers up hopefully at the yard and the line of cars, but there isn't anyone there except Duane carrying cans of bleach in from the outhouse, and Mrs McKechnie recollects that she never did like Duane, what with the hardcore magazines he keeps out back in the store and the looks she's seen him giving the waitresses, and that not having to talk to Duane again will be a whole heap of fun. The travel bag is nearly full now, with just a lamé windcheater waiting to be packed in somehow, and Mrs McKechnie considers it for a while, remembering finally how Eugene gave it to her at Thanksgiving a while back, and wondering if she'll care to be confronted with it in three months' time in LA. But there are going to be worse things, Mrs McKechnie thinks, than remembering Eugene watching her pull open a mound of tissue paper. She rolls the windcheater up into a ball, squeezes it inside the plastic bag lying on the window sill, stows it away.

In the kitchen Duane thinks about the girl he met two nights back at the Winnebag, and wonders if she'll come and see him like she promised. Over by the grill Joe the black cook is talking his religious stuff, which is something Duane doesn't care for, but he figures that it isn't anything he ought to mention since the two of them are working together. 'You see Duane,' Joe is saying in that heavy voice of his, 'sin is all around us. Sin ain't something we can ignore.' 'Yeah, sin,' Duane says politely, hoping Mrs McKechnie or someone will come in and give him a different job, but the white door to the diner stays shut and Joe shakes his head again and goes on: 'Isn't a man in this state can say he don't know something about sin. Not you, not me, nor the Reverend Johnson at the Tabernacle.' Joe can go on for hours like this. There is a line of fresh eggs running across the groove of the draining board, which need to be made into batter, and Duane starts busting them one by one into a glass bowl, making a little flourish with his hand like one of those TV chefs on the cable channels, thinking all the while about the girl and what kind of tits she has, and what he'll say to her. 'And that sin is ours to deal with,' Joe goes on. 'Ain't nobody else's.' Looking out through a space in the steamed-up window, Duane sees a pair of bikers in leather jackets strolling around Larry Frazier's forecourt and sucks in his breath enviously, wondering for a moment what it would be like to speed round the county on a Harley Davidson with the girl from the Winnebag clamped to your spine, maybe, and not giving a shit about anything. 'So what you gonna do Duane?' Joe says, urgently but somehow still not looking at him, 'how you gonna fix that sin?', and Duane blushes, that way he has when anybody talks to him, and nods. 'I'm working on it, Joe,' he says.

In the diner the breakfast customers are thinning out. The crowd that follows is more ramshackle: kids in baseball caps and Pirates T-shirts; middle-aged women in stretchsuits; a swarm of teenage girls. Lila takes orders: coffee, donuts, shakes. A highway patrolman in a soft hat comes and drinks a hot chocolate standing up by the bar, chats to the teenage girls. As Lila fills him up with a second chocolate he says: 'Coupla cars out there blocking up the exit to the highway.' 'Ain't my problem,' Lila says, 'you want me to fetch the boss?', but the highway patrolman shrugs and lights a cigarette. There is a kid sitting in one of the chairs by the children's activity area playing with a toy Cadillac. When he sees Lila he rolls the Cadillac carefully towards her so it stops an inch or two from her feet. For some reason Lila stops, puts down her tray full of dirty coffee cups and fragments of pie, and rolls it back.

Behind the perspex window Mr McKechnie makes phone calls. His lawyer. Another lawyer the first one recommended. Two suppliers he owes money to. All the time Mr McKechnie

118

does this his leg itches and hurts, so that by the time he calls the bank there are little purple stars of pain shooting up in front of his eyes like Fourth of July fire crackers. For a long time the receptionist keeps him on hold, but finally he gets put through to the guy who wrote him the letter and they talk for a while. The guy sounds too young to be doing this kind of job, Mr McKechnie thinks, too young and too nervous. At one point he says, 'We're not talking about carrying a debt here, we're talking about foreclosing', and Mr McKechnie wants to yell at him until he recollects that the guy has a job to do and that talking to him like this is the way he does it. Outside bars of sunlight go skittering across the empty tables, and Mr McKechnie suddenly feels tired of talking. He puts down the phone and eases himself gently out of the chair, figuring that maybe he'll walk over to the bungalow and see what Ella thinks of it all. On the wall by the door there is a picture of the diner like it was twenty years back when Mr McKechnie bought the land, just a lean-to with a couple of chicken-runs and a flat-earth car lot, and Mr McKechnie stares at it, transfixed for a second by the memories it throws up, of him and Ella, and the guy named Henderson they had to do the decorating, how there was a state congressman came in one time and Ella never even noticed, the time two bikers held up the till, rain coming in endlessly over the distant Kentucky mountains.

In the bungalow Ella lights another cigarette from the smoking butt of the one in the ashtray. There is more smoke billowing over the trees and over Larry Frazier's forecourt, but Ella doesn't notice it. For some reason she starts thinking about the diner, and about maybe it might have worked out if they'd got permission for the motel, or the freeway extension hadn't gone through Dade County forty miles away. Can't make a living out of kids and dirt farmers, Ella thinks. In her head she can see the bright glow of the LA street lights. She picks up the travelling bag and takes it out onto the porch, seeing nothing except the white blur of the cigarette moving

119

in her mouth, scuff marks on her boot tips, old pieces of paper flapping up over the timber floor.

In the diner Lila is down to her last two dollars' worth of nickels. Neither of the other waitresses has any, so she decides to ask Mr McKechnie for the float. Through the kitchen door she can see Duane telling Joe about this new girlfriend of his, about how Joe can get an eyeful when she comes in to see him today, so Lila reckons there is no point looking there. Placing her heels carefully on the gravel path she sets off across the yard.

Moving out of the kitchen door Duane sees the girl from the Winnebag sitting down at a table near the main entrance. 'Hey,' he says, so loudly that the waitresses turn and look at him, 'hey there.' The girl from the Winnebag smiles a little, and then a big guy coming back from the counter with two coffee cups, stops and puts a hand on her shoulder, and Duane stares at them both, his mouth half open, the broom clutched in his hands like a soldier's rifle, frozen in mid-air.

In the bungalow there is a stale, sweetish smell. Flies whirl in the hall and outside the closet door. From where she stands in the porch Lila can hear Mr McKechnie moving around some room in the back of the place, like he was picking things up and letting them drop on the floor. Lila coughs a couple of times, wondering if she should go back, but then Mr McKechnie comes limping through the doorway. There is a kind of glaze over his face, as if he doesn't know who she is, and Lila thinks of Bob, that last time in the clinic, with the tubes running out of his mouth like a crazy motorway intersection. Mr McKechnie stands in the doorway for a moment and looks around him kind of helplessly. 'It's OK,' Lila says, feeling stupid because these are the only words she can think of, 'It's OK,' and the two of them look at each other, curious and a little surprised, while the gray smoke blows in the window and the car-tyres squeal and whinny in the dirt.

Standing in the slip-road next to the drawn-up Pontiac, Mrs McKechnie says: 'Reckoned you mightn't show.' 'Thought wrong then,' says Larry Frazier easily. He is a tall, brown-haired guy in his late twenties with a thin moustache. Leaning forward to put the travelling bag in the car a thought seems to strike him and he straightens up. 'Hey. You tell your old man about this?' Mrs McKechnie nods. 'Well, he sure as hell isn't going to come running after us,' Larry Frazier says, and for some reason Mrs McKechnie remembers the sound the car hoist made as it snapped and the look on Mr McKechnie's face in the split-second before it fell. She starts laughing, standing there in the road, while the cars slide by and the wind lifts the dust a little and Larry Frazier looks at her uncertainly, like a clamouring kid who, placed finally in the fork of the tree, is scared into silence by the rolling, endless distance.

CUTS

TOWARDS FIVE THE late afternoon stupor left him and he became aware of his surroundings once more: of the low, subterranean room with its rows of high-backed chairs; grey, queerly illumined shop fronts glimpsed obliquely through the area window; the curved metal trays with their cargoes of protein sachets and cologne bottles. Each detail of the basement's decor was set in sharp relief by bright, flaring light. Northwards towards Oxford Street a clock was striking the hour and he listened without interest to the chimes rising above a tide of quieter, unfocused sounds: hairclippers, the steady drone of the drying machines, a murmer of conversation.

Outside it grew dark. The woman whose hair O'Brien had been examining for the past ten minutes shifted slightly in her chair and made a small, irritable movement, like a spaniel having its coat combed for fleas. She said:

'I thought you were asleep just then.'

Knowing that he could be seen in the mirror, O'Brien made a deprecating gesture with his hand. The woman went on:

'Just before you started putting on the lotion. A glazed look. Miles away, I'd say.'

'I'm truly sorry,' O'Brien said quickly. He decided to emphasise the Leinster brogue because he sometimes found that this encouraged women to regard him more favourably. 'A tiring day, if you take my meaning.'

'Miles away,' the woman repeated. O'Brien felt her scalp twitch under his fingers. She smiled slowly as she spoke but for some reason he was alarmed by the intonation. To

122

forestall anything that might be construed as a reproach he picked up an electric dryer and listened with feigned anxiety as it stuttered into life. Then as a further precautionary measure he glanced over to the square clerical desk by the door, but Mr Trafford had disappeared and there was only an assistant arranging the mass of papers into neat, rectangular piles.

The woman said something else, but O'Brien lost it in the hum of the dryer. To avoid her gaze he pretended to be distracted by a pile of newspapers and magazines which lay on the floor next to the chair's height-adjuster and the coil of electrical cables. Straightening up he said:

'Would you like a book to read?'

When she did not reply he went on: 'Surely now? Many of our clients like to have a book to help them pass the time.' Always call them clients, Mr Trafford had said, it gives the place a better tone. Grocers' shops have customers.

The woman frowned, saw the pile of papers – they were free magazines of the kind distributed at underground stations – and relaxed her features. 'Oh, you mean a *magazine*? For a moment I thought you meant a proper book, like Dickens or someone.' The idea appealed to her and she laughed loud enough for the man next to O'Brien to turn round and stare. 'I thought you might have a library down there that you lent out to people.'

O'Brien grinned into the mirror. Relief at the woman's good humour fought with a sense of foolishness. It was stupid of him to say book when he meant magazine. It was because of his mother: 'Mrs O'Brien's book' they had said at the newsagent's when he went to collect her copy of *Ireland's Own*. For a moment he remembered the newsagent's shop with its pink and white canopy and the bottles of stout kept cooling in the tank until another memory came and drove it away, a memory of something he could not quite locate, that was somehow connected with his present surroundings but floated away and hung vaguely above them. Mr Trafford came through the swing doors in a burst of cold air, holding the evening newspaper under his arm. O'Brien waited for the dust to career towards him and swarm around his legs, and he moved his feet up and down uneasily as if he were testing his weight on cracked floorboards.

'You're very quiet now,' the woman said. O'Brien shrugged. He had a range of gestures for when the effort of talking grew too much for him. Out of the tail of his eye he looked over at Mr Trafford, who stood to one side of the big desk holding the newspaper up in front of him at arm's length and flapping the sheets to and fro. The worst thing about it was that Mr Trafford with the paper reminded him of Keenan. With the thin black hair combed back over his head and the way he had of sticking his elbows out as he walked it could almost be Keenan coming into the room and reading ostentatiously in front of him. The memory grew sharper and he remembered suddenly what it was that he had been thinking about earlier in the afternoon before the tiredness overwhelmed him: Keenan, Keenan and the old days.

The woman moved her head slightly. O'Brien's hand hovered for an instant above a clump of dark, grimy curls and then came to rest again. He felt better now, definitely better, as if he had just solved a problem in one of those puzzle books you saw fellows looking at on the underground, or seen the correct results in a football pools coupon snap miraculously into place. Over by the desk Mr Trafford was still reading the newspaper. O'Brien saw that it was open at the page where the advertisement was. You had to hand it to Mr Trafford; it was a fine racket he had going here, what with the advertisement in the newspaper, the headed notepaper and the fancy white tunics he made them wear. There was a copy of the advertisement sellotaped to the glass of the swing doors so that people could read it on their way in, with the words *Trafford Hair Clinic* printed in big letters. It offered free consultations, specialist staff and an end to misery and uncertainty.

Outside in the street it was quite dark. Through the area window O'Brien watched truncated legs walk backwards and forwards. Somewhere in the middle distance a siren began to sound and a bright, flickering light came boomeranging off the walls, making the roomful of white-coated men stir uneasily. O'Brien remembered travelling in an ambulance once with Keenan. It had been a joke because Keenan had known the ambulance driver, and so they had gone with him and helped to deliver some old ladies to a day centre. The woman yawned, a wide, full-throated yawn, so that O'Brien could feel the skin around her neck tighten. It occurred to him that he ought to say something that would make her want to stay sitting in the chair. Dimly, like a radio heard through a noisy room, he remembered the speech which Mr Trafford had made on the salon's opening day. 'Flattery, that's how we make our money. You have to instill confidence in the client. Make him think that what you're suggesting is for his own good. Nobody should leave here without a cut at the very least.' Mr Trafford's methods were persuasive: it was rare for anyone who entered the clinic to spend less than twenty pounds.

The woman was stirring again. O'Brien wondered if she sensed his nervousness. Or perhaps she thought that he had discovered something dreadful about her hair. Judging the moment right and letting the brogue creak softly into his voice he said: 'That's a fine head of hair you have in any case.'

The woman smiled, as if she was used to compliments of this sort. She said: 'I used to think so once. But it's thinning out, you must have noticed.'

O'Brien looked at her closely, the first time that he had done this since she had sat down. She was about forty, he decided, but the bad skin made her look older and she had what Keenan used to call a 'Derry front'. Keenan had had a joke that all the women in Derry had large chests. He had had other jokes about girls from County Clare and Roscommon sheep farmers. O'Brien shortened the focus of his eyes, so that the room ceased to be a blur of elongated white shapes and became a series of hard, intelligible objects. There was still something troubling him, though, down in the pit of his mind, and he looked over again at Mr Trafford, who had placed the newspaper squarely on his desk and was considering the sports page, but the ratchet-wheel of his memory obstinately refused to click. The woman said: 'So what would you advise me to do? Seeing that it's thinning and the colour's starting to go.'

O'Brien reviewed the possibilities. You could go too far, suggest an expensive rinse with highlights only for the person to shake their head and leave. He began cautiously: 'A bit of nourishment, perhaps, to give strength to it. A bit of a trim now. Our clients usually find that that's the agreeable thing.' The woman looked disappointed, as if she had expected something more than this, some bizarre preparation that would magically transform her, and for a moment O'Brien thought that he had failed. But then she gave a small, resigned sigh and settled herself back in the chair.

'Some nourishment and a trim then,' she said. 'That won't cost much will it?'

O'Brien smiled his broadest smile, the smile of victory. 'An inconsiderable amount,' he pronounced. He ran his eye quickly over the woman's figure, sensing shabbiness in the creased skirt, noting a boot-heel come askew. He would try for fifteen pounds, perhaps, or twelve.

It was nearly half-past five. In an hour they would close. Mr Trafford often spoke of staying open until eight or nine and plundering the Christmas crowds, but the late-night shoppers were reluctant to be enticed downstairs to luxuriate beneath the basement's haggard light. Picking up the scissors, flicking them expertly against his tunic to detach the tiny residues of oil and grease, O'Brien felt nervousness well up uncontrollably within him. To try and anaesthetise it he wondered about what he ought to do that evening, after he had taken the bus back to Brondesbury and had his tea. He could go down to the White Oak and see if any of the fellows were about, or he could stay and watch television. But then quite often only a few of the fellows were there, or only the ones that he disliked, and he had divined that Mrs Ellingford resented him watching television because she could hear the noises through the wall. For a moment he almost despised himself – a grown man of fifty-one still living in a boarding house with a vanload of teenage navvies fresh off the boat from Rosslare – but this made him feel shamefaced, because they were good fellows, all of them, and one or two even went to Mass, which was the mark of a good fellow, surely, and it was wrong to sneer at them.

Above his head the strip light faltered, died and then sprang into life once more. Holding the scissors at right-angles, O'Brien cut carefully along the line of hair which rested on the nape of the woman's neck. Occasionally he grasped it in a fan between his fingers or smoothed a vagrant strand back into place with his thumb. In the mirror he could see the woman watching him intently, her eyes fixed on the movement of the blades. O'Brien realised that his nervousness had reached a wholly unprecedented pitch. He wished that he could light a cigarette, but Mr Trafford had a strict rule about smoking. He tried to focus again on what it was that was disturbing him. It was not Mr Trafford, or the memory of Keenan, but something else. He prodded tentatively at a small hank of hair above the woman's ear and watched it fall airily onto the sleeve of his tunic. The woman shifted the angle of her face in the mirror, so that he could see the long line of her cheekbone, and without warning he realised what was the matter. For a second the shock was so great that he felt slightly dizzy and had to lean up against the chair back to steady himself.

The woman looked at him reproachfully. 'Your hands are shaking.'

'Oh, it's nothing,' O'Brien said. 'Nothing at all.'

'Do you feel all right? You look very pale.'

'A little giddiness,' O'Brien assured her. 'Nothing at all that you could be concerned about now.' To prove his invincibility he made a brief, feeble movement with the scissors. The woman stared at him. 'Well, if you're sure.'

O'Brien blinked hard, still alarmed at how much the recognition disconcerted him. He took two deep breaths, carefully exhaling to steady himself. Mr Trafford, he noticed, had stopped reading the sports page and was gazing at him, not angrily but with a kind of mild curiosity. He set to work again hurriedly, stabbing at the protruding tufts of hair and thinking about his discovery. He had been right, he realised, to remember Keenan and the old days because it was then that it had all happened, going to the house out West in Greenford or Hillingdon with Keenan and a fellow called Flaherty who worked on the roads. 'There'll be some grand girls there,' Flaherty had confided, 'that I can assure you.' He remembered seeing her for the first time in an empty, deserted kitchen lit by a raw bulb, where he had gone to see if there was anything else to drink, and later in another room, with yellow light seeping in under the closed door and the noise of the party booming beneath them, the woman telling him to be careful of her dress. He thought very hard, choosing and then rejecting a number of colours, but he could remember nothing about the dress.

There was only a little hair left to cut. O'Brien was relieved to find that he had not made too bad a job of it. A few wisps hung down in a cluster above the woman's shoulder and he gathered them up in his fingers and smoothed them out. For a short time he wondered if he should say something, make some remark that would immediately disclose all this knowledge to her. He could imagine her mouth falling open and her eyes staring incredulously if he did. But what was there to say? 'Do you remember the room in the house in Greenford or Hillingdon, and Keenan and Flaherty, and you telling me to be careful of your dress?' You could not say a thing like that. It was just not possible to say a thing like that.

As he brooded on this the woman said: 'You've cut me.'

O'Brien stared at the white expanse of her neck. He said slowly: 'Some mistake, I assure you.'

'You have. You've cut me. I told you your hands were shaking and now you've cut me. Look.'

There was a small trail of blood glistening along the lobe of her ear. O'Brien watched, fascinated, as a drop fell lightly onto the towel around her shoulders. He said hurriedly and in an undertone: 'I have a bottle of TCP here you know. That's the safest thing.' From a box by the mirror, kept against such emergencies, O'Brien produced cotton wool, disinfectant, a box of sticking plasters. As he did so he smiled but the woman seized the cotton wool from him and pressed it against the wound. 'You're clumsy,' she said furiously. 'Stupid and clumsy. I should never have come here.'

O'Brien found that he could not meet her gaze. He stood meekly to one side as she threw the towel onto the chair and with brisk, jerky movements put on her coat. Mr Trafford's gaze of mild curiosity had altered, he saw, to one of definite annoyance. For a moment he wondered about asking her for a reduced payment and then thought better of it for he saw that she was too angry to listen to him. He waited for a long time until the sound of her footsteps moved away before raising his head. When he looked up he saw her staring at him from the swing doors, beyond the neat rows of chairs and the flaring light, so that there was no doubt about her recognising him. She stayed like that for a long time, curious and uncertain, until a group of women with parcels and umbrellas came rapidly into the salon and she was caught up in them and disappeared. O'Brien, lowering his head to the level of his shoulders, picked up a broom and began to arrange her hair in neat piles across the white, marbled floor.

FANTASY FINALS

TWENTY MILES ALONG the M6 the mini-van broke down. They stood in a semi-circle on the hard shoulder rubbing their hands together against the raw Pennine dawn, while Alex hobbled the five hundred yards down the motorway to call the AA. Coming back from the emergency phone, hearing the surge of the oncoming traffic as it flew dangerously towards him, he saw them loitering stiffly in the pale early light, drinking tea out of flasks and swapping cigarettes. There were red and white scarves knotted over the back of the van, with a slogan that Alex hadn't seen until now – ALEX FERGU-SON'S RED AND WHITE ARMY – sprayed in shaving foam on the rear windscreen. They were good lads, Alex thought. Hell, they were the best. Half an hour later, slamming the bonnet down into its frame, the AA patrolman noticed the scarves and the piled Umbro bags. 'Are you some kind of sports team?' he asked.

High up in the Hotel Pompadour, with its dizzying views out over the level Hertfordshire plain, the boys killed time: lingered by the shining surface of the fifty-metre swimpool, drank half bottles of Bollinger in the Marie-Antoinette Lounge or strolled moodily through the lush pasturages of Axminster and polished pine. A handful – always that intent, stolid handful – kept to their suites and trained.

'OK. Words that sound the same but with different meaning. One: contraceptive and town in South-west France?'

'Condom.'

'*Check*. Two: baby's nappy and eighteenth-century poet?'

'A what?'

'Eighteenth-century poet is what it says here.'

'Diaper.'

Trevor smiled. 'Nice one, Leroy. You want to me try you on Chemistry? You were weak on that in the semis.'

'Go ahead.'

'A white crystalline dextrorotatory sugar found in the form of xylon in wood and straw?'

Leroy beamed in a smile made famous by a hundred fan-posters, souvenir programmes and TV docs. 'Xylose,' he mouthed happily. '*Xylose*.'

Ten miles south of Birmingam they stopped at a Happy Eater for coffee. Coming back from the phone again – if Doreen didn't return those library books this morning they'd get another sodding warning letter – Alex noticed that there was something wrong about the ellipse of hunched, muscular shoulders, the double row of bony, cropped heads that occasionally banged together as their owners bent over the narrow table, the better to apply themselves to the platefuls of chips and the monstrous, glistening donuts. What was wrong was that there was only ten of them.

'Where's Andy then?'

In the long, uneasy silence that followed only Gary was prepared to catch Alex's eye.

'He couldn't come boss.'

'Why couldn't he come?'

'Said he didn't feel like it . . . Besides, that Sharon – you heard they got married? – said he ought to go to the sales with her and her mum.'

Christ! You know what this means?'

The faces hung and stared, fists halfway to swollen mouths, eyes popping over the formica. They knew he was a hard bastard, Alex reflected, but they respected him.

'It means,' he said, 'that I'll have to play myself.'

Supine on the leopardskin sunbed, mobile cradled in the nook formed by head and splayed elbow, Ken Fantoni listened to the poolside chatter.

'How much did you get for that interview with *Hello*?' Trevor demanded.

'Which interview?'

'The one about you and Greta Scacchi. The one where you reckoned she . . .'

'Oh, *that* interview . . . Ten.'

'Barry got fifteen for that piece about how he remembers stuff with mnemonics.'

'*Fifteen*!' Leroy shook his head sternly. 'I'm going to have to talk to Ron about this.'

'Wow!' Trevor breathed admiringly. 'You never told me your agent was *Ron*.'

Even now, Fantoni reflected, even now, four hours before the game, with a hundred thousand people on their way to the stadium, with security fighting off the tabloid reporters in the foyer, with the agents' phones burning white-hot with ever more outrageous demands for camcorders, round-the-world flights and virtual reality machines, it was hard to resist a certain complacency. The papers – *Quizmaster* and *Brainbox* – had been sceptical at first, but three months later here they were with the world at their feet. Inevitably, they'd had their share of the breaks. Buying Carlsson from Trondheim had been a lucky one, what with that question about Ibsen in the third round. And who'd have thought Wayne – Wayne of all people – would have memorised a complete list of the English county towns? Fantoni glanced at his watch: ten minutes until the Sky TV crew arrived. Ignoring the respectful nods from the boys, from Barry and Wayne and Trevor, staked out in all their boxer-shorted splendour, he lumbered off to the Louis Quatorze Suite, where only last week, the hotel had hastened to assure him, a Saudi prince and his retinue had been accommodated for the night.

Nosing their way eastward along the North Circular, caught up in the ebb and drift of the Cup Final traffic, Alex listened to the voices from the back seats.

'Fucking good idea of someone's to pick the same day as the fucking Cup Final.'

'Think the Red Lion'll win?'

'Stands to reason dunnit? He's unbelievable, that Carlsson. I saw him in the League against Thetford Dog and Ferret. Ten questions about Brookside and he got the fucking lot.'

'And he's fucking Norwegian as well. Makes you think.'

Even now, Alex reflected, even now, with a full-strength side – well, nearly a full-strength side, with Ryan let off his paper round for once – it was hard to believe that they weren't going to get steamrollered. Unexpectedly, they'd had their share of the breaks. Chelsea not turning up in the third had been a bonus, though. And who'd have guessed Roy's dad would have been owed a favour by the ref in the fifth? Alex glanced at his watch: ten minutes until the time he'd promised to phone Doreen again. Ignoring the V-signs from the boys and the glimpse of the two brothers, Paul and Gary, hunched over their tattered copy of *Gentleman's Relish*, he eased the van into the nearside lane and started looking for a phone box that took money rather than sodding phonecards.

'Naturally I'm very proud of the lads,' Fantoni told the reporter from BSkyB. 'I mean, I found Wayne making notes out of the *Bloomsbury Guide To English Literature* the other day at training: I don't think you can ask for much more commitment than that . . . Terry? Now don't get me wrong, Tel's done a great job with the Trowel and Hammer lads – the way they came back against the King's Head in the semis was brilliant – but I think there has to be a question mark over their in-depth knowledge. Politics. TV and Leisure. Entomology. These are all areas where we'll be looking for an early advantage. Of course, I'd have paid two million for Darren Guscott if I'd had the chance, but you've got to remember the lad's only nineteen and he's never going to get those seventies pop questions is he?'

'Fingers crossed love,' Alex told his wife. 'This is the big one.'

133

In the hush of the Wembley tunnel, a minute before they stepped out into the bright, coruscating glare, Fantoni stole a look at his team – Wayne taking a last-second glance at his pocket edition of *Who's Who in Showbiz*, Leroy and Barry pooling information on Danish coastal resorts, the subs, Darryl and Maurice, nervously combing their hair in hand-mirrors. Hearing the boom of the taped music, pumped from a hundred speakers high above the concrete – they were playing 'The March of the Gladiators' – Fantoni thought he was going to cry. He remembered his early days, crouched in the corner of a sweaty pub in Shoeburyness while his dad, old Frank Fantoni, failed to answer questions on pre-war film actresses, his humble apprenticeship as unpaid coach to a non-league winebar in Macclesfield. And now this! Somewhere in the distance a bell rang. Staring resolutely in front of him, Fantoni strode out to meet the wall of dense and noiseless sound.

When they got to the ground, a bare, grassless rectangle flanked on both sides by teams of girls playing six-a-side hockey, the West Ham team were already warming up. A dozen spectators smoked cigarettes or bickered cheerlessly. Alex, regarding them gloomily, noted that they were big lads all right and hoped things wouldn't get out of hand. For a second he felt a brief pang of nostalgia for his old hobby, but the local Boys' Brigade branch had closed now and they hadn't wanted him as a Scoutmaster. Trudging across from the changing room, the reek of disinfectant still hanging in the air, he watched Eric point disparagingly at the pitch. '*Merde*!' he said – somehow Alex could never get over the fact that Eric was French – 'They might at least have shifted the dog turds.'

In the end it all went the way Fantoni had predicted. Before the cameras' dense, vaporous stare, beneath the urgent baying of the crowd, the Red Lion took an early lead through Carlsson's knowledge of the Hanseatic timber trade and lost it again when Leroy failed to define the word 'paronomasia'.

With one question to go the Trowel and Hammer were a point behind. As Guscott stepped up to the dais, his pale teenager's face twisted with tension, the crowd fell silent.

'Which group in the early 1970s had three singles which entered the charts at Number One?'

Guscott whinnied slightly, gazed in anguish from right to left, guessed wildly: 'Abba?'

Amid a mounting crescendo of noise the tuxedo'd MC shook his head. 'Sorry son. The correct answer is Slade.'

'Lost six-nil,' Alex informed Doreen. 'No, they were big lads. Eric and Paul got sent off for fighting . . . They're keeping Nicky in overnight for observation.' Outside rain fell over the grey London streets. 'Eleven o'clock then, but I promised Roy I'd drop him off at the station, and you know Ryan's mum doesn't like him staying out late.'

In the hospitality suite Fantoni graciously accepted his fifth daquiri and tried to concentrate on what the interviewer was saying.

'So what about Europe, Ken? Do you think you can repeat this success on the international stage?'

Fantoni yawned. He was thinking of changing his girl-friend. Mitzi was OK but you couldn't take her to the European Cup Final could you? What about that girl who read the ITV weather? He'd ask Ron about it.

'Ken?'

'Definitely, Alan. Munich Bierkeller. Estaminet Georges Pompidou Marseilles. I know they play a different style over there – Economics, Art and Literature, they have university professors turning pro these days – but I'm confident we can beat these Continentals at their own game . . .'

135

VIVAT REX

EVEN NOW, A quarter of a century later, I can still remember when it all started, back at the impersonators' convention at Fresno, with the old silver-haired announcer emceeing at the mike, the crowd – farmers' kids in grey denim overalls with their girls wearing plunging polka dot dresses up from the country for the day – hustling up to the front of the stage, and Billy Ray cracking walnuts with his fingers in the big hospitality tent and saying that there were two contestants come as Jack Kennedy but what the hell could you expect in California anyhow? Billy Ray was my manager in those days and he'd been coming to the impersonators' conventions since way back in the fifties, coming with stiff-necked Iowa insurance salesmen who looked like Ike or Nixon, middle-aged Republicans with mortgages and families, desperate for a shot at the big-time, but he was starting to let the business slide now and talking about condos on the beach or a ranch out in Nevada, so it was a bonus if he paid any attention to what was going on up on stage. 'Just do your stuff kid,' he'd say easily, whenever I asked him about gesture or intonation – and these were things I wasn't sure about then, wasn't sure about until a great deal later – 'Just go ahead and do your stuff.' The other entrants, the cheery housewives whose husbands had told them they looked like Elizabeth Taylor, the pale teenagers whose music coaches had said reminded them of John Lennon, had brought their families along – rows of snub-nosed children, fathers in seersucker suits ready to cheer each twitch of the beloved's hand. I hadn't brought anybody – my folks didn't approve of

136

impersonators' conventions so much – so when I got up there was only me, the lazy-eyed college kid who played piano and a sea of neutral, uncomprehending faces.

I had one definitive advantage, though: I could sing. Most of them couldn't. The impersonators' circuit was in its infancy then and the bulk of the amateurs thought that all you had to do was to look the part. This meant that you had guys who were the dead spit of Dean Martin climbing on stage and simply clamming up, or standing around and signing autographs in the hope that they wouldn't be asked to open their mouths. But I'd been practising. I knew just how long to string out the '*Weeeell* . . .' at the beginning of 'Heartbreak Hotel', exactly when to throw in that dynamite '*Uh*' before the words 'Lay offa my shoes'. I gave them 'Hound Dog' and 'All Shook Up', and by the time I went into my jitterbug routine at the end of 'His Latest Flame' (three months in front of a mirror to perfect) it was all over bar the shouting. Earlier on I'd been worried by a Barry Goldwater lookalike in a tuxedo and a woman who could have been Debbie Reynolds's twin sister, but I don't think they even bothered to show up for the awards ceremony. I took first prize, the fifty-dollar cheque, the voucher allowing me twenty minutes free air-time on the local radio station, and the fathers in the seersucker suits and the sullen kids forgot for a moment that Mom had sung flat and looked foolish and whooped and hollered as if the lights had just come up at the Las Vegas auditorium and the man himself, sweat pouring down his glassy forehead, was raising his face to greet them.

Billy Ray wandered out of the hospitality tent then, wiping the walnut flakes off his chin with a big, scrawny forearm, and stood looking at me with a kind of puzzled wonder. He was out of his league, Billy was, and he knew it. Most of his protégés up until then had suffered from some fatal, disabling flaw: the John Wayne double reduced to abject terror by the sight of a horse, the Ella Fitzgerald replica – legs, hairdo, everything – compromised only by a husky baritone. Compared to Big John and Ella and all the others I was flawless, inviolate, unstoppable. 'El,' Billy confided after the show – I'd told him it was important for my self-confidence that he stopped calling me Vernon, but he could never bring himself to go the whole way – 'get the feeling you're going places boy.' Well, I could have told him that, Billy Ray with his Lone Star baseball cap and his shy Texas drawl, and I wasn't surprised when he hauled me into his office a day or so later to meet a couple of businessmen ('Real important guys, El. Showbiz management') who'd flown up from Tennessee on purpose to see me.

I can recall that day precisely – better than the Vegas appearances, better than the time I got to meet Jimmy Carter on the lawn at the White House and even signed a couple of autographs for his grandchildren – the dusty sunlight falling over Billy Ray's rickety pinewood desk, the far-off hiss of the cars on the interstate freeway, Billy Ray all nervy and flustered and sending out for cigars and pitchers of orange juice. When I walked into the room the elder of the two guys – who looked like a Southern grandee at around the time of the Civil War – whistled through his teeth and said: 'Reckon you struck gold here Billy', while the younger one – he was sweating into a three-piece suit and complaining about the air conditioning – smiled and cocked his eye, as if he'd finally figured out the answer to some nagging problem that he'd been concentrating on for years. Billy Ray chattered on in that shy, respectful way he had – he'd been a District Attourney's clerk before the war and you could see it in the way he never sassed anybody – but it was mostly to the younger one. The elder guy just stared at me, while the smoke from Billy Ray's cigar stole across the room towards us and hung over our heads until the fans caught it and whirled it away. Finally he said: 'Don't mind my asking this do you boy? That a wig you're wearing there?' I shook my head and he whistled some more and nodded. 'Uh huh. And the teeth? I got a hundred-dollar bet with Eugene here says that's a false set.' I smiled. 'Had them a matter of twenty-seven years, sir. Don't know how you reckon on accounting for that?'

Looking back I can see that it was then that my real life began, back there in Billy Ray's thirty-dollar-a-month suite with the cigar smoke hanging in cotton wool clouds under the fans, and that the preceding years had been of no account when set against this smooth, inexorable destiny, a vague preliminary best forgotten in the reckoning up of sterner duties. I can remember shaking hands with Eugene and the Colonel, saying goodbye to Billy Ray, heading back to the rooming house to pack my two suits and my three neckties as if I were a kid who had somehow walked into a magical toyshop full of dazzling sempiternal light, where the dolls leaped up out of their boxes to shake your hand, whirl you round in an ecstatic waltz, leaving you draggled and confused but unswerving in your conviction that the dream couldn't end.

Flying in towards Memphis in a grey dawn, as the plane swooped low over the narrow ramparts of the tobacco fields and the Colonel twitched and mumbled in his sleep, Eugene filled me in on the daunting protocol of my new existence. 'Now, I know your real name, and Colonel Tom knows it, but that's as far as it goes OK? You ever hear a limo driver or a guy on the staff call you anything less than "Mr Presley", then I'll kick his ass. Fire him too, if I reckon he's safe and won't talk to the papers.'

'And what about him? What does he call me?'

Eugene's shot grey eyes keeled crazily in their sockets. 'Oh, you don't ever get to meet him son. Noway nohow. Larry, kid who was doing your job a while back, now he got set on meeting him. Bust into his private annexe one night with a crate of beer figuring on saying hello. Now Elvis, he just yelled like it was his mother's ghost. Had to get the medics in and sedate him. So no, you don't ever get to meet him son. Unless he asks, that is.'

The wheels hit ground, Colonel Tom came heavily awake, in the distance the Memphis rooftops glittered in the early sun, and a new life came swarming up to greet me.

That was the last I saw of the Colonel, mostly. Sometimes early in the morning when I was skimming leaves off the surface of the swimming pool – it was in the shape of a guitar, too, just like all the magazines said – or at night when

I was catching a late movie in the TV room – watching *Jailhouse Rock*, say, for the seventeenth time – I'd find him staring at me with a kind of queer, calculating intensity, like Uncle Sam on the recruiting poster, but though I'd nod and smile he'd never speak, just drift away as if I wasn't there. So it was Eugene who got things settled, fixed me up with a bungalow at the back of the main complex, made arrangements for the plastic surgery – my nose needed a little straightening and the Colonel had expressed a slight reservation about the point of my chin – and the voice coach and looked over my schedule. I took things gradually at first. In my second month they put me on a radio show where I was discussing new record releases ('Just say your favourite record's "The Old Rugged Cross" Eugene instructed, 'only El's been having a little trouble with the Baptist Church just lately.' A month later I went to a Grammy Award dinner and got to sit next to Diana Ross. Eugene was terrified about that, because he reckoned Elvis and her had met once before a couple of years back and really hit it off, but it was nothing I couldn't handle, and when either by chance or design she upset a glass of wine over my white pant suit I just murmered: 'It ain't nuthin', ma'am.' After that Eugene and the Colonel started to trust me. I did TV shows, a special film they sent out to the troops in Vietnam, and a Vegas walkabout. I got photographed trying on buckskin gear in Madison Avenue, on horseback with Roy Rogers, shaking hands with a candidate in the Republican primaries. 'I'm just a plain country boy from Tennessee,' I told him, 'but I'd like to tell you sir that the Good Lord's on your side.'

Eugene enthused about this last touch. 'Got to hand it to you boy, you're a natural. Reckon we could put you live on the primetime network shows and nobody'd notice the difference. Don't it worry you though?'

'Why should it worry me?'

'Think about it. You look like him. You talk like him. You goddamned sing like him. You could *be* him.'

'No,' I told him – truthfully, as it happened – 'it doesn't worry me.'

140

Hectic, restless years. I have album upon album of stills photographs to remind me. All those dumb late sixties films, those monstrous TV shows, the pre-recorded Christmas messages for the fan-clubs, it was me, all of it. The real Elvis, meantime, was reduced to the status of a bit-parter, a walk-on, wheeled in on the rare occasions when I couldn't make it. I got better and better, to the point where you couldn't tell us apart. In fact, if anything I looked more like Elvis – he was getting fat now, apparently, and hitting the booze – than Elvis did. Still naive and credulous about my part in the whole Graceland set-up, I once questioned Eugene about this mounting role reversal.

'So what does Elvis Aaron' – we called him that to distinguish him from me – 'what does Elvis Aaron actually do?'

Eugene frowned. 'He does the big Vegas sessions. He gets to meet the President. Leastways, when he's sober he does.'

'Eugene,' I said, suddenly biting at the thought which had been crackling away in my head all these months. 'You don't need him. It's me you need. Admit it.'

Eugene flicked me that lazy, inscrutable smile of his. 'You didn't say that boy. You didn't say that and I didn't hear it.' He paused. 'Guess I can fix you a Vegas show, though, if that's what you want.'

I wanted it. I did seven nights in the Las Vegas auditorium and *Variety* talked about 'a star reborn'. After that Eugene gave me everything I asked for. It was the mid-seventies by now, in any case, and the real Elvis wasn't in any shape to protest – he'd got into drugs in a big way by this time, everybody said, weighed eighteen stone and mostly didn't know who he was any more. Curiously, it was in these later days that I finally got to meet him. The limo had just delivered me back from the studio late one night – I was laying down some tracks for an album to be called *Elvis Sings Gospel* – and, coming into the wide Graceland foyer, there he was slumped in a chair, looking like a fat white ghost that was too old and too decayed to bustle out haunting. I hurried by – I was wearing my purple suit and carrying the sequinned cape he used for his TV shows and I was afraid he'd be upset – but he just rolled an eye up from beneath the furrowed crevice of his forehead and muttered: 'That's a good-looking set of clothes you got there boy.' He fell asleep again then and I tiptoed away.

Elvis Sings Gospel sold half a million copies. *Time* magazine said it was 'a welcome return to form by an artist whose decline had long been thought irrevocable'.

And then he died. Sprawled out over the king-sized bed with his face turned purple, clutching a fistful of barbiturates. Eugene let on, confidentially, that he and the Colonel had been expecting it for some time, but I was devastated. At the meeting the three of us had before the death certificate was signed I grasped in vain at the only straw of at hope that seemed to offer itself.

'Eugene. Colonel . . . He. He doesn't have to die, you know.' I looked appealingly from one to the other, got a faint gleam of recognition from Eugene – I could tell he was on my side – but Colonel Tom just stared at me. 'I loved that boy,' he said – it was the first time I'd heard him speak for years – 'and I intend to devote the rest of my life to his memory. I can tell you're suffering from shock, Vernon, and perhaps you ain't responsible for what you're saying, but if I were you I'd take a look at your contract.'

I took a look. There was a big paragraph under the *In the event of death* heading. For a time I wondered about selling my story to the papers or writing a book, but as Eugene pointed out no one would believe me. In the end, rather than follow the self-sequestration option, I went for 'facial restructuring' as they called it: half an inch off the nose, reset cheekbones and a hair rethink. There's still plenty of money left – Colonel Tom settled up handsomely when he found out how upset I was – but the time hangs heavy down here in Florida. Sometimes the local bar and diner stages a talent night, so I put on the cape and the pantsuit and do 'Hound Dog' or 'Blue Suede Shoes' and occasionally, just occasionally mind, some drunk kid will holler out 'Elvis Lives'. But he's dead now. And I'm dead too. I died a long time ago, back at the impersonators' convention, with Billy Ray cracking the walnuts between his fingers, and the proud fathers cheering, and the cigar smoke curling through the dead, empty air.

FLIGHTS

AT WEEKENDS OR on the long summer evenings when Francine went to her aromatherapy class or sat around the house sewing stitches into a fat embroidery sampler, Dorfman took the car and headed west: out beyond the point where the freeway slid on towards Des Moines and the state border, off through the low flat terrain of dust and scrub and the network of side-roads that led inexorably to the airport. At first no more than an incidental diversion, a change from the familiar tables at Schwab's or the cool subterranean rumpus-rooms of the country club, the journey had, he realised, assumed the status of a settled habit: as much a part of his routine, Dorfman thought, as the pink life-insurance forms that lay over his desk in the study back home, or the shiny jars of linseed oil Francine had bought the time they had vacationed in New Mexico, now forgotten and unused in the workroom, something fixed and irrevocable in his life. Occasionally, he had tried explaining this to Francine, never with success. 'Standing out by the runway watching a plane take off,' Francine had reasoned. 'What kind of a way to spend an evening is that?' 'Just something I do, baby,' Dorfman had countered warily. 'Just like you going to see Mrs Fogelberg. Isn't any harm in it.' Francine had resented this reference to the aromatherapy class, seeing in it lack of respect, a brazen male disregard for salutary feminine activities, and for a time Dorfman had tried to alter the pattern of his evenings, driving east to the marina at Dyersburg, going bowling at the big sports centre at Phoenix

Rock. Such substitutes were, he quickly decided, an inadequate recompense. The white sail-boats, the ponytailed farmers' daughters gossiping in the sports centre bar – these were frail, insubstantial ghosts. It was the aerodrome, the control tower rising up to greet him from beyond the distant cornfields, the great metal birds like stitching in the sky above his head, that were real.

There was even, Dorfman thought, thinking it now as he stowed the convertible away in its familiar parking space and stood in the car park letting his feet make little rivulets and runnels in the gravel, something vaguely proprietorial about his obsession, a sense in which his own personal development had mirrored the wider traffic of the skies. Dorfman had grown up with the aerodrome. He remembered in fifth grade taking time off from helping his dad with the car showroom – old man Dorfman had had a Pontiac franchise for thirty years – to cycle over and watch as the bulldozers shovelled humps of tarmac this way and that over the dusty amphitheatre of the site, returning a little later as a high school student to stare at the inaugural ceremony, where a state senator stepped gallantly into a rickety Cessna trainer and was flown off to a convention in Sioux City. And then on through the late teens and twenties, the place lay anchored deep in his consciousness, a kaleidoscope of memory twisted together and given a single point of focus: standing in the metallic reception area watching his mother come back alone through the checkout the year his dad had got sick and died on vacation in Florida; seeing the first of the giant DC10s come in to land, a silvery scrap of metal growing larger by the second; the time the airport company had fixed a deal with Pan-Am and got made a stopover point on the coast-to-coast routes. They'd started building the motels then, and the vanilla-painted shopping arcade. Ten years on, Dorfman didn't recall a time when the airport hadn't been there, the phantom, impersonal city in which it reposed rising up to meet the pallor of the surrounding scrub, the naptha beacons streaking the pale Iowa sky with artificial light, couldn't remember in fact what previous entity it had managed to supplant. He had tried asking Mr Kopechnie, indisputably the oldest person he knew, but without satisfactory results. 'Used to be a golf course or something,' Mr Kopechnie had suggested, eyeing Dorfman's executive briefcase and his shiny salesman's suit with practised caution. 'Anyhow, what sort of a question is that?' And Dorfman, avoiding Mr Kopechnie's eye and hefting the executive briefcase out of one hand and into the other, had been forced to admit that it was no sort of question at all.

It had started raining as Dorfman got out of the car, and he backed instinctively into the concrete shelter at the rear of the park where there were cigarette machines and Seven-Up dispensers and a strew of cans and aluminium fast-food trays lying over the asphalt floor. Two kids, a boy and a girl in leather jackets, broke apart as they heard him approach and stared frostily at him. Dorfman glared back. The girl's jacket had a stencilled motif on the back that read WHOMP THAT SUCKER. He watched it recede beneath the overhang of cement and breezeblocks, hearing a gust of fugitive chatter blown back on the breeze. Dorfman hated kids. It was one of his special prejudices, something for which he reserved a rare, intense hatred, which Francine – disloyally, Dorfman thought – declined to abet. 'Asshole kids' he would murmur, standing rigidly by the downstairs window as some gang of high school desperadoes loitered purposefully by. 'But honey,' Francine would insist, looming up through the grey early-evening light to tug at his wrist, 'they ain't doing anybody no harm.' 'You wouldn't understand,' Dorfman told her, proud in spite of his irritation. 'But honey,' Francine would demur. 'All they want to do is to have a little fun, just like the rest of us.' There was no arguing with such indulgence, Dorfman thought, no way of compromising with this gross intrusion into the security of the suburban man. He lit a cigarette and smoked it for a while, kicking at the detritus around his feet, willing the serenity he had felt as he steered the car along the approach road twenty minutes back to return.

There were, Dorfman knew, a number of ways of spending time at the airport, each of which harboured its own particular satisfactions. He could go and talk to the guy who ran the security desk, a grizzled ex-cop who remembered Dorfman from the days when he drove a patrol car and would occasionally volunteer details of abstracted contraband or mid-flight delinquency. He could take a wander down the shopping mall, empty now and gaping in the mid-evening shutdown, and stare at the racks of Fox Brothers suits and the rows of pale Reebok trainers, or go and stand in the arrivals lounge and trade back-chat with the limousine drivers waiting to meet the 1900 flight from Denver. The weighing up of these possibilities, each one glimpsed momentarily in his head like frames cut from a reel of film, brought easy consolation. Appeased, his resentments damped down and anaesthetised, he moved on through the wide corridor, the sight of his short, stubby body caught suddenly in one of the big wall mirrors oddly reassuring, the confirmation of an identity that the sight of the two lickerish teenagers had somehow called into question. Halfway into the mall, a queer sense of resolution forming in his head, he stopped at the McDonald's concession and bought a frankfurter so he could loiter for a while in the big, gleaming lounge, where cigarette butts lay piled up in the massive iron ashtrays and there were pictures of ancient, flat-bellied Dakota transports lining the walls. The old negro who worked the cashdesk looked up sleepily as he passed. 'That's right Mr Dorfman,' he nodded, and Dorfman nodded back, the familiar clink of the fifty cent piece he tossed into the empty saucer acting on him like the sight of a final jigsaw piece slotted neatly into place. By the time he emerged again into the mall, silent now except for a skinny, white-coated janitor scooping up dirt with a broom, the sense of resolve had hardened into something sharp and tangible. Emboldened, Dorfman set off through the tangle of side-alleys and high NO ENTRY doors that led to the hostesses' lounge.

Of all the airport's vagrant diversions, the sense he sometimes got of roaming along a corridor full of agreeable rest rooms, it was the hostesses' lounge that Dorfman found most beguiling. No clue to this emerged from its decor or contents. It was a narrow, L-shaped room, staffed by a single tired barman, with a neon sign above the door saying NO PUBLIC ACCESS, though no one, Dorfman reflected, had ever questioned his presence there. The girls clustered at one end of the chromium-plated bar, chattering to each other and lighting their cigarettes off a patent cigarette lighter that the barman had left to one side of the soda pump, or occasionally sauntering over from their stools to jam dimes into the fake Wurlitzer jukebox. Hunched over his can of Budweiser in the far corner of the room, Dorfman had conducted an exhaustive survey of the hostesses. At an early stage he had divined that they weren't local girls. They came from Eugene and San Francisco, spoke in unfamiliar West Coast accents and flicked mock insults like 'airhead' and 'space cadet'. Dorfman, who had once read a disparaging newspaper article about social life in California, surmised that these were Valley girls. He regarded them warily but with fascination, like exotic migrant birds blown off course to land in some meagre downtown garden. Occasionally, in the intervals of complaining about the shortness of their shift-breaks or venturesome cabin staff, they made vague acknowledgments of Dorfman's presence. 'Hey Dorf!' they would say. 'Give us a cigarette will ya?' Or 'Hey Dorf! Next flight to Seattle leaves in an hour. Why don't ya come with us hey?' And Dorfman, conscious of the dense, ketchup-coloured stain spreading across his face, would smile his slow, mock-grimace, unsure if he was being made a fool of or not.

There was a new girl in the hostesses' lounge that night. Dorfman watched her out of the corner of one eye as he plundered complimentary pretzels out of the hospitality bowls or glanced out of the window at the big long-haul jets taxiing on tarmac strips near the perimeter fence: small, oriental-looking, with one of those level eyebrow-nudging fringes that made him think of *The World of Suzi Wong*. Hearing odd fragments of chatter skimming back over the bar, he noted her habit of sticking an interrogative 'no?' on the end of questions: *We have time to go shopping in Dallas, no? That boyfriend of Laraine's is bad news, no?* Filipina?

148

Thai? Dorfman couldn't differentiate Eastern speech patterns. He surmised that she was a Filipina. Francine, who staffed affirmative action committees and stitched solidarity blankets for the street children of Third World dictatorships, disliked Asian women. 'You're not gonna believe this hon,' she had told him, 'but none of them have pussy hair. Can you imagine that?' Dorfman, who had browsed his way around a certain school of pornography categorised by the hardcore stores as *Asian Babes*, wasn't inclined to argue the point. Staring grimly down at his drink, the noise of a circling 747 suddenly drowning out the conversation and rattling the windows in their frames, Dorfman broke open a packet of Merits and started feeding them into his mouth. The Asian girl was smoking too, he registered, thin cigarettes like bird bones he had once seen on the beach at Nantucket. For a moment Dorfman thought about Mr Kopechnie and his fierce blue eyes, the stacks of inky proposal forms, the arc of Mr Kopechnie's sprinkler which always drenched the calf of his pants however prudently he sauntered up the path. Then he dismissed the image from his mind. The barman was having a telephone conversation that could have been drugs. In fact, listening to the worried undertone, the precise situational details, Dorfman was sure it was drugs. Embarrassed, he stared stonily in front of him, the way he did when commanded to watch one of Francine's public service channel docs on female circumcision in the Yemen or read a *Newsweek* article on testicular cancer. The girls were beginning to disappear now, gathering up their vanity bags and their cigarettes, peeling off in ones and twos to secret recesses in the drome where even Dorfman had never penetrated. He had a vision of himself, spectral and unseen, stalking the airport at night, prowling the deserted corridors, peeking into the empty franchise huts in the mall, listening at the door of the women's comfort rooms where the only sound would be the noise of a dripping tap. Their leisure over, the girls grew sharp and professional once more, whipping up sagging lipsticked smiles with the aid of hand mirrors, pinning up drifts of vagrant hair. It was in this general redefinition of

149

spirit and costume – like some medieval raiding party, he thought, easing on their hauberks and chain mail while pageboys scurried and the womenfolk gnawed their knuckles – that he got to meet the new hostess. 'This is Dorf,' one of the girls said, as Dorfman hovered halfway between his Jack Daniels and a three-quarters empty schooner of cashew nuts. 'He hangs out here whenever he can get the old lady's teeth out of his ass.' And Dorfman smiled unreliably, not sure whether he desired this limelit introduction or whether anonymous skulking better suited a purpose about which he was still undecided. But the girl smiled back, bobbing her head so that the fringe, sweeping upward and then returning to its vantage point like a line of filings obeying the magnet's call, assured Dorfman of the existence of about ninety dollars' worth of designer haircare. 'And do you work here Mr Dorfman?' she asked. There were further gusts of merriment. 'You wanna watch Dorf,' her companion loudly advised. 'Sure,' someone else chimed in. 'Fucks like a rattlesnake with a firehose dick.' Head lowered, Dorfman watched them go, out through the white door, stout shoes clattering on the metal carpet (it was only in movies that hostesses got to wear high heels), not sure whether to be cheered by the intimacy of this kind of joshing or marvel at the weird, lopsided vision of himself that it conjured up. Dorfman the stud, Dorfman the terror of the boudoir. According to Francine. Dorfman had 'a negative attitude to female sexuality', whatever that meant. Alone in the silent room, the barman disappeared into some remote and unguessable closet, he cherished his glass while behind him the white fuselages bounced and shimmied into the darkling sky.

Later Dorfman wandered back along passageways aflame with burning light to the car park. Around 2100 the local flights ended. The rest of the big coast-to-coast stopovers not expected until midnight, there was a lull in the drome's activities, a fall in the pulse-rate. Deserted except for the odd scrubbing janitor, the franchise booths reared up at him, their swathes of pantsuits and denims frozen behind plate-glass security grilles. Someone had taped a sticker to the convertible's rear window that said NUCLEAR WASTE – THIS STATE'S DISGRACE. Dorfman peeled it crossly away, sighing when the yellow paper stuck to his fingers. If there was one thing Dorfman hated more than kids it was bleeding heart Dudley Doright Democrats. He sometimes had visions of himself armed to the teeth with Uzis and Sten guns stalking the walls of a stockade housing drums of spent uranium rods and loosing off pot-shots at the seething longhairs thronging at the gate. As he swung out onto the freeway extension, the moon veered up suddenly from behind the distant control tower and he stared at it, baffled by the shafts of white, coruscating light. Back at Rockefeller Drive, the house was shrouded in darkness. Dorfman stowed the convertible carefully in the car-port and stumbled his way into the kitchen, where shiny milk cartons gleamed out of the murk and there was a smell of lavender water. Dorfman was used to these vagrant odours, by-products of Francine's aromatherapy habit, rearing up unpredictably to confuse him: the gypsophilia on the stairwell, flurries of burnt almond wafting over the back porch. He fixed a mug of coffee and sat in a high-backed chair to drink it, thinking of the crowded runways, bright metal wings shearing through an opaque sky, the Asian hostess's calm and welcoming smile.

Dorfman collected model airplane kits: Wellington bombers, Messerschmidt ME109s, Heinkel IIIs with cigar-shaped fuselages. The boxes lay piled up in the lean-to shed at the back of the house where Francine kept her stores of sourgrass pickle, discarded exercise bikes and noxious experiments of Mrs Fogelberg's in see-thru carafes. Most evenings and nearly every weekend Dorfman spent a couple of hours in the lean-to, nostrils depressed against the overpowering reek of pickle and tiger balm lotion, streaking tiny tracks of glue onto aeliron hinges with a match head, painstakingly lowering into place the transparent covers of machine-gun turrets. Dried out and complete, markings and insignia patiently transferred, painted up according to approved box-lid colour schemes, they hung from ceiling wires or reposed in neat lines on Dorfman's work table: a proud, gleaming squadron ready to scramble at a second's notice and fly up menacingly on his behalf. There was family precedent for this hobby, and also for its historical focus. Old man Dorfman had flown Superfortresses out over Japan in the war. There was a picture of him hanging in the upstairs closet, in leather flying jacket, backed up against the hull of his plane, the Red Sox Express, next to the stencilled outline of a baseball pitcher. Staring at it, as he crouched balefully over the can, Dorfman felt only a vague, tremulous envy of the kind he experienced leafing through the mail order subscription copies of *Aircrew*, *Windsock* and *Flight Monitor*, the consciousness of an entire teeming universe out there beyond the horizon, distant yet beckoning, and eternally out of reach.

Half-past seven the next morning found Dorfman in his lean-to, brooding over the construction of a Fiesler Storch, a weird kind of late-period Nazi scout plane, which for some reason had a blunt fuselage and the cockpit shifted way down near the wing-engine. *Special care should be taken in the alignment of the tailplane*, the instructions cautioned, and Dorfman, who had already spilled half a tube of glue over his grey handyman's apron and lost a propellor blade somewhere in the floor's inch-thick coating of sawdust, could believe it. Outside pale midsummer mist dispersed airily off the back-yard lots and gardens. From the kitchen Dorfman could hear the brisk, purposeful sounds of Francine fixing herself a cup of acorn coffee or a bowl of hi-fibre wheaties. Dorfman, who had breakfasted an hour earlier, felt the three bratwurst sausages and their attendant garnish of mustard and corn-bread hang heavy on his stomach. From further away, but not that far, he could hear the *ticka-ticka-ticka-thump* of Enzo Manzoni, eldest son of the neighbouring Manzoni household – globular wops who ran a restaurant in town – listening to rap music. Dorfman's brow creased over. Frown-ing at the twin sections of the Storch's fuselage, gleaming up at him like the two halves of the cod steaks Francine sometimes grilled on Sunday nights, he used his free hand to stir the pile of proposal forms that lay on the chair. Not much of a harvest for a week's hard calling, Dorfman had to admit. A woman out in the corn country wanting to insure her vacation. A gay couple in Sioux City enquiring about health insurance (it wasn't even worth processing the forms, Dorfman knew). A few premium top-ups from previous clients who'd bought their wives jewellery or splashed out on a new car-port. That left Mr Kopechnie. Sometimes Dorfman wondered why he carried on visiting Mr Kopechnie, who at eighty-one must have been the worst risk for a life policy any ABO salesman had ever encountered, knowing all the while that the explanation had nothing to do with insurance. Like Dorfman's old man, Mr Kopechnie was an airforce vet. Hell, the guy had flown Wildcats in the South Pacific, idled on the carrier foredecks waiting for the Kamikazes to come blazing out of the sun. Together they embarked on long, serious conversations about the way a B–25's undercarriage retracted or the exact shade of paint you might colour the underside of a Mustang bent on a night mission. Dorfman had tried asking Mr Kopechnie about the Kamikaze attacks. 'You mean they just . . . blew themselves away?' 'That's right,' Mr Kopechnie would nod. 'Only took enough fuel for a one-way trip. This weren't no baseball game.' And Dorfman would bow his head, uncertain whether the figure of speech was a rebuke to one who had not experienced the tumult of the South Pacific or simply Mr Kopechnie's own awe at his spangled youth.

Outside in the yard there was an anguished, turbulent commotion that sounded like someone who weighed a hundred and eighty pounds falling over a stack of empty kerosene cans. A bit later Francine's mild, innocuous – but not for that reason any less infuriating – voice came quavering through the door. 'You in there, hon?' By way of an answer Dorfman shifted the alignment of his feet, the better to peer down at the tiny plastic homuncule wedged between his fingers, and stuck out his tongue. 'Come on, hon.' Francine's voice came again, the half-coaxing, half-exasperated tone reminiscent, Dorfman realised with bitter disgust, of other, more intimate encounters. 'What you doing in there?' 'Beating off,' Dorfman mouthed noiselessly. Straightening up, he flicked the doorcatch with his thumb. 'Heck is going on here?' he enquired with what was meant to sound like belligerence but in fact ended up way down on the scale of craven timidity. Staring at Francine's plump, guttering face, the features even at this hour giving the impression of melting away into her Eco-Freak sweatshirt, Dorfman was struck by how many times in their six-year relationship she had confronted him in this way, looming menacingly before him as he drowsed over late-night TV, pawing him awake from the airy valleys and deltas of the night to recount dreams about Charlie Manson and Sharon Tate. 'Hey look,' Francine said seriously. 'I have to talk to you OK?' Bridling instinctively at the blank, serial killer's stare, she went on: 'About tonight, yeah? Only Mrs Fogelberg figured I might like to have supper after the class. Is that OK or do you want to think it over?' Bending to dab a tiny fleck of flesh-coloured paint onto the homuncule's upturned face, Dorfman thought about it. Francine having supper with fat klutz Fogelberg meant an extra-curricular trip to Mr Kopechnie. Or a visit to the airport. Or, if he kept himself to a pretty tight schedule during the rest of the day, a trip to Mr Kopechnie *and* a visit to the airport. Dorfman straightened up. The day was looking good. The day was looking shit-hot. 'Could take in a burger at the drive-by,' he said doubtfully. Francine gazed back, intent and solicitous. 'Well if that's what you want, hon. Else I could leave you something. You fancy some of Mrs Fogelberg's home-made pastrami we had the other night? Or maybe I fix you some bean chowder?' Dorfman shook his head. Looking down at the body of the German airman, thirty seconds later, he was alarmed to find that in his annoyance he had somehow managed to wrench the head clean away from the torso. Guilt flaring in his eyes, the gabble of Enzo Manzoni's rap music pounding in his head, he bent reverently to repair the damage.

Eleven hours later found Dorfman goading his convertible up the sharp incline that led to Mr Kopechnie's bungalow, one among a plateau of retirement homes populated by pot-bellied ex-insurance salesmen and their loaf-haired wives. Weak early evening sun catching on the wing mirror flashed into his eye and made him jam the visor down hurriedly with his hand. It had been a bitch of a day. No, Dorfman corrected himself, a *motherfucker* of a day. First there'd been a flat tyre two miles outside of Hudsonville. The vacationing farmer's wife had disappeared someplace leaving an idiot son who declined the pink proposal form Dorfman had tried to press upon him. The meeting with the gay couple in Sioux City – two leathery forty-year-olds with peg teeth and beaten-in faces, had turned into a funeral parlour nightmare of blood counts and haemoglobin deficiencies. Finally, something he'd had for lunch had disagreed with him and he'd spent twenty minutes with his pants round his ankles in a layby outside of Tidewater squirting ochre shit into a drainage ditch. As ever the sight of Mr Kopechnie's front porch, gained after the usual clenched-teeth clanging of gears, had a sedative effect. There were times, Dorfman thought, when Mr Kopechnie's bungalow, like the airport, had assumed the status of a fixed point in his, Dorfman's, life. Other things might alter, as indeed they had continued to alter during the five and a half years Dorfman had paid calls in this part of town, but Mr Kopechnie's front porch with its single parking space next to Mr Kopechnie's venerable chevy, remained the same: sprinklers drenching the lush, virid lawn, the line of motionless cypresses, Mr Kopechnie's dog comatose under a tree. Mr Kopechnie himself cross-legged in his garden chair with a copy of the *Iowa Free Citizen* stretched out over his lap. Watching the old guy lever himself out of his chair and come hastening lopsidedly over the grass – Mr Kopechnie had had a hip replacement three years back which imparted a queer circularity to his gait – Dorfman bent his head in what he supposed was a kind of respect. Mr Kopechnie, eight-two next Fall, had seen it all: Capone, Prohibition, Hoover, the Old Deal, the New Deal, the Japs strafing Pearl Harbor, Roosevelt dying, and on into the monochrome hinterlands of the fifties: Monroe, 'Nam, the Moon landings, Nixon, Reagan and the barbarities of the startling present. Jesus, the guy was a walking almanac of American history, a man who always remembered what he was doing at those significant moments in time, the day the big bomber headed east into the Nippon sun, the afternoon the presidential motorcade sped into Dallas. To Dorfman, who had tried self-laceratingly to determine what he had been doing when he heard the news about Lennon getting shot and narrowed it down to getting fired from a travelling salesman's job in Albany or failing to make out with a girl called Cissie Matupelah, these were stern credentials. Still more awesome was the fact that, indubitably, Mr Kopechnie looked the part. Six foot tall and ramrod-straight, with white, side-styled hair, facial skin still holding up, and none of your Reagan-era vanity tucks and creases, he looked how Dorfman imagined an ageing rancher in a Gary Cooper movie ought to look: invincible, ironical, tough.

As Dorfman blundered into the arc of the sprinkler, felt the sting of icy water rip through his pants leg and hurriedly blundered out again, Mr Kopechnie moved easily out of the deep shadow of the cypress tree. 'Figured you might drop by,' he said seriously. 'Take a Coke, maybe, or a beer?' There was a pitcher of ice on the garden table, Dorfman noticed, and a couple of tall glasses with lemon twists. 'Got a six-pack of Bud in the chiller,' Mr Kopechnie went on. 'Just say the word.' Oppressed by the memory of his twenty-minute stake-out athwart the drainage ditch, Dorfman settled for Coke. Seated in one of Mr Kopechnie's spindly garden chairs, the thin stanchions digging into his buttocks, stretched polyester crowding out his bulky thighs, he felt simultaneously elated and cast down, cheered by the grave reservoir of peace that would lap around him for the next half-hour, depressed by the inevitable professional dead-end. From the vantage point of the insurance salesman, Mr Kopechnie was a walking disaster area, a kind of LA faultline snaking across Dorfman's career. Once, two years back, he'd actually got as far as figuring out a quotation for Mr Kopechnie, based on Mr Kopechnie's living until ninety and receiving the minimum death benefit, and the premiums had weighed in at four hundred dollars a month, leaving aside the thrice-yearly medical check. Plus they hadn't liked it at the office either. 'Jesus, Dorf,' Guyland had whistled, as he cast his eye over the panels of neatly framed statistics. 'Quit fooling around with eighty-year-olds, huh? I mean, what's in it for him, with the premium at five grand a year? Ten to one the guy has a fucking actuary for a nephew and they'll sue us for entrapment. Just forget it.' But Dorfman, who had worked out that the salesman's commission on a ten-year policy of the kind suggested to Mr Kopechnie would raise approximately ten thousand dollars, didn't feel like forgetting it. Not quite. Awareness of the policy and its occasional resuscitation fell across their conversation like the cypress shadows.

Meanwhile, there were other, sunnier bowers where he and Mr Kopechnie could linger. 'Hey,' Mr Kopechnie said sharply. 'Knew there was something I means to show ya. Here now.' Reaching into the big metal chest beneath the table, he pulled out a squat, oblong cardboard box. 'What do ya reckon of that?' Dorfman turned the container over gingerly in his hands, eyeing the four-colour illustration and the red and white AIRFIX logo in the corner. That was another thing about Mr Kopechnie. Dorfman knew that no matter how many collectors' conventions he attended, no matter how many ads he placed in *Windsock* or the *North American Aeromodellers' Association Journal*, the chances of him walking off with a first issue World War II RAF Blenheim fighter bomber for under two hundred dollars were rather less than Tom Harkin's in the Democrat primary. 'It's beautiful,' he said slowly, struck by a pang of envy so intense that for a moment he stopped looking at the box and gazed upward beyond the trees, as if he expected the Blenheim's real-life equivalent to sail into view above his head. 'It's a special kind too,' Mr Kopechnie went on. 'Night fighter markings and camouflage. Silver-grey on the undercarriage. Flying low to beat the radar. Catch that baby over your shopping mall just before dawn and you'd wonder what hit ya.' And for a second Dorfman imagined the scene: the forest of upturned faces, tracer bullets zinging across the tiled patios, the sluice and spatter of spilled blood; opened his eyes to find calm Iowa sunshine sinking away into the foothills of the fading day. 'Hey,' he said unconfidently, just before he got up to go. 'Don't suppose you had time to think about . . . about what we discussed last time I was round or nothing?' Mr Kopechnie, regarding him stoically, shook his head. 'Sure. I done some thinking, and, fact is Dorf, I don't see the reason for it.' 'No?' 'Surely not. If Wilma was alive, then maybe there'd be some point to it. But seeing as . . .' He made a tiny gesture with his hand of the kind Dorfman encountered a lot with his elderly clients: it meant terminal illness, funeral parlours, widow's weeds. 'You got kin though ain't you?' Dorfman found himself saying. It was an old trick from out of the salesman's manual: *make your target feel guilty about any dependent relatives he or she may have*. 'Thought you said you had a kid?' Mr Kopechnie frowned, the keen-eyed rancher seeing smoke signals along the trail. 'Sure,' he admitted. 'But Spence now, he ain't shown up in years. Jesus, if I went and left him life insurance the lawyers wouldn't even know where to address the cheque.' Dorfman smiled his careful salesman's smile, the smile of reduced rates, absent signatures and unforeseen death. At the car Mr Kopechnie bobbed awkwardly and thrust the cardboard box through the open window onto the passenger seat. 'Here,' he said, 'I'd like you to have this.' 'Hell no, Mr Kopechnie,' Dorfman heard himself saying. 'You can't give me a thing like that.' But Mr Kopechnie was inexorable. 'You're a kind of guy I like, Dorf,' he explained. 'You got respect for old people like me, guys that served our country in its time of trial. I want you to know that I appreciate that.' Still Dorfman found himself prodding the box back in the direction of Mr Kopechnie's long, curved fingers. In the near distance, beyond the car-port, he could see the arc of the sprinkler beating down on the sodden turf, Mr Kopechnie's dog slinking off to some bolthole by the trees, empty glasses side by side on the table. 'Go on, take it,' Mr Kopechnie commanded. Revving the convertible's flatulent motor, waving one hand negligently out of the nearside window, the box glistening up at him from the seat, Dorfman found himself crying tears of mingled pride and shame.

Back home, Dorfman stowed the convertible in the car-port, resisted the temptation to take the Blenheim straight into the workshop, and slunk into the house. There was no sign of Francine. On the kitchen table lay a hunk of Francine's home-baked cornbread, parched and adamantine from the sun, and a platter of black-bean chowder. Mindful of his earlier problems at the roadside, Dorfman junked it airily down the waste disposal chute and decided to hit the chiller. Munching on a hastily constructed cold pork and sauerkraut sandwich, he played back the half dozen or so messages on the ansaphone. No surprises. Two members of Francine's Tai Chi group wanting to reschedule a class date; Guyland from the office; one of the gay guys from Sioux City asking about medical cover restrictions on pre-senile dementia. The last message – an unidentified female voice – cut off almost as soon it began talking. Out of curiosity Dorfman played it back a couple of times, losing whatever it was that was being said in the slurp and crackle of static before retreating to the lounge to cast a critical eye over a mail order video called *Wildcats over Korea*.

Francine came back at eleven, red-faced and perspiring and bearing a paperback titled *Body Essence: Smelling Sensuality the Swedish Way*. 'Sorry I'm late, hon,' she apologised. 'Only Mrs Fogelberg's husband got back from his realtors' convention and we just sat around talking. How was your chowder?' 'Great,' Dorfman lied. 'Fuckin' A.' Francine regarded him fondly. 'Hey,' she said. 'Mrs Fogelberg reckoned she'd seen you last week.' 'Oh yeah. Where was that?' 'Over at the drome is all. You know she does a class at the recreational centre there? Said she saw you out on the spectator's gallery watching the flights come in.' Embarrassed by this revelation, which somehow reminded him of being caught naked in the bathroom ogling a copy of *Playboy* magazine by his mother, Dorfman peered stonily back. 'Yeah, well it's my hobby.'

'Funny kind of a hobby, Mrs Fogelberg said, for a guy that never went on a plane in his life.' For some reason Dorfman, who had once travelled on vacation to Tucson in a greyhound bus rather than face the traffic of the skies, meekly conceded the rebuke. 'Hey,' he exhaled desperately, not caring what they talked about as long as it avoided the airport, 'how was your class?' 'Uh huh.' Francine's attention was gone now. She fussed round the room tidying magazines, wrinkling her nose over the remains of Dorfman's sauerkraut. 'It was OK.' She giggled. 'Actually hon, tonight we did sex and smell.' 'Yeah?' 'I mean, for instance,' Francine went on, 'did you know there are thirty-seven separate olfactory responses associated with the act of love?' 'Is that so?' For once Dorfman was dumbfounded, in spite of himself. 'Tell me about 'em.'

Later that night, unaccountably, they had sex. To Dorfman, playing it back on the VCR screen of his mind early the next morning, the encounter seemed to have taken place in fathoms of icy water: the sky spinning in the remote distance, furry limbs thrashing in the ooze of the ocean floor, heads breaking the surface for an instant and then disappearing once more. Afterwards Francine went to sleep immediately, her head slumped back over a pillow, while Dorfman roamed disconsolately round the downstairs rooms fixing himself cups of coffee which he failed to drink, switching on the video and then switching it off again, padding into the workshop for a last gloat over the Blenheim. From across the way came the *chugga-chugga-chugga*, the *dadawa-dadawa-dadawa* and the *plinka-plinka-plinka* of Enzo Manzoni's rap music. Dorfman shouted 'Wop sonofabitch' quite loudly, secure in the knowledge that old man Manzoni was off licking the floors of his restaurant. Back upstairs he discovered that Francine had turned the overhead light on and was staring brokenly at the gap in the stairhead into which he emerged. 'Oh hon,' she said sadly, 'I'm so *worried* about you.'

Remembering the words by chance a week later as he cruised

160

gently down one of the approach roads to the airport, Dorfman realised that Francine was not alone in her concern. He, too, was worried about himself. Specifically, he was worried about his job. Business was down, way, way down, and Guyland back at the office was chewing his ass. Daily and by phone. In vain Dorfman had countered the remonstrances about unfilled quotas and loss-making accounts with an upbeat assessment of possible medical scenarios faced by the gay couple in Sioux City. Guyland was wise to smoke-screens of this kind. 'Forget it, Dorf. Two fags who met ten years ago in a bath-house, shit-scared of taking the test. What else you got? Engaged couples with bubonic plague wanting to cover their Diamond Wedding. Stop wasting my time huh?' Dorfman, assimilating this advice in a hallway packed out with Francine's sports gear and a bunch of RAF Short Stirling kits that had arrived that morning from a mail order firm in Teddington, England, had wanted to say: *Look, what makes you think people want your lousy insurance? And what makes you think they want it from me*? Plus a few remarks about the deodorant-proof stains that edged out from the underarm of Guyland's shirt and the reek of garlic that lingered round his upper body after he came back from the dinner hour stake-out at the Robespierre Grill. Instead, seeing Francine's awesomely tracksuited form surging up at him from the hall mirror, Dorfman had confined himself to neutral, even-tenor salutation. 'Yeah Neville,' he had whispered solemnly into the cradled receiver. 'OK Neville, I'll check it out.' Or not.

Meanwhile, pushed up against the epicentre of this bewildering spiral of fucked livelihoods, there were compensations. The Asian hostess's name was Ascension. Oddly enough, Dorfman's guess had been bang right: a Filipina, from a city in the South Dorfman had never heard of called Gobernador de Leon. There were no jobs for twentysomething girls in the Philippines. Ascension had explained matter-of-factly. Two of her sisters were currently working as bar hostesses in Manila. A third was HIV.

Ascension was naive and confiding. 'You must have an

important job, *no*?' she suggested to Dorfman early on in their conversation, 'to be able to come here just when you want, huh?' And Dorfman had obligingly sketched in a farm manager's job out in the cornfields, negotiating contracts with the wheat mills in Chicago, running his eye over the files of Massey-Ferguson tractors at the Iowa farmers' conventions. Ascension – and they'd only had drinks twice, that and an early evening saunter round the spectator's gallery – was the kind of girl you said things like that to. Her trust, he'd already discovered, was limitless, credulity-defying, unreal, embracing all known forms of religious observance and superstition. She believed in the healing powers of stackfuls of Catholic saints, in the efficacy of charm bracelets, horoscopes, astrologer's charts, the lot. To Dorfman, who had discarded belief in the numinous in his early teens the year the Globetrotters had gone down before the Oakland As, this kind of inclusiveness was curiously engaging. There were other things he liked about Ascension too: being four feet eleven inches tall (at five six Dorfman felt a stupendous, swaggering giant beside her); smiling at him a lot, peppering her speech with Filipino colloquialisms; not minding about the time he spilled a Seven-Up down the side of her hostess's tunic.

Stowing the car down in the long-stay bay (you never knew), nodding to the burly security joe, Dorfman made his way briskly through the shopping mall towards the hostess's lounge. There was no guarantee of Ascension's presence here. She worked short-haul domestic flights mostly, East-West stopovers, with occasional long-haul excursions out of LA and San Francisco to the Antipodean. Even here, balanced above a complex world of time zones and mid-flight refuellings, her ingenuousness persisted. 'It must be pretty exciting, going round the world for a job,' Dorfman had ventured, halfway into the first round of Cokes he'd dared to buy for them, thinking as he did so that maybe five days a week in the air, eating airline food and crapping into a tin bucket behind the foc'sle (though a non-flyer himself, Dorfman had heard the stories) sounded like a disaster area.

'Sure,' Ascension had volunteered. 'You know my sister, the one in Manila? (there was some complex factor that differentiated the two bar hostesses, but Dorfman could never remember what it was). 'When I tell her I travel all over the world, wear a uniform, and get paid, she say she not believe me.' Amazingly, Dorfman's luck held. No one he knew lurking around the malls (and in the wake of Francine's data about Mrs Fogelberg he had resolved to be fucking careful, OK?), waved on by the goons at the NO PUBLIC ACCESS barrier, the hostess's lounge deserted save for the trim, tiny figure posed neatly over the shining surface of the bar's end. 'Hi,' Dorfman said throatily, checking the whereabouts of the barman (head down and tut-tutting over some piece of pump apparatus), edging into the empty space alongside of her in a gesture that was meant to impress any unnoticed third party with its studied casualness, but in fact only succeeded in conveying terminal anxiety. Ascension blinked in a way that to Dorfman's Disney-soaked consciousness recalled nothing so much as Bambi registering the advent of the Great White Hunter. 'It's great to see you, Dorfman,' she said relaxingly. Dorfman whinnied back. 'It is?' 'Sure. You know, when I wake up this morning back in the motel I think maybe this is a sad day for me, no?' Dorfman shrugged. Ascension patted the rim of her glass with a delicate movement. 'And how is *Senora* Dorfman and the little ones at home?' Rather to his surprise, Dorfman had invented a thin, Vassar-schooled wife and two crop-haired sons to go with the farm manager's job. 'They're fine,' he admitted, and then, seeing that something else was required, improvised a line about Wayne (they were called Wayne and Archie – shit, he ought to write them down in case he forgot) having measles, but the doctor saying it was OK. 'You are a good man, I think, worrying about your family in this way,' Ascension deposed. Dorfman nodded his head. One or two of the other hostesses were drifting into the lounge now; pale, haggard sirens flaked from fourteen-hour flights from Lima and Montevideo. Dorfman doled out cautious waves, hoping that nobody would speak to him: nobody did. Back at his side Ascension pulled an olive out of

163

the complimentary platter and split it in two with a gleaming incisor. 'But maybe in the end I find that, yes, this is still a sad day for me.' Yeah?' Dorfman's voice radiated concern, glowed and boiled and gave off seething fumes of empathy. 'Why's that then?' 'Oh is just that I get this letter from my mother, no?' Ascension volunteered meekly. 'Is that so?' Dorfman wondered dreamily. Outside the planes trawled and laboured over the tarmac surround like giant scorpions.

'This is Kent,' Francine said carefully in a tone about half an octave higher than the one she used to order Dorfman to find the VCR switch or fetch in the groceries from the car. Dorfman, stumbling into the room with a pained expression on his face, saw a line of rising ducks and a photo of some vaguely imbecilic kid on the far wall. From the davenport by his knee a fat guy in shirt and suspenders rolled expertly onto plump, slippered feet. 'Name's Errol Fogelberg,' he said. 'Any time you want to sell your place just give me a call, OK?' Dorfman nodded. Years of piecemeal social interaction had taught him that the confraternity of fatmen is a myth, that the one thing a bulging two hundred-pounder with a stomach jutting over the waistband of his pants detests is a replica of himself. 'Yeah,' Mrs Fogelberg came in, winding carmined fingers round a pitcher of iced vodka-tonic, 'and Errol's mom always reckoned she called him after Errol Flynn. Can you imagine that?' Mr Fogelberg joined in the laughter at this. Watching him, Dorfman thought it sounded like tired laughter, a sitcom watched too many times. The dinner party had been Mrs Fogelberg's idea, 'Just so you boys can get a notion of what we get up to on our evenings off.' On another davenport in the far corner of the room, so far in fact as to suggest that they occupied a subsidiary status – would get up without warning, say, and start serving the meal – sat a couple named Harris, the male half of which Dorfman figured he just might have met at an Elk convention.

'You like vodka, Kent?' Mrs Fogelberg hazarded. 'Or Errol says there's beer in the chiller.' Dorfman shook his head. For once in his life he was content for Francine to do the talking. He had things on his mind.

The first of these, predictably enough, was Ascension. Directly behind the hostess's bar, down a flight of stairs and along a corridor marked AIRPORT PERSONNEL ONLY there was a row of rest rooms where cabin crew sometimes grabbed an hour's sleep during refuelling or crashed out after winging in from the Pacific. Here, greatly to his surprise, on three of the preceding seven afternoons, Dorfman had found himself lying on the starched sheets of a tiny truckle bed clasped in Ascension's fervent embrace. Not having any yardstick for his own or Ascension's behaviour, it was difficult to know what to make of this experience. The closest he could come up with was watching an adult movie from the decent obscurity of a cinema back row and then suddenly being requested to climb up onto the screen and take part in the celluloid thrash and gouge. He had tried talking to Ascension about this, without success. Five minutes later found her dressed, the red check airline scarf pushed firmly back into the top of her blouse, the blanket folded, only the faint tang of sweat in the air a reminder of what had passed between them.

The second thing, much less predictably, was Mr Kopechnie. Two evenings ago he had had the old guy on the phone, breathless and jittery, wanting to know if he could come over. As it happened, Dorfman was booked for the next couple of days, but he'd marked the visit down in his engagement book for the afternoon of the third day with a rare tremor of anticipation. Old people sometimes got weird ideas, Dorfman knew, his experience honed by the memory of Francine's great-aunt Eulalie, who, dying after years of juleps and cornbread on the Dorfmans' patio, had left thirty thousand dollars to some longhair community in Wisconsin.

Back in the luridly-lit front room, Dorfman watched Mr Harris – who, it transpired, worked in air-conditioning – lugubriously engulf a pretzel from a dish offered to him by Mr Fogelberg. 'Go on,' Mr Fogelberg exhorted him frighteningly, 'take two.' The talk, Dorfman divined with an odd

165

sense of recognition, had turned to the airport, and in particular to the thrice-weekly aromatherapy relaxation class (billed as 'Smell and Surrender') conducted by Mrs Fogelberg among the airport personnel. 'Sure,' Mrs Fogelberg was saying, stabbing the air with her unlit Merit, 'the people I feel sorry for are those poor girls. Pilot on a 747, OK that's a career. Those hostesses now, they're so blitzed they don't know where they are. I've had girls come to my classes half an hour off a red-eye from Taiwan thinking they were in Baltimore.' 'Some hot babes down that aerodrome, OK,' Errol Fogelberg corroborated in a sinister undertone, laying his hand on Dorfman's shoulder. 'Guy I know made out with a hostess was pissing razors inside a week. Doctor reckoned it was some weird kind of Vietnamese NSU the antibiotics hadn't gotten round to fixing yet.' Dorfman stared at the hand, which continued to rest inert on his shoulder like a museum waxwork he'd once seen of the Kennedy family in which old grandma Rose extended a white glove towards the brawny upper arm of her eldest son. 'How's business?' he whipped back urgently, determined to throw lardass off the trail. Errol Fogelberg's dead, submarine eyes tracked back and forth. 'Fuckin' less than zero is all. I got apartments down in Sioux City going for under the price of a trailer, and even then it's only Rican turdbirds want to buy.' Later they moved to the diner and ate coleslaw salad followed by swordfish steak and bilberry pie. Two huge cylinders, burning at each end of the table, filled the room with a pungent, cloudy aroma. 'Thai joss sticks,' Mrs Fogelberg explained. She had dense, hairy forearms that reminded Dorfman of *An American Werewolf in London*. 'I find they have a mellowing effect.'

From the back of the rearside window of the rest room there was a view out over the southern stretch of the reserve runway. Here small craft – Cessnas and De Havilland trainers – jockeyed and manoeuvred over the flat, men in blue overalls manhandled sanitation trucks, security jeeps trundled purposefully towards the control tower. Waking from the

166

snatched, cathartic sleep of mid-afternoon, Dorfman was grateful for this spectacle, the series of small components that guaranteed the efficiency of the larger machine. By his side Ascension slept on, hands gripping his shoulders blindly, like a baby. Naked beneath the thin coverlet, she seemed astonishingly vulnerable, like some rare crustacean cunningly enticed from its shell. Curiously, at these times Dorfman found that he tended to think of Francine, not the Francine of discarded embroidery samplers and aromatherapy classes, but an older – or rather younger – Francine with whom he had haggled over linseed oil on vacation in New Mexico or squired to drive-in movies down in the corn country back when the world was young. It was weird, Dorfman thought, what time did to people, making thin guys fat (Dorfman had been a hundred and forty pounds when he met Francine), fat guys thin, turning smiling women who favoured sex in hot tubs into joss-stick sniffers and pickle fanciers. Time, which had taken a square mile or two of cornfield and turned it into a metropolis of the air, had in the same grim procession of years turned Dorfman from a butter-haired urchin in sneakers watching a senator unveil a commemorative plaque into a pumice-skinned forty-year-old cheating on his wife with a doe-eyed Filipina who cried over a bad horoscope and carried a picture of John Paul II in her vanity bag.

There was no doubt about it, Dorfman thought, twitching aside the frail sheet to get a better view of the dense hummocks of Ascension's torso, time had definitely made him bolder. The Blenheim kit that Mr Kopechnie had given him grew in leaps and bounds. In place of his usual timid dabs of paint, his hour-long stake-outs while paint dried, Dorfman found himself streaking in huge green undulations of camouflage on the upper wings. Then the other night, reversing the convertible into the car-port, Dorfman had caught sight of Enzo Manzoni slouching into the family driveway with a swatch of CDs cradled under his arm. 'Hey you,' Dorfman had yelled at a surprisingly loud volume. 'You play any more of that nigger jive disturbing the peace tonight, I'm gonna bust your ass y'hear?' 'Oh yeah?' Enzo Manzoni, who was three inches taller than Dorfman and pitted so lavishly with acne that the scars might have come from some secret society initiation rite, had sneered back, while sharply skedaddling into the family lair, 'I tell my old man about you, shithead.' But, queerly, silence had prevailed throughout the following night.

To others, though, Dorfman dimly comprehended, time brought only a swift, avenging sword. Mr Kopechnie, found on his back porch two nights ago, had seemed a man transfixed by the crowding years. Dorfman had arrived at the bungalow to encounter a scene which nothing in his previous dealings with Mr Kopechnie had prepared him for: sprinklers turned off (the edges of the lawn were already a parched yellowy-green), the dog gone, Mr Kopechnie a hunched, rickety old guy labouring up from his cane chair like an old ghost. 'What happened to the sprinklers?' Dorfman found himself asking, conscious for the first time in Mr Kopechnie's presence of the dry skin of his calf. 'Sprinklers?' Mr Kopechnie looked dazed but somehow devious, as if their absence was part of a cunning masterplan he wanted to explain to Dorfman but couldn't quite remember. 'County environmental service team came and fixed a water meter the other day on account of the drought is all.' Dorfman nodded, swinging the flat executive briefcase against his knee, aware of the sounds brought by the sprinklers' removal, bugs grinding in the privet hedge, somebody's stereo system playing classical music in the next house. 'Thing is,' Mr Kopechnie said hurriedly, 'Spence's back.' Dorfman raised an eyebrow. 'Oh yeah?' Despite never having met Spencer Alberquerque Kopechnie, Dorfman knew all about him, knew about the coke jags and the financial disasters. 'Broke his daddy's heart,' people who knew Mr Kopechnie politely suggested. 'Sure. Living in a trailer park down in Brownsville with some Rican girl. It ain't for me that I'm doing this Dorf, you understand . . .' Dimly Dorfman perceived that Mr Kopechnie was talking about his life insurance policy. 'You're sure about this, Mr Kopechnie?' he enquired, the unreason-ableness of storing up money for some retard who lived on a

168

trailer park with a Rican bedwarmer suddenly flaring up inside him. 'Sure I'm sure,' Mr Kopechnie said crossly, no longer, Dorfman realised, Gary Cooper playing an elderly rancher, but like an exceptionally frail grasshopper. 'He's my own kin ain't he?' Inside the house, where stale air blew over the dusty vestibule, and a huge 1:32 scale model of a Grumman Wildcat hung at chest-height from the ceiling, they stared at the pile of pink forms, stabbed fingers at the lines of small print, collected beers from the chiller and brought them back. 'It sounds kind of complicated,' Mr Kopechnie had said mildly, cutting short Dorfman's explanations of compound interest and accumulated benefit. 'No sir,' Dorfman had told him, smirking in spite of himself. 'It ain't complicated at all.'

By his side Ascension snuffled wildly and came dramatically awake, pawing at Dorfman's chest with her tiny hands until he gently repulsed them. 'Forgive me, yes?' she said, opening her eyes at last, 'only I have this bad dream.' 'What sort of dream?' Dorfman enquired, still thinking of the sad, pendulous droop of Mr Kopechnie's throat muscles. 'Oh, this bad plane crash, maybe, where everyone get hurt and killed.' 'You ever been in a crash?' Dorfman asked, anxiously pulling on his pants. 'A bad one I mean?' Ascension shook her head. 'I am a fortunate person,' she said simply. Dressed and sobered, they regarded each other nervously. 'Hey,' Ascension proposed, 'let's go up and see the planes, no?' Dorfman accompanied her along the staircase of chrome and steel in the direction of the gallery, wondering a little at the choice of venue. Ascension usually preferred a coffee diner deep in the bowels of the drome or a saunter down one of the food halls, anywhere in fact where she wasn't liable to be noticed by one of the other hostesses. 'You see, Kent,' she had explained seriously. 'They are nice girls, but they would be jealous, no, if they know that a man in your position preferred me to them.' On the square rooftop they watched DC10s disappearing into the afternoon glare. Dorfman frowned at a couple of kids messing with plastic straws. His mind was on other things: Mr Kopechnie; Ascension's narrow thighs; telling

Francine. Looking up he saw tears coursing down Ascension's plump, doll-like face. 'What's the matter, honey?' Dorfman exclaimed, throwing a fat arm around her shoulders. 'It is not polite of me to tell you,' Ascension sniffed, 'not when you are so good and kind.' The kids messing with the plastic straws were staring interestedly at them. Dorfman frowned some more. 'Relax,' he said. 'Just relax and tell me about it, OK?'

Five minutes later Dorfman felt competent to sit some kind of high school paper in *Filipino social structures with particular reference to domestic misfortune*. Ascension's mother, Mrs Boyet, was dying, or at any rate dangerously ill. To pay for her treatment, Ascension's sister – not the one with HIV but one of the hostessing ones – was seriously in debt to a local mafia chief. Further, unspecified, trouble involved a delinquent Boyet cousin named Augusto. Plus the mortgage payments on the family shack in downtown Gobernador de Leon were three months overdue. The cost of rectifying all this, not to mention Ascension's return ticket home, weighed in at a cool four thousand dollars. Slightly to his own astonishment, Dorfman found himself agreeing to pick up the tab. As he did so he registered what could only be described as a look of veneration on Ascension's mute, lachrymose face. 'I know you would do this,' she explained. 'You did huh?' 'That's right. Ever since my coffee snack with the other girls this morning I know you would do this.' Silently she extracted a thin, curling slip of paper from her vanity bag and flicked it across. 'Fortune cookie,' she said proudly. Dorfman read: A *friend's generosity will make your day*.

In the office the low hum of air-conditioning drowned out the distant voices. 'Nice work, Dorf,' Guyland beamed, all smiles now that the deal was done. 'You want the commission now, or with your pay cheque?' Dorfman watched the rank ooze of Guyland's armpits edge out another centimetre or so. 'Now,' he said. 'OK.' Guyland smiled again. Facing the wide screens in the corner of the room, two clerks played computer ice-hockey. 'I'll fix it,' he said. 'Between you and me there's only forty grand come in the place this month, so we can sure as fuck use it. Hey, you want to take a vacation or something?' Dorfman shrugged, a newer, shrewder Dorfman, who wasn't taking any shit from Guyland or any other of the dorks at ABO. 'I'll think about it,' he temporised. Weirdly enough, Dorfman had already been thinking about it, ever since a phone call from Ascension two nights ago had put the idea in his head. 'I was thinking,' Ascension had said, 'maybe you like to come with me no?' Dorfman had had a sudden crazed vision of himself gingerly negotiating the tangled corridor of a 747 in mid-flight, honking into one of the grey paper bags, cradled into his seat in a delirium of fear as the landscape banked and shifted beneath him. 'Go to Gobernador de Leon with you?' 'That's right. Is a great idea, no?' And Ascension had babbled happily on, about the great time they'd have taking her sister's kids to the coast and the attractions of Gobernador de Leon nightlife. Brooding over the receiver, as the sound of one of Francine's New Age relaxation tapes boomed and juddered from the upstairs landing, Dorfman had thought about it, emerging from the half-minute or so's mental turmoil, with a furious sense of resolve. There were things happening in his life, he realised, gleaming vistas and walkways of opportunity that required of him only the courage to place that first, hesitant foot on the mat. 'And it would be a way to say thank you, no?' Ascension hurried on, 'to say thank you for bringing this happiness into my life.' Dorfman had just managed to croak his assent and slam the phone down before the sight of Francine, towel wrapped around her mountainous haunches, en route for the shower had blown this reverie away. Driving back from town along the freeway, the Black Flag tape pounding from the car stereo – somehow he'd gotten back into all that punk stuff – Dorfman found his sense of purpose spectacularly renewed: on course, the flight path mapped out before him, the wide, promising world taking shape beneath his grasp.

Back home a stench of lavender oil hung over the stairs and five of Francine's swimsuits – billowing garments like bell

171

tents – dangled from the dryer. Francine lay on the davenport sewing stitches randomly into her embroidery sampler. Without looking up she said: 'I just got back from Alicia's, Mrs Fogelberg's. She's real worried about Errol.' 'Uh huh,' Dorfman riposted. 'What he do, lose weight?' Francine put down the sampler and regarded him with liquefying cow's eyes. 'Honey, you wouldn't make jokes if you could see how upset she is. She said: "He's fooling around, I know he is", and when I asked how she knew she said he was always putting the phone down when she came into the room, and there was three cheques at a florist in Sioux City showed up on his credit card in the last month.' 'Uh huh.' Dorfman lowered himself into a chair, thought better of it and hoisted himself out again. 'That's too bad.' Ignoring Francine he stalked off into the workroom, where the Blenheim lay sharp and glistening on the bench. Holding the tail-plane reverently between his fingers, Dorfman whistled. Only the undercarriage and a few pin-head traceries across the transparent dome of the gun-turret and the thing was finished. He wondered if they had kits in the Philippines, and what Ascension might say if in their first trip around the markets of Gobernador de Leon he asked to be taken to a model store. Back in the lounge Francine had the Eagles on the stereo and was singing along to 'Hotel California'. Dorfman wondered about telling her there and then, slamming in fact after fact like a champ boxer matched against some numbskull contender – Ascension, paradisial afternoons, the long-haul flight to Manila – as she reeled before him, thought better of it. The phone rang in the hall and he slipped out nervously to answer it, only to find Francine already trading lugubrious gossip with Mrs Fogelberg. As he passed on into the kitchen, Francine put her hand over the receiver and whispered: 'She says she found a packet of condoms in his jacket.' Dorfman shook his head almost jauntily and went to make himself a bacon and sour cream bagel. For once, he figured, it wasn't his problem.

At midnight the phone rang again. Cowering in pyjamas

172

under the haggard glare of the hall light, Dorfman listened to Ascension imparting details of an evening flight two days away. 'It will be OK no, you and me?' she suggested, and Dorfman nodded his head, enveloped suddenly in wide, aquamarine spaces where Stuka dive bombers chased and zapped him, and from his bunker on the hillside AirReichs-marshall Goering sent squadrons of Messerschmidt 109s to blow his ass away. 'Are you OK, darling?' Ascension wondered, 'I worry maybe you hang up on me, no?' 'Sure I'm OK,' Dorfman breathed. 'Fuckin' A.' The silence of the night throbbed around him. Back upstairs he found Francine had switched on the light and was flapping abstractedly through a book called *Dead Meat*: *Animals are our Buddies too*. 'Who was that, hon?' 'Oh, turdbird Guyland from the office about some rescheduled meeting is all,' Dorfman lied. Seeing the droop in Francine's lip he smiled inadequately. 'You OK?' Francine shrugged. 'I just thought it might be Alicia. Only Errol was due back from the realtors' convention in Chicago, and she said she didn't know if she could keep her hands off the cleaver.' Dorfman settled himself unhappily back between the covers. 'Yeah, well some people overreact.'

Forty-two hours later Dorfman stowed the convertible in the airport parking lot, remembering the things he had failed to do. Like telling Francine where he was going (and at present a brief letter left on the kitchen table represented the sum total of his disclosures). Like telling the office. Like even making arrangements for the fucking car. The stub of his airline ticket protruding from the top left-hand pocket of his shirt and a tightly packed handgrip (sneakers, pants, a couple of Hawaiian shirts – it was supposed to be hot out there, OK?) provided no sort of reassurance at all. What was he going to do about the fucking car? As the drome's front porch loomed towards him he veered off forlornly towards a pay phone in the alcove at the side, praying he'd get the ansaphone. He got the ansaphone. After what seemed like a lifetime, Francine's voice began on the message, a message about regrets, absences, speaking after the tone and replying at earliest

173

convenience. While it played, Dorfman wondered what he was going to say. In the end he simply bellowed: 'The car's at the fuckin' airport, OK?', slammed down the receiver and lit out through the airport's high, welcoming doors. He clock at the entrance to the shopping mall said 8.03. The flight left at 10.15. He'd promised to meet Ascension in the hostess's lounge at 8.30. In two hours' time, Dorfman realised, he'd be strapped into his seat while the girls recited safety routines and the control tower lights winked in the middle distance. He'd once asked Ascension timorously: 'What do you do if somebody freaks?' 'Freaks?' 'In mid-air, I mean. If someone can't handle it.' Ascension had rolled her eyes. 'Oh, drink, pills. One time, you know, we had a guy shook so much that the co-pilot have to come and hold him down in his seat.' Dorfman figured that the half-dozen or so Jack Daniels he reckoned on downing before take-off plus a vial of Quaa-ludes he had in his valise would see him through. But what would it be like at the other end? He'd tried getting Ascension to dilate on social life in the Philippines, only to be rewarded with a series of first grade geography primer out-takes: 'There are many poor people in my country'; 'There are many unhappy people in my country'; 'Many people in my country not like Americans'. That last revelation in particular, was just dandy news. It was 8.06. Anxiously Dorfman started prowling the malls, nodded to the security Joes, bought a cappuccino at the coffee diner and drank it looking in the window of a record and tape store. For a moment Mr Kopechnie's face floated up into his mind, and he hoped the old guy would be OK, what with Spence back home in the trailer park and waiting to collect. In the distance, beyond wide-frame windows, the sky was darkening. Dorfman watched it with pained, palpitating unease, his guts dissolving into a stew of uncertainty and fear.

In the hostess's lounge, cool grey light skimmed over the chrome surfaces of the bar; there was no one around. Dorfman had a curious sensation of time stopping, of existence splayed our before him, subject to none of its usual frets and prompts, inert and malleable. He breathed deeply to steady himself, laid his fists on the bar and regarded the plump knuckles with startled detachment. Straightening up from behind his cash machine, the barman said: 'You Dorfman?' Dorfman nodded expectantly. The barman flicked a thin white envelope across the bar. 'This one's for you then.' Dorfman ferried the letter over to a side table and read it in the soft aquarium shadow. In it Ascension told him that he was a liar, that she never should have believed him, that she was ashamed (of both him and herself) and that she had taken an earlier flight to Manila. There was no mention of the two thousand dollars Dorfman had presented her with two days before. *And yet though you are such a bad man I hope you will have a happy life*, the letter signed off. 'Bad news, huh?' the barman diffidently suggested. 'Got it in one,' Dorfman agreed. 'Fuckin' ball breakers, those hostesses,' the barman deposed. There was an odd, complicit gleam in his eye. In answer, Dorfman moved purposefully towards the bar. 'I want to get drunk,' he said.

Arriving home at 2 a.m. he found Francine sprawled in a deliquescent state at the foot of the staircase, together with a half-empty bottle of vodka and a paperback entitled *Channelling Your Rage*. In the incoherent and accusatory conversation that followed, Dorfman learned that he had Mrs Fogelberg to thank for the unravelling of his plans, an eagle-eyed Mrs Fogelberg who had encouraged confidences from the tearful ornament of her aromatherapy class. 'And the worst thing,' Francine had said, 'the worst thing was the lie. Telling her you were some big-shot with a farm in the corn country. In any case, what kind of retard would believe that stuff?' 'You wouldn't understand,' Dorfman proposed. 'Oh Kent, baby,' Francine had cried, 'don't leave me.' 'Who said anything about leaving for Chrissakes?' Dorfman demanded. In the distance he could hear the rumble of music: *chunka-chunka-chunka, badaway-badaway-badaway, linka-slinka-trinka*. Dragging into the workshop a minute later, he flicked the light on and sat down heavily in a chair, edging out his foot so that it rested on a jar of linseed oil that Francine had brought back from New Mexico all those years ago. On impulse Dorfman picked up the jar and threw it on the floor. As the glass smashed, he heard the sound of Francine coming to investigate. Prompted by some fierce, ungovernable whim Dorfman seized the Blenheim and brought one fist down viciously on the fuselage, watching the plastic shiver and break between his fingers, the tiny figures go skittering out from beneath the shattered cockpit. 'Oh hon!' Francine wailed from the door, and Dorfman stopped and stared at her, thinking of the plane tacking away, out across the silent ocean, deep into the welcoming night.

ESSEX DOGS

THEY CAME OVER the hill as the dawn rose up from under the horizon, and the light turned the colour of orangeade – hard, heavy light mixed with the sodium glare of the streetlamps.

'This is going to be a good day,' Hennessy said, his high voice squeaking over the noise of the engine. 'One of the best.'

It was half-past six, quarter to seven maybe. The new watch Maxine had given him for Christmas never kept proper time, Kennedy acknowledged. Out of the window he watched scudding early traffic move past the road signs to Grays and Thurrock, Canvey Island. Beneath them, further down the hill, deep in mist, the Essex villages slept.

'Going to be a great day,' Hennessy said again, as if he badly wanted to believe it. 'You'll see what I'm saying.'

A bit later a rattle from the back of the truck told Kennedy that he'd forgotten to fasten the tools down the night before. Hennessy pulled into a layby and he walked round to the tail-gate, lifted it up, and tied the forks and shovels together with a piece of rope he found there. Standing by the wheels, pulling the tail-gate down again, he could see Hennessy through the rear window smoking a cigarette and reading the newspaper they'd had in the cab since last week.

It was still cold. Back in the cab Hennessy had switched the heater on and the windscreen was starting to steam up. Kennedy wiped it cautiously with the back of his hand; the smoke from Hennessy's cigarette crept into the corners of his eyes and made them water. He wondered if Hennessy was cross about the tools. Hennessy was like that sometimes about small things. A trail of sugar, say, pitting the brown surface of his coffee, and he'd push the cup away. Maxine said it was stupid, Hennessy being *fastidious* like that. He remembered her saying the word, then pushed the thought away.

As Hennessy bent over the wheel and edged the truck slowly out onto the road again – there were coaches now, and the early traffic heading for London – another thought, not really considered since the afternoon before, rose in his head again.

'Maguire is it? Today I mean?'

Hennessy didn't turn his head. 'The very same,' he said.

It was eight o'clock by the time they got to Shoeburyness. By now the heavy lorries had gone, and the car park outside the cafe was empty. Inside he watched Hennessy craning over the counter, staring shortsightedly at the dirty menu, big and untidy in his teddy bear coat with the lining coming away down one side. Kennedy assumed that he'd cheered up. They ate bacon sandwiches and drank tea out of mugs while a radio played at the next table. Kennedy read a Southend United fixture card that hung on the wall and a clump of pinned advertisement cards: *Greyhound, 3 yrs, fast, pedigree, £180 ono; Great Dane puppy's £50; Fridges, white goods, top prices paid.*

'You still seeing that Maxine?' Hennessy asked carelessly as the radio played 'Sitting On The Dock Of The Bay'. Kennedy thought about this for a moment, wondering why Hennessy was so interested. Hennessy's life was a mystery. In fact Kennedy hardly knew where he lived. When they met it was always in pubs, Hennessy looking up from his pint and waving, fixed in the halo of smoke. In the end he shrugged, in that offhand way you could interpret how you liked.

'Ah well . . .' Hennessy said. Kennedy had seen him talking to women sometimes: he looked a bit smarter then, and he used his hands more.

Maguire was late, much later than he'd ever been.

178

Hennessy tried calling him twice on the mobile, but there was no answer. 'Probably at the yard,' Hennessy said vaguely. When he arrived it was nine-thirty and they were clearing the plates away, and a man with a broom was trying to sweep up the cigarette ash that Hennessy had dropped on the floor near his chair. Kennedy tried not to look self-conscious as Maguire walked down the path between the tables. Instead he watched Maguire's tan work-boots clearing a passage through the dust.

'What'll you take then?' Hennessy asked.

Maguire looked around the cafe, not exactly furtively but with a kind of low-level watchfulness.

'I'll have a glass of milk.'

Hennessy couldn't believe this. 'Are you serious?'

'A glass of milk,' Maguire said to the waitress, without looking at Hennessy again. He sat down in the chair next to Kennedy. 'What's cooking then boys?'

Kennedy looked at some more advertisement cards: second-hand prams, rock groups who needed bass guitarists, minicab firms wanting drivers. He left Hennessy to do the talking. The milk came and Maguire drank three-quarters of it at a swallow and then stared at the rest. Kennedy was never certain whether he liked Hennessy or not, but he knew he didn't like Maguire. Maxine had met Maguire once, one evening when she'd been able to get a babysitter and they'd gone out. She said he gave her the creeps.

'So,' he heard Hennessy asking, 'where is it today then?'

'Saffron Walden,' Maguire said. 'You'll know it when you see it. Big place on the outskirts. Lots of ground, too. Five thousand square feet if it's an inch.'

Hennessy looked thoughtful. Kennedy knew that at times like this he tried to impress Maguire. Sure enough, he said: 'No worries, Mac. We'll take care of it.'

'Of course you'll take care of it' Maguire said. 'Four o'clock mind. Phone if there's a problem.' Back in the truck, Hennessy wanted to talk about Maguire. 'Funny guy isn't he?' he said. 'Jesus, a right funny one. You know he drinks milk in pubs even? That's right. Seen him ask for it and no

179

one bats an eye.' They moved on into the sun, towards a line of container trucks heading for Tilbury. There were gulls crowding in the wind over above the telephone wires: Kennedy watched another gust gather them up and disperse them into the bright air. 'I mean, I like the guy; Hennessy was saying, 'but I wouldn't want to *socialise* with him if you know what I mean.'

Past Chelmsford they turned north towards the retirement villages: rolling drives glimpsed between pillared entranceways, sleek lawns within high walls. Hennessy drove purposefully, as if he really had a destination. 'Always look as if you know what you're doing,' he'd once said to Kennedy, 'as if you had a *right*.' Near Great Dunmow they found what they were looking for: set back from the road, half an acre of lawn, a carless drive. Hennessy drove the truck noisily up to the front door and reversed it into the gravel. They climbed out and examined the silence for flaws – a dog, say, at the back of the house, a lawn-mower a quarter of a mile away.

'Deserted,' Hennessy said. 'Can't ever be sure though.'

Five minutes later, after Hennessy had squinted through the letter box and seen a week's post piled up on the mat, they got to work. Kennedy took the bigger of the two spades and marked out the grass in metre-width squares, Hennessy levered the turves out of the ground with his big turfknife, and they manhandled them onto the back of the truck. 'Six inches at least,' Hennessy told him when they'd done the first dozen or so, and Kennedy put his full weight on the spade so that only the handle stuck out of the ground. It was amazing how quickly you could dig out a lawn he thought. In twenty minutes a space the size of a cricket pitch had gone; in half an hour Hennessy reckoned they were three-quarters done. 'No need to rush,' he said. 'Jesus, they're not coming back are they?' Kennedy shrugged. In all the months of doing this they'd never worked out what would happen if anyone came back.

There was soft rain coming in now, blowing over from Harwich and the Hook. They stood by the truck smoking cigarettes and brushing away the clods of earth. Kennedy thought again about Maxine and what she'd said the last time they'd met, sitting in the front room at her house with the baby playing on the carpet. *You are unreliable. And you hang around with Hennessy and Maguire.* Actually she hadn't said that but Kennedy could read her thoughts. He looked at the watch again and found it had stopped at 10.15.

There were some children's toys lying at the edge of the gravel drive: a miniature tricycle, two or three wooden bricks, a plastic sword. Kennedy prodded them carefully to one side with his foot. He wondered what it was like to have children, taking them to the park and things like that. He tried to remember his own parents taking him to a park, but lost the image somewhere: perhaps his parents hadn't been the kind of people who took their children to the park. Hennessy flicked his cigarette onto the gravel and said out of the corner of his mouth, 'Here comes trouble.'

Kennedy's eyes were confused by the rain and the angle of the ground: it took a minute for him to work out that the flapping, mackintoshed figure labouring across the field towards them was an elderly woman. When he saw this, his shoulders relaxed. You never had any trouble with old women. All they wanted was an explanation. You could just say politely *Sorry love, we're nicking this stuff*, and they'd nod and go away. 'Leave this to me,' Hennessy was saying as the woman approached.

Smashed red veins under a Sou'wester hat. That odd, vague look they had. They straightened up to hear what she said, trying to look authoritative, legal.

I was just looking out of my window, and I thought . . . Really had to ask what was going on . . .'

'Quite all right, madam,' Hennessy said. 'No cause to be alarmed. From the council.'

'But . . . Mr Frobisher on holiday too . . . *Sure* he would have said . . .'

'That's right, madam.' Hennessy had her by the arm now, Kennedy noticed, polite but firm. 'Very short notice. No way you could have known.'

'Oh well . . .' She hovered round them for a bit, looked on

in a puzzled way from the corner of the drive. Kennedy smiled at her reassuringly once or twice. They watched her progress back across the wet grass with silent unease.

'Interfering old bitch!' Hennessy suddenly shouted. He was really angry, Kennedy could see. 'Mr Bloody Frobisher! Let's get out of here.'

Luckily they had most of the turf on the truck. Bending down to pick up the last strip Hennessy lost his temper and kicked out savagely at the toy tricycle, which lifted a yard or so in the air and snapped in two as it hit the ground. Turning into the road they saw the old woman standing by the gate watching them. 'Up yours!' Hennessy shouted defiantly as they whipped past.

The dusk was coming up now, rolling in over the low, sodden fields. It was too late to get to Saffron Walden, Hennessy said. In the distance, firefly lights from the motorway winked through the shadows. Kennedy wondered about asking if they could stop at a call box so that he could phone Maxine, then thought better of it. 'You should have seen the look on that old bitch's face when I shouted at her,' Hennessy said, his red hands gripping the wheel. 'What did I tell you?' He was in a better mood now, honking his horn at the oncoming traffic. 'Listen,' he said, 'this is what we do, right. First the pub. Then go find Maguire. Get some sleep and then tomorrow we'll head over to Saffron Walden and deliver. What do you say?' For a moment Kennedy thought about Maxine. Maguire's stiff face looming up through the grey light of the pub. Then he saw Hennessy's boot hitting the tricycle again, and the fractured, descending arc, saw, too, the child's disbelieving face as he found it. 'No,' he said, shaking his head. 'Not tomorrow.'